PRAISE FOR *WHAT IS MINE*

"Unsettling from the very first page, *What Is Mine* is an emotional thrill ride about two women's desperate attempts to keep their families whole. Lyn Liao Butler has packed this story with page-turning suspense, culminating in a grand finale of explosive surprises."
—Megan Collins, author of *The Family Plot* and *Thicker Than Water*

"*What Is Mine* features Lyn Liao Butler at her very best. This twisty page-turner plays on every parent's darkest fears by evoking a scenario in which nothing is as it seems, and no one can be trusted. In the crowded field of domestic thrillers, Butler delivers!"
—Don Bentley, *New York Times* bestselling author of *Forgotten War*

"Captivating from the very first line, Butler masterfully builds a world full of suspense. With careful twists and shocking reveals, *What Is Mine* is a must-read novel."
—Nekesa Afia, author of the Harlem Renaissance Mystery series

"Relentlessly suspenseful and heartbreakingly chilling! Butler's stealthy, diabolical storytelling and her brilliant sleight of hand kept me guessing from page one—then rocket ahead to places readers will never predict. A gripping page-turner about family and obsession and, most terrifying, a tale of how far people will push to get what they want. Clear your calendar—you will not want to put this down!"
—Hank Phillippi Ryan, *USA Today* bestselling author

PRAISE FOR *SOMEONE ELSE'S LIFE*

"A skillful by-the-numbers thriller with its share of nice touches."
—*Kirkus Reviews*

"Well-developed characters and plenty of local color add to the slowly simmering plot, which builds to a strong and unexpected climax. Alfred Hitchcock fans will be satisfied."

—*Publishers Weekly*

"Chilling from page one, *Someone Else's Life* is an unputdownable descent into two women's parallel lives. With genuine jaw-dropping twists and enough seeds of doubt to populate a very wicked garden, Butler's debut thriller is a breath of fresh Kauai air."

—Eliza Jane Brazier, author of *If I Disappear*

"Lyn Liao Butler has mastered the art of full-body-tense suspense in this fresh take on the 'stranger in the house' concept, which will have you racing to the end even as your blood pressure increases and you have to remind yourself to breathe."

—Amanda Jayatissa, ITW Thriller Award–winning author of *My Sweet Girl*

"A chilling and immensely readable psychological thriller, *Someone Else's Life* simmers with menace as an unsettling encounter reveals the darker side of paradise and the fractures in a seemingly perfect life."

—Heather Chavez, author of *Blood Will Tell*

"*Someone Else's Life* is the read that every thriller lover needs. Atmospheric and character-driven, this story of two women's parallel lives at times disturbed me, then brought me to tears within the same page. The slow build that Butler executes seamlessly translates into a satisfying ending that took me by wine-soaked surprise."

—Elle Marr, Amazon Charts bestselling author of *Strangers We Know*

PRAISE FOR *RED THREAD OF FATE*

"I couldn't put this book down. A masterful story of sorrow, secrets, and unexpected romance. Ms. Butler writes with humor, compassion, and honesty. Simply wonderful. I can't wait for more from this gifted author."

—Kristan Higgins, *New York Times* bestselling author of *Pack Up the Moon*

"Lyn Liao Butler does it again! I was anticipating Butler's second book after devouring *The Tiger Mom's Tale*, and *Red Thread of Fate* did not disappoint! With a poignant tale and beautiful prose, Butler once again whisks us onto a powerful journey of loss, sorrow, but ultimately a journey of quiet strength."

—Jesse Q. Sutanto, critically acclaimed author of *Dial A for Aunties*

"Lyn Liao Butler is quickly becoming a go-to author for heartfelt, complex stories. *Red Thread of Fate* has everything—family secrets, mystery, identity. The rare blend of suspense and humor makes this story hard to put down. I can't wait to read what Butler writes next!"

—Saumya Dave, author of *What a Happy Family*

"A heartfelt contemplation on the course of our lives—what is fate, what is the result of the choices we make—coupled with a central mystery that will keep you reading late into the night. It seems Lyn Liao Butler's fate is to entertain with absorbing stories and compelling characters that linger long after the final page."

—Steven Rowley, *New York Times* bestselling author of *The Guncle*

PRAISE FOR *THE TIGER MOM'S TALE*

"*The Tiger Mom's Tale* is a heartfelt, delightful read. Lyn Liao Butler's story of Taiwanese and American identity had me turning pages and laughing (and drooling over the delicious descriptions of food)."
—Charles Yu, author of *Interior Chinatown*, winner of the 2020 National Book Award

"Unembellished and forthright, *The Tiger Mom's Tale* is a touching story that illuminates intricacies of race, ethnicity, traditions, and stereotypes . . . Filled with potential book club discussion topics and perfect for fans of YA novels by Jenny Han, *The Tiger Mom's Tale* will unleash timely dialogue about identity, family secrets, and cultural divides."
—*BookPage*

"Sharp and humorous, *The Tiger Mom's Tale* is a scenic debut novel with a cast of complicated characters sure to bring laughter and discussion to your next book club. I can't wait to read what Lyn Liao Butler writes next!"
—Tif Marcelo, *USA Today* bestselling author of *The Key to Happily Ever After*

"An absolutely absorbing story . . . *The Tiger Mom's Tale* grabbed me from page one and never let me go. I highly recommend this book to fiction readers, especially those who like plucky, get-back-up-again female leads, stories set in New York City, and those with settings on less familiar terrain."
—*Fresh Fiction*

"*The Tiger Mom's Tale* is a breathtaking debut from a compelling new voice in women's fiction. With captivating characters and vivid descriptions of mouthwatering meals, Lyn Liao Butler whisks us from the bright lights of New York City to the bustle of Taichung. A story of belonging, betrayal, and the bonds between family that can never be broken, *The Tiger Mom's Tale* is a deeply emotional and satisfying read."

—Kristin Rockaway, author of *She's Faking It*

"*The Tiger Mom's Tale* has it all—family drama, scorching love, vivid transcontinental settings, and culinary scenes that made me drool. A charming, engrossing debut from Lyn Liao Butler."

—Kimmery Martin, author of *The Antidote for Everything*

"With a keen eye for detail and a lush appreciation for the joys and comforts of food, Lyn Liao Butler delves into the complicated bonds of family, the endurance of sisterhood, and the fundamental yearning to connect with our heritage."

—Allie Larkin, internationally bestselling author of *The People We Keep*

"This is a story of complex family relationships, standing up for oneself, and the power of forgiveness."

—Book Riot

"Butler's riveting debut follows a half-white personal trainer who reconnects with her Taiwanese family after her biological father's death . . . Butler weaves in convincing descriptions of Lexa's navigating of the dating scene and the fetishizing of Asian women, and depicts a fascinatingly complex antagonist in Pin-Yen, who by the end must contend with the effect of her past actions. Butler breathes zesty new life into women's fiction."

—*Publishers Weekly*, starred review

"Filled with mouthwatering descriptions of food, a messy family, and a bit of mystery, this is a heartwarming story of one woman's search for her place in the world."

—Bust.com

WHAT
IS
MINE

OTHER TITLES BY LYN LIAO BUTLER

Someone Else's Life

The Tiger's Mom Tale

Red Thread of Fate

Writing as Lyn Liao

Crazy Bao You

WHAT IS MINE

A Thriller

LYN LIAO BUTLER

THOMAS & MERCER

Published by Thomas & Mercer, Seattle

www.apub.com

Amazon, the Amazon logo, and Thomas & Mercer are trademarks of Amazon.com, Inc., or its affiliates.

ISBN-13: 9781662513008 (paperback)
ISBN-13: 9781662512995 (digital)

Cover design by Ploy Siripant
Cover image: © Krakenimages.com / Shutterstock; © busliq / Shutterstock

Printed in the United States of America

*For my parents, who are thankfully nothing
like Hope's parents*

PART 1

Hope

1

The day of
5:16 p.m.

It was the absence of sound that made Hope realize something was wrong. She'd been cooking dinner with the thump, thump of Luca's basketball outside as background noise. Tomorrow was his last day of school, and Luca was excited for the start of sports camp. She'd been humming to herself as she stir-fried the mapo tofu in the pan. Leaning forward, Hope inhaled the spicy scent of the fermented bean paste, chili sauce, and ginger in which the tofu and ground beef simmered. Luca had requested the dish for dinner. She'd considered it a win, especially since he'd recently started calling her Ayi, or "aunt" in Mandarin, a sign that he was finally starting to come out of his shell around her and Shaun.

The rice cooker clicked, and Hope turned to it just as the back of her neck prickled. Her eyes narrowed as she took in the kitchen. The gray-and-white marble countertop was littered with ingredients for dinner. One of their dogs, Toby, a white-and-brown dachshund mix, milled around her legs, hoping for food to drop on the floor. Everything was in place, but she had the distinct feeling something was missing. She cocked her head, ears straining for any sound.

Silence.

It was quiet, too quiet. No thwack as the basketball hit the hoop's backboard. No thumps as Luca dribbled. No shouts of victory whenever he made a long shot. She rushed to the window overlooking the driveway.

Empty.

Rationally, Hope knew there were many reasons Luca might not be there. He could have gone into the garage to get something. He could be in the backyard playing with his dog, Mochi, whom they'd adopted for him six weeks ago. He could have gone across the street to shoot baskets with one of Jalissa Caine's boys. But deep down, that kernel of doom that had lodged itself in her stomach ever since her younger sister, Cassidy, Luca's mother, had died reared its head. Dread washed over her, and she ran for the front door.

"Luca?" she called, praying he was in the garage. She rounded the corner of the house and found the driveway empty.

Hope scanned the garage and backyard.

No boy.

No dog.

"Luca!" she called again, louder this time. When she got no answer, she turned in a circle, frantic. "Mochi?"

Hope prayed for an answering woof, or a shout from Luca, maybe from the woods surrounding their house, but there was nothing. She ran to the end of the driveway, looking both ways.

No one.

Not even one of Jalissa's four boys, who always seemed to be outside. Hope's heart galloped in her chest as her mind immediately jumped to the worst-case scenario: someone had taken Luca.

"No, no, no." Hysteria bubbled inside. She doubled over, placing her hands on her thighs. He couldn't have been taken. Theirs was a safe neighborhood, where kids played in the streets and no one locked their doors. But there *had* been that teenager's accidental death last year . . .

Don't panic. Luca was here somewhere. He'd done this a few times before. Taken Mochi on a walk without telling them, once not returning until an hour later. They'd been frantic then too, and had explained to him he couldn't disappear like that. He'd been frightened, said he was sorry. He wouldn't do it again.

Hope was new to this whole parenting thing. Had Luca not understood it wasn't safe to walk his dog by himself at nine years old? She tried to calm herself. He wasn't dead or kidnapped. Any minute now, he'd appear in front of her, and she and Shaun would laugh about it later, how she'd overreacted when Luca had just taken Mochi for a walk again and forgotten to tell her. They'd hug him and say how glad they were he was all right, but they'd be firmer this time. Make him understand that it wasn't okay to disappear like this. But then Hope stilled. Luca hadn't come into the house to get Mochi's harness and leash, which always hung on a hook by the back door in the kitchen. How could he have taken Mochi on a walk without the leash?

Seconds ticked by and still no boy or dog. "Okay, it'll be okay," she said out loud, as if that would slow the thundering of her heart. "Maybe he's at Jalissa's house."

She ran across the street to the Caines' and pounded on their front door, ringing the bell repeatedly.

No answer.

She looked in their driveway and realized Jalissa's giant van was gone.

Panic clawed at her as she fought to remain calm. She ran back toward their house and knocked on their next-door neighbor's door. When kindly old Mr. Alden answered, she blurted out, "Have you seen Luca?"

"What's that, dear?" Mr. Alden was slightly deaf, and he cocked his head to the side.

"Luca!" Hope shouted. "Have you seen Luca? Did he walk by with Mochi?"

"Oh." Mr. Alden paused. "No, I don't think so. I'm watching *Jeopardy!* Does Luca want to come watch with me?"

"No. I don't know where he is." Hope's voice trembled.

She couldn't have lost Luca. He'd been through so much already in his short life. He'd *promised* he'd never leave their property without telling her. She turned to scan the street again, praying with all her might that she'd see him standing in their driveway, wondering why she was being so dramatic. But it was still empty.

She darted back to their property without saying goodbye to Mr. Alden, intent on getting her keys so she could search for Luca by car. Surely she'd find him right down the road. She reached their driveway just as Shaun's SUV pulled in. She was at his side the moment he opened the door. "I can't find Luca or Mochi."

"What?" Shaun took her in his arms, leaving the driver's door open.

For a moment, she allowed him to envelop her in his warm embrace before she pushed him away. "He's gone, Shaun. Something happened. Someone took him."

"Let's not panic. Maybe he went to Jalissa's house. Or he took Mochi out again without telling you." Shaun's voice was calm, which only made Hope more frantic. Didn't he understand the urgency of the situation?

"I checked Jalissa's already. No one's home. Mr. Alden hasn't seen him either." Hope paced back and forth in front of Shaun, wringing her hands. "He didn't come in for Mochi's harness and leash. He'd never take Mochi on a walk without them."

Shaun's lips tightened, and Hope could see she was finally getting through to him. "Okay, we'll find him. He's got to be around here." Shaun turned back to his car. "I'll drive around, look for him. Call Jalissa—maybe she took him with her somewhere and thought he told you. And call his other friends."

"He doesn't *have* any other friends." Hope made a noise of distress in her throat, and Shaun met her eyes.

That was the problem. Luca had been living with them for two months, and his only friends so far were the Caine boys, especially Andrew, who was his age. Hope could think of no one else to try.

"Okay. Just . . ." Shaun stopped, floundering for words. "Call anyone you can think of. I'll let you know when I find him." He gave Hope's hand a squeeze and got in the car. A few seconds later, he was gone, down the road past Mr. Alden's house.

Hope ran for the front door to get her cell. She paused on the porch, staring at their doorbell. They'd talked about getting one of those Ring doorbells with a camera, now that they had a child living with them. Dammit, why hadn't they installed one? Then they could have seen what happened.

Mentally kicking herself for this mistake, she looked over her shoulder one last time, hoping against hope that she'd see Luca and Mochi walking toward her on the street. But there was nothing, only the basketball sitting under the hoop.

Hope got hold of Jalissa, who said she hadn't seen Luca since that morning. Hope started calling all their immediate neighbors, but got mostly voice mails. Only one person picked up, and he was still at work. Growing more frantic, she called Shaun.

"Did you find him?" she blurted out before he could even say hello.

"No." Hope heard the distress in Shaun's voice. "I've been driving up and down the roads around the lake. No sign of them." He paused and then said, "Maybe you should call the police."

Police. Hope's heart pounded in her ears as she hung up and dialed 911. She couldn't believe they were calling the police. But it felt like forever since she'd realized Luca was gone, and there was no sign of him. When the operator answered, Hope closed her eyes and told them her nephew was missing.

Within minutes, two patrol cars had shown up, followed by more until a half dozen official vehicles sat in their driveway and in front of their house. Shaun had come back after the second wave of vehicles arrived.

The tall officer questioning them had kind eyes, his gray uniform crisp and pressed. Hope couldn't remember his name. He'd told them when he first got there, but her mind was splintered in a million directions.

"What is the boy's name?" he asked.

"Luca," she said. "Luca Wen. My nephew. You need to go out and search for him!" Hope shot up off the couch. Why were they all standing around here at the house? Shouldn't they be sending people out right this minute?

"Mrs. Chen, Mr. Chen." The man (what was his name?) turned to each of them. "We'll do everything we can to find him. But we need information first." The man's voice was patient, his face compassionate, but Hope was distracted by a memory—Cassidy teasing her when Hope had married Shaun. She'd said all Hope had to do was switch out the *W* in Wen for *Ch* and she had her new last name.

"How old is he?"

Hope snapped her attention to the officer. "Nine." She sat back down, her mind now trying to conjure up the man's name. If she could only remember his name, then Luca would come home to them, safe and sound.

"What does he look like?"

Hope didn't answer, because the officer's name was on the tip of her tongue. Something about a song, music?

"Dark-brown hair, long in front, short in back. Dark-brown eyes. Half-Chinese/Taiwanese, half-white," Shaun said, after a pause.

"Where did you last see him?"

"Hope said he was playing basketball in the driveway," Shaun answered again.

"What was he wearing?"

Shaun turned to Hope.

"Um, dark-blue basketball shorts and a gray T-shirt," Hope said. And then she blurted out, "Harmon!"

The officer looked at her.

"Sorry." Hope ducked her head, embarrassed but also grateful she'd remembered his name. That meant Luca would return any minute now, right?

"You believe he had his dog with him?" Officer Harmon continued the questions after a moment. When Hope nodded, he asked, "What kind of dog?"

"She's a Chesapeake Bay retriever mix, mostly white with brown spots on her ears and one brown patch near her tail. About twenty-five pounds," Shaun told the officer.

Hope's attention was distracted by the door opening as another officer left the house, talking into his radio. Her vision blurred, and for a moment, she wondered if this was all a bad dream. None of this was real. She'd blink and be back in the kitchen, the mapo tofu ready and Luca waiting eagerly for his bowl.

"Any distinct markings on his body?"

Hope's head whipped toward Officer Harmon. "No." *Oh god, why did he ask that?*

"How long before you realized he was gone?"

Hope pressed her lips together. "Maybe ten minutes? Maybe more? I don't really know. I'm sorry." She'd been so engrossed in her cooking that she couldn't be sure.

"We need a recent photo of him and the dog." The officer gave them an email address to send the pictures.

Shaun pulled some up on his phone and sent them immediately.

On and on the questions went. Hope hated that Luca had been reduced to these statistics, rather than a lonely boy grieving the only family he'd had before coming to live with them.

"His mother, my sister, died recently. She was only thirty-two. He just came to live with us about two months ago. He's had a rough life." Hope contributed this hoping to hurry up the process.

"Rough how?" Officer Harmon asked.

9

"They . . . um, moved around a lot." Luca had told them that he and Cassidy had traveled all over the country, renting whatever apartment Cassidy could find or even sleeping in her car if they couldn't afford a place. Hope looked around their modest house. It wasn't big, only a two-bedroom, two-bathroom in a lake community at the top of Westchester County, about an hour and fifteen minutes north of New York City. But to Luca, it must have seemed like a luxury home.

"Wen." Officer Harmon's voice brought Hope's attention back to him. "Like Cassidy Wen, who was found in a car at the trail a couple of months ago?"

Hope's heart sank. He knew about her sister. "Yes. That's her."

He was now looking at her with a combination of pity and understanding. "And Luca is her son?"

"Yes," Shaun said, when Hope failed to reply.

"Can you tell me more about their circumstances before Luca came to live with you? Maybe someone from his previous life took him?" The policeman looked from Hope to Shaun. "Is there anyone Luca would go back to?"

Hope shook her head. "My sister left this area soon after Luca was born. I lost track of them all this time. She was . . . troubled." She swallowed, fighting tears as she thought about Cassidy. "I don't know much about their lives these last nine years."

Hope had never gotten over Cassidy disappearing right after Luca was born. She'd looked for them, wanting to help because Cassidy had struggled with drugs and alcohol since high school, but they'd vanished, just as Luca had tonight.

As Shaun told the officer the little bit they knew about Cassidy and Luca, Hope stewed in her misery. How could she have failed Cassidy again? She'd always blamed herself for not trying harder before Cassidy disappeared. Her sister had been a wild child, rebelling against their immigrant parents' strict Chinese/Taiwanese upbringing. Even though Hope and Cassidy had been born in America, their parents still clung to the old ways from Taiwan, where their mother had grown up, and China, where their father was raised.

Was there something Hope could have done to change Cassidy's fate? Had someone really taken Luca, or had he run off with Mochi? Every second that passed meant Luca was getting farther away from them. She couldn't let him disappear for good like Cassidy had.

"Does he have a history of running away?" The policeman's voice broke into Hope's thoughts. "Any chance he took off on his own?" His tone was gentle, but his question made Hope's pulse jump.

"No." She shook her head vehemently. "He wouldn't do that." But would he? How well did she really know her nephew? They'd been thrown together just two months ago, when the police had shown up at her doorstep to tell her that Cassidy had died. "Please, can you start searching? If he and Mochi are still nearby, we're wasting time."

"Can you put out an Amber Alert or something?" Shaun asked.

"There are certain criteria that have to be met before an Amber Alert can be issued. We need to be sure the child has been abducted, and that there is sufficient evidence either of a struggle or . . ."

Officer Harmon stopped when Hope drew in a sharp breath.

"I didn't hear a struggle. Mochi didn't bark." She turned to Shaun, and her eyes flooded with guilt. "If someone had taken them, wouldn't Mochi have barked?"

Shaun didn't answer, but he moved to Hope's side.

Officer Harmon conferred with a woman who had walked up to him and then turned back to them. "We've sent people out already. We'll also search your home, with your permission, in case he's here somewhere on the property. But in order for an Amber Alert to be issued, we have to believe that the child is in imminent danger of serious bodily injury or death, and that there is enough descriptive information about the victim and the abduction in order to aid in the recovery of the child."

Hope and Shaun exchanged a glance, fraught with worry. "What can you do, then?"

"We'll be issuing a BOLO, be on the lookout, to other agencies. Rest assured we will do everything within our scope to find him." The officer turned sympathetic eyes to Hope, but it only made her feel worse.

Shaun answered more questions and then gave the police permission to search their home, even though Hope had already done that before calling their neighbors. She trailed after them, knowing that Luca wasn't hiding under his bed or behind the couch. He'd been in the driveway when he disappeared, not in the house. But they had to follow procedures. More calls were made, radios crackled, and the officers coordinated an official search for Luca. Helicopters would be dispatched, and police dogs sent over to try and pick up Luca's scent. They would start in a six-mile radius and work their way in toward Hope and Shaun's house.

"Can I set up a search party with some neighbors?" Shaun asked. Hope could see how stressed he was by the way he was biting his lips. He always did that when he was worried. She knew he cared about Luca too. When Shaun had found out how much Luca loved basketball, they'd played together whenever they could. They'd go for hikes with Mochi on the weekends, leaving Hope home alone with Toby to read or work in her vegetable garden. They walked the dogs together around the lake, and Hope had even found Shaun helping Luca with his homework when she'd been stuck late at work.

"Not yet." The police officer shook his head. "We'll be asking your neighbors to stay in their houses for now, so as not to muddy the scent for the dogs or trample on any potential evidence." He turned so that his look included Hope. "I know you've already started calling neighbors, but keep calling anyone you can think of who knows Luca. Even people from his past, his classmates, anyone he's had contact with recently. Keep us posted." He paused and nodded at them. "We'll find him."

But an hour later, there was still no sign of Luca. It was as if he'd disappeared into thin air.

2

Hope sat at the dining room table, scrolling through her phone, occasionally calling a number, but so far, no one had seen Luca. The police were following all protocols for a missing child. It was a multiple-agency effort, with the town, county, and state police involved. Hope and Shaun were to keep their cells on them at all times, in the hope that either Luca would call or someone else would phone in a demand. They didn't have a landline at home, so they only had to worry about their cells. The police dogs had just come by, and Hope had given them clothes that Luca had worn yesterday.

Across the table from her, Shaun put down his cell. "None of the neighbors we know have seen him." He'd been going through the contact list provided by their lake association, which listed all the families and their phone numbers.

"We got a hold of the school," Officer Harmon said. "They gave us Luca's bus driver's info. We've sent someone out to his house to question him."

Hope nodded. They were clutching at straws, but they had to be sure they talked to everyone who knew Luca. It was a small list. She had remembered how the bus driver, Mike, had seemed to take a special interest in Luca. She felt bad siccing the police on people who were probably innocent, but they had to be sure.

"Jalissa said the last time she saw Luca was this morning, waiting for the bus with her boys." Hope played with her phone. "I called on Mr. Alden again and he hasn't seen Luca in a couple of days. Beth and John farther down said they haven't seen him in a while. Who else does he know?"

"Did you try Tessa?" Shaun asked.

"No." Hope looked up. "Maybe he took Mochi to visit them." Her heart galloped as she pulled up Tessa's number in her phone, hoping with all her might that Luca had walked to visit the Conrads and their dog. Even though he knew he wasn't supposed to do that by himself. But she would forgive him, if only they found him.

"Who are they?" Officer Harmon asked.

"A couple who adopted a dog that we fostered." Shaun pointed out the window. "They live on the other side of the lake. I took Luca and Mochi over to visit a few weeks ago."

"Please, please be there, Luca," Hope muttered under her breath. She held the ringing phone to her ear. *Pick up, pick up, pick up.* But it went to voice mail and her heart plummeted. She left a message, hoping Tessa would call her back soon.

"We'll send someone over to see if they're home." Officer Harmon picked up his radio. "What's their full name and address?"

Hope was about to tell him when her cell rang. She looked at the phone display. "It's Tessa." Picking up the call, she said, her voice frantic, "Tessa? Have you seen Luca?"

"Hello?" Tessa's voice was faint.

"Luca is missing. We can't find him. Is he with you?" Hope squeezed her eyes shut tight, willing Tessa to say yes.

"No, I haven't seen him." Tessa paused, and Hope deflated like a balloon. "Robert hasn't been doing well." The other woman's voice grew fainter. "I thought the end was near. We're not home. We're on our—" She broke off, and Hope could hear the other woman sucking in a breath. Then she was back, her voice stronger. "He rallied, though. He's doing so much better. Maybe there's a chance . . ."

"I hope so." Hope's heart softened at the desperation in the woman's voice. Robert had prostate cancer, and it had come back with a vengeance recently. Stage 4 this time, and his prognosis wasn't good. That was one of the reasons the couple had wanted to adopt a dog. Tessa needed the support of an animal to get her through this hard time.

"I know so." Tessa's voice was determined. "They say part of the fight is thinking positive, right? So that's what I'm going to do."

"I'm sending positive vibes to you both." Hope looked at Shaun and Officer Harmon, shaking her head. She felt so sorry for Tessa. She hadn't known the Conrads before the adoption, but ever since, she'd found out that Tessa often volunteered at the children's events for the lake, even though they didn't have kids themselves. Hope couldn't even imagine how heartbreaking it was for Tessa to watch her husband fading away before her eyes.

After a moment, Tessa said, "Thank you."

"If you hear from Luca, will you call us?" Hope blinked to fight back her tears. She wasn't sure if she was tearing up over Tessa and Robert's plight or the fact that Luca wasn't with them. The disappointment was crushing, making her more frantic to find her nephew.

"I will."

Hope hung up, and her shoulders slumped in dejection. What if the police were right and Luca had left on his own? How far would he get with no money and a dog in tow?

Hope looked at Shaun with defeat. "I can't think of anyone else. Why hasn't he called us?"

They'd made him memorize their phone numbers and address. Surely, he would call soon when he realized it was past dinnertime? He always looked forward to every meal. Poor boy. Could Mochi have gotten out of the gate, and Luca had chased after her? But if so, why hadn't they come home?

Shaun made a face. "Maybe we should start calling people who we think might have taken him?"

"You mean like that racist neighbor up the street who always yells about getting the Chinks out of the neighborhood when we walk the dogs by his house?" Hope looked at Officer Harmon. "I don't think he likes us."

The officer nodded grimly. "Give me his address. We'll send someone to question him." His radio burst to life with a series of crackles.

Hope narrowed her eyes, thinking out loud. "Wasn't there an email recently about a registered sex offender who had moved into an apartment complex near here?" Maybe he had taken Luca and . . . She squeezed her eyes shut, refusing to let her mind go there.

Or maybe it was that creepy man from work, the one who was always hanging around her office, supposedly asking about the class schedule? Hope was the group-fitness manager of a nearby gym, and the man had developed a crush on her about a month ago. Hope had been polite but dismissive, thinking he was harmless. Now she wondered if maybe she should have told someone about him. Could he have followed her home one day and taken Luca to get her attention?

She told Officer Harmon about him, and when Shaun started going through a list of the kids who took the bus with Luca, in the hope that maybe he had befriended one of them and gone to their house, she walked out of the kitchen. Toby, who hadn't left her side, followed. She went to the window by the front door. A small group of newspeople had gathered on the corner by their house. Hope pressed a hand to her chest, wondering why this was happening. How had Luca and Mochi vanished without a trace? And on her watch?

As Hope stood there gazing out, she heard the whomp whomp of a helicopter and looked up. It circled overhead, searching for Luca from the air. This was really happening. Luca was gone, and it wasn't a simple misunderstanding or him losing track of time.

Something touched her on the elbow, and she jumped. She whirled around to see Shaun standing behind her.

"Hey. We'll find him." His voice was soft, yet Hope could hear the fear behind it. He was a man of action, and she knew he was feeling helpless right now. Like she was.

"Where is he?" Hope bent down and picked up Toby, clutching him tight against her, as if trying to crush the anguish deep in her gut. "Do you think he might have run away with Mochi?"

Shaun heaved a deep sigh. "I don't know. I wonder . . ."

"It's my fault."

"You can't watch him 24-7, Hope." Shaun dropped his hand. "He was just in the driveway."

"I know but . . ."

They shared a look, and then both looked out at the street. The helicopter blades continued to thrum, and more news crews pulled up at the corner. Officer Harmon had stayed, while most of the others had left; he was their liaison with the police department, keeping them updated on what was going on. Shaun paced the hall behind her, while Hope stayed glued to the window, willing Luca to come walking down the street and end this nightmare.

Shaun suddenly pivoted and headed for the front door.

Officer Harmon looked up from where he stood just outside the foyer in the living room. "Where are you going?"

"I can't just stay here. I'm going out to look for him." Shaun shoved his hands into his jeans pockets.

Hope's head jerked around to stare between her husband and the officer. "We're supposed to stay put." The public information officer assigned to them was organizing a press conference for them to speak to the media soon.

"I have to do something." Shaun grabbed his keys, which hung on a hook by the front door. "I'm going to drive around. Check the park, the library, anywhere that he might go to. I know him better than the police. Maybe they're not looking in the right places."

Officer Harmon conferred with someone on his radio, then nodded at Shaun. Shaun squeezed Hope's shoulder and planted a kiss on her lips before he left the house. Hope walked into the living room, and then back into the foyer. She couldn't sit still. How could she rest when Luca was gone? She kept looking at her cell, willing it to ring. Where was Luca? What was happening to him right this moment, as she stood here in their house, helpless?

The doorbell rang and Hope jumped. Maybe it was Luca. She ran to the front door, her heart thundering in her chest, but Officer Harmon held up a hand. He opened it, and when Hope saw it was Jalissa, she deflated in disappointment.

"Hope!" Jalissa peered around the officer. Her dark hair was pulled into tiny braids that fell over her shoulders. "I'm her neighbor, Jalissa Caine," she said to the man.

The officer turned to confirm with Hope, who nodded. He stepped aside to let Jalissa in. "I'll just be outside," he said, and then walked out the door, leaving Hope and Jalissa in the foyer.

"I came as soon as I could. I'm so sorry!" Jalissa reached out and pulled Hope into a hug. Hope could see the newspeople milling around at the curb, cameras pointed at them as the officer walked down the front walkway. She pulled Jalissa inside and shut the door, her black hair sticking to her cheeks, which were suddenly wet with tears.

"It's my fault. I was inside when he disappeared," Hope whispered, as they walked into the living room and sat on the couch. Toby climbed up the ramp to be by her side.

Jalissa looked at her fiercely. "It's not your fault. We'll find him, okay?" Jalissa had moved to the States from Kingston, Jamaica, with her family when she was twelve, but her Jamaican accent always came out when she was excited or stressed. "Where's Shaun?"

"He's driving around." Hope bit her lip. "I thought it was safe for Luca to play out there by himself, with Mochi watching. Your boys are always outside, and no one has taken any of them." She wrapped her arms around herself. "If a boy had to be missing, why couldn't it be one of yours? You have four, you can spare one."

The minute the words were out, she regretted them. She slapped a hand over her mouth. She was usually so calm and collected, the one others leaned on in times of crisis, but now she was falling apart and saying horrible things.

"I'm sorry," Hope muttered behind her hand.

Jalissa's expression softened. "It's okay. I know what you mean. I get it."

More tears streamed down Hope's face, and she buried it in her hands. This too was new. She almost never cried, not even when Cassidy and Luca disappeared all those years ago. Back then, she'd been determined to find them, channeling her grief into action. But Luca disappearing on her watch was making all her walls crumble. What kind of aunt was she to lose him? What kind of sister?

Jalissa didn't say anything, just let her cry, but she went into the bathroom and got some tissues for Hope. She sat next to Hope and rubbed her back as Hope's mind tortured her with one horrific scenario after another.

"I'm staying with you until Shaun gets back," Jalissa said. "I told Jack he was on his own with the boys."

Hope met her neighbor's eyes, and they shared a small smile. Jalissa's boys ranged in age from five to fifteen, and they were a handful. Lively, rambunctious, and with such huge appetites that Jalissa had joked once that she spent more time in the grocery store than she did at home.

Jalissa opened the tote that was still slung over her shoulder. "I brought some Ting. Things always seem better with a Ting, no?"

Hope let out a short laugh and accepted the cold bottle of Jamaican carbonated grapefruit juice. She was grateful for Jalissa's presence right now, glad she didn't have to sit here alone, her thoughts torturing her. "Have they found anything?" Jalissa asked. "Jack got home before me and said they asked to see our front-door security camera footage." Hope shook her head. "Yours is the only house with a camera on this block. They told us only one car drove by in the time when Luca was outside, and it was a neighbor from up the hill. He said he saw Luca playing basketball."

"Oh." They exchanged a look. There were only four houses in this section of the street: Hope and Shaun's and Mr. Alden's on one side, an empty house directly across from Shaun and Hope's, and the Caine house next to that. On either side of these four houses were long expanses of woods, with at least two hundred yards until the next house in either direction.

Hope took in a shuddering breath. She wanted to hide in her bedroom until Luca was found, but she couldn't do that. She needed to stay strong, and do everything she could to get Luca back. She would not let another family member disappear.

A loud knock suddenly sounded on the front door, and like a shot, Hope was off the couch and at the door, pulling it open. Jalissa was right behind her. Officer Harmon stood on the porch, his radio crackling.

"What is it?" Hope's eyes searched the street, hoping to see Luca, but he wasn't there. She looked back at the officer. She could tell by the look on his face that they'd found something. And judging by the frown he aimed at them, it wasn't good.

Hope clutched Jalissa's arm as she felt the blood drain from her face.

3

"Did you find him?" Hope's voice trembled.

The officer shook his head. "No, but one of the dogs picked up his scent in the woods on the other side of Mr. Alden's house." He paused. "They found some blood. Not a lot, but—"

"No." Hope's gasp cut him off, and she rushed to go out the door.

"Mrs. Chen." Officer Harmon stepped in front of her, preventing her exit. "You can't go there. And it wasn't a lot of blood. They also found a key chain with some sort of drink with a straw in it."

Hope's eyes widened. "Bubble tea. Purple, with little dark balls on it?"

He nodded. "Yes. It's Luca's then?"

Hope pressed her lips together as tears sprang to her eyes. "He has . . ." Her voice broke, and she cleared her throat. "He's got a key chain collection. He had that bubble tea one clipped to his shorts when he went out to play basketball."

Officer Harmon gave a nod, then spoke quietly into his radio. He turned back to Hope. "They're checking out the scene. It was found slightly down the hill next to the path that leads to the street that the lake is on, the one behind your house."

Hope looked behind her, as if she could see the lake from where she stood. "If Luca was there and went down that way, someone could have taken him away in a car from Lake Circle."

Officer Harmon nodded. "We'll be checking the front-door cameras of the residents down there."

"The path leads right to the lake community clubhouse. Does it have a camera?" The clubhouse was located on the lake next to their beach, where they often had parties and meetings.

"We checked with the association president, Nancy Meza, and she confirmed that it doesn't." Officer Harmon shook his head. "If Luca had gone down there, we might have seen where he'd gone."

Jalissa tsked. "We really need to get one." She was on the board, and Hope knew she would get this done. But it was too late for Luca.

"Mrs. Chen." Officer Harmon's quiet voice had them both turning back to him. "We need to consider the possibility that Luca ran away. So far, we've found no evidence that he was abducted. The blood we found could have just been him tripping and skinning his knee or arm. And you said he was really attached to his dog, so the fact that the dog is missing too . . ."

Hope's hands tightened into fists at her side. "He didn't run away." But in the next moment, her conviction wavered. What if he had? What if he hadn't liked living with them and wanted to go back to whatever life he'd had with Cassidy? He was only nine, though, so where would he have gone if he really had run off?

Officer Harmon shifted his feet as he shot her a sympathetic look. "We're keeping every avenue open. But if you can remember anything about his past, where or who he might go to, we can look into it. Oh, and we spoke to all the neighbors you mentioned."

Hope's eyebrows lifted. "Anything?"

The officer shook his head. "Mr. Russo, the neighbor you told us about, the one way down the street on the next corner, he has dementia."

Right—the man who always spewed racial slurs at them whenever they walked their dogs by his house. Hope turned to Jalissa and found her neighbor shooting her a sympathetic look. She'd told Jalissa about him.

"He has full-time nurses," Officer Harmon continued. "The one currently on duty says he often gets away from them and likes to stand at the edge of his property hurling insults at his neighbors. While he's not politically correct, he also has no idea what he's saying and isn't sound of mind enough to have kidnapped Luca. His family has given consent for us to search his house." He paused for a breath. "We'll keep you posted if we find anything."

"Okay." Hope looked at her phone, which she still clutched tightly in her hand.

"Okay," the officer echoed. "I'll be back in a bit." And with a nod, he stepped off the porch.

Hope closed her eyes. *Please, let us find him soon. Please.* She didn't know who or what she was praying to, but right now, she would have given her soul to the devil if it would bring Luca back.

When she opened her eyes, her mind focused on the fact that the searchers had found Luca's key chain in the woods next to Mr. Alden's house. She walked to the window in the living room, which was adjacent to the old man's home. Could he have had anything to do with Luca's disappearance? He'd been nothing but kind to them, but wasn't it always the most unassuming person who turned out to be the killer or kidnapper?

Hope's eyes scanned the parts of Mr. Alden's house that she could see above the fence that separated their properties. In the ten years that they'd lived here, Hope couldn't think of ever seeing a single person visiting Mr. Alden socially. He never talked about family, no children or grandchildren or close friends. Why was he always alone? Hope tilted her head. The setting sun cast shadows from the trees against it, and the windows glinted in the fading light. Soon, it would be dark, and she couldn't imagine Luca out there somewhere in the night by himself.

Could Luca be in her neighbor's house right this minute? Maybe the whole "kindly neighbor" thing was an act. Maybe Mr. Alden took and kept children in his basement against their wills.

Part of Hope knew she was scraping the bottom of the barrel being suspicious of their neighbor, who'd been nothing but nice to them. But Luca was gone and everyone was a suspect now.

"Hope." Jalissa's voice had Hope turning toward the front door. "There's a man standing outside your house. Officer Harmon is talking to him." Jalissa beckoned with a hand.

"What? Who?" Hope rushed to Jalissa's side. She took one look and then dropped onto the floor, crouching beneath the window.

Jalissa stared down at her. "What're you doing?"

"It's him," Hope whispered, even though there was no way he could hear her. She carefully lifted her head and peered out the window. The man stared intently at their front door even as he spoke to Officer Harmon. Hope backed away from the window before straightening up.

Jalissa followed her into the living room. "Him who?"

"That creepy guy from my gym." Hope scrolled through her cell. "I need to call Shaun."

Jalissa stood by with her forehead furrowed. Hope didn't have time to explain. She dialed Shaun and put it on speakerphone. As soon as he picked up, she started talking.

"Shaun. That guy I told you about is standing in front of our house right now. Do you think it was him?" Nervous energy made Hope drum her fingers on her thigh.

"What guy?" Shaun sounded as confused as Jalissa looked.

"That guy! George." She *knew* George had something to do with Luca's disappearance. Hadn't she just been thinking maybe he'd followed her home, and now here he was, outside her house? "The one from the gym I told you about? Keeps popping up everywhere I am in the building?" She should have reported it when she noticed his excessive interest in her.

"He's at our house?" Shaun's voice raised.

"Yes. I know he took Luca." Hope looked toward the front door. "If he's hurt him . . ." Her chest heaved as emotions took over her body.

"Where's Officer Harmon?" Shaun asked.

"He's talking to George." Hope took in a breath. "I'm going out there, find out what's going on."

"I'm coming back now." And Shaun hung up.

Hope strode to the front door and pulled it open, Jalissa behind her. She ignored all the cameras and people that swung in her direction and focused on only the man. About average height, he had light-brown hair shaved close to his head. There was nothing remarkable about him, just an average man who would blend into any crowd. Someone who, Hope now thought, wouldn't be suspected of kidnapping a little boy to get her attention and would be smart enough to come back to the scene of the crime to throw suspicion off himself.

When he caught sight of her, his face lit up. He waved in greeting, and then Hope was moving toward him. If he'd done anything to Luca, she was going to tear him apart with her bare hands.

"Hope, I heard the news." George's face showed nothing but concern, yet Hope narrowed her eyes as she drew up in front of him. Someone shouted a question at her from behind, but she ignored them.

"What news?" Hope studied his face, trying to figure out if he was guilty.

"About your nephew. That he's missing." Sympathy flooded George's face. "I came to see if I could help." He took a step toward Hope, but Officer Harmon stopped him.

"How do you know where I live?" Hope's forehead furrowed in concern. *Did he really follow me?*

"They gave the address of the clubhouse if we wanted to pick up flyers to hand out. And I heard some people say you live up the hill, just one block away from the clubhouse. I started walking and saw all the people gathered over there." He waved a hand to the crowd at the corner.

"Why are you really here? You don't know me. We're not friends. Did you take him?" Hope felt Jalissa place a hand on her arm, but Hope's entire attention was on George.

"What? Of course not." His forehead creased, and he threw Hope a hurt look. "I came to help. If I'd taken him, would I be here now?"

Hope's eyebrows lifted. "Yes, if you were trying to throw suspicion away from yourself."

Officer Harmon held up a hand. "Okay, wait. You told me you were a friend of Mrs. Chen's." He looked at her. "What's going on?"

"This man has been following me around the gym for the past month." Hope pointed at George. "I thought of him earlier when we were thinking of people who might have taken Luca. I don't like that he just showed up in front of my house."

George protested, holding up his hands. "I was just trying to help."

Jalissa pulled gently on Hope's arm. "Let's go back inside." Hope didn't budge, and Jalissa pulled a little harder. "Let the police take care of him."

Hope resisted at first, but Officer Harmon gave her a reassuring nod and she finally let Jalissa lead her back inside. The truth was, she was afraid of what she would do if she thought George had something to do with Luca disappearing. It scared her, that she would do *any-thing* she had to, to get Luca back. She couldn't bear the thought of failing Cassidy again, this time by losing her son.

Once in the house, she stood at the window next to the door as Jalissa said she'd clean up the kitchen. Hope had left it a mess from the dinner Luca never got to enjoy. She stared at George talking to the officer. Was he guilty? And if not, what was his interest in her? Why was he here? If it wasn't him, was it someone else she knew?

Hope turned to walk to the kitchen and then stopped. She listened to the sounds of Jalissa tidying up, dishes rattling as she put them in the dishwasher. Hope frowned, her mind working. What about Jalissa and her husband? What if they were the ones who took Luca? Hope's body stilled as she suddenly remembered something from a few years ago. Hadn't there been rumors about Jalissa's husband, Jack, back then? Something about being involved in shady business and gambling debts? Hadn't they separated for a while when Jalissa threw him out of the house? This had been before their youngest was born. Hope had never paid attention to the rumors since she was friendly with Jalissa. But now she remembered the fights the Caines had had, the shouting coming from their house, and she wondered. Had Jack gotten himself involved in something sinister and taken Luca? But for what reason? There was no ransom note so far, and even if there were, it wasn't as if she and Shaun had money. Shaun worked in digital marketing at a nearby hospital, and she worked for a gym. They didn't make the kind of money needed to pay off debts to bad people. And if a boy was going to be taken for ransom because of Jack, wouldn't it make more sense to take one of his four boys? After all, the Caines had the biggest house on their street, completely remodeled just a few years ago.

Hope shook her head. Her imagination was running wild. But at this point, she trusted no one. Not even Jalissa.

4

Shaun walked through the front door fifteen minutes later.

Hope ran to him. "Anything?"

"Nothing." Shaun raked a hand through his black hair as Hope deflated. "But Officer Harmon just told me that George has an alibi for the time when Luca went missing. He claimed he was at the gym. They're checking surveillance cameras now and are questioning people."

They stared at each other for a moment until Jalissa came toward them from the kitchen. "Shaun. I'm so sorry about Luca."

They exchanged a hug, and then Jalissa gestured to the front door. "I need to get back, get the youngest two into bed. They usually go to sleep around eight thirty."

Hope nodded, and when Jalissa hugged her, Hope tried to quell the pang of guilt at having suspected her friend before. There was no way Jalissa and Jack were involved in Luca's disappearance. Was there?

As soon as the door closed behind Jalissa, Hope's cell rang, making her heart jump. But one glance at it had her hopes plummeting. It was her parents. Hope knew Shaun had called them earlier to tell them about Luca's disappearance, but she'd been too preoccupied to speak to them then. Besides, she didn't know if they even cared.

They'd been upset about Cassidy's death, sure, as it had brought back so many bad memories, but they hadn't been interested in getting to know their grandson. When she'd suggested that they come visit or that she could bring Luca to California to see them, they'd deflected, saying now wasn't a good time. Hope had known her parents were cold, but for them to not even want to get to know Luca now that he was back, well, that hadn't sat well with her.

She thought about not answering, but at the last minute, her finger accepted the call.

"Hope-ah? He back?" Her mother's gruff voice filled her ears.

Hope walked to the couch and sank onto the cushions. "No."

"Oh." And then nothing. Her mother had nothing else to add about the disappearance of their only grandchild.

The silence hung like a heavy mantle, and Hope realized she had nothing to say to her mother either. It made her sad, but at the same time, this was the way it was in their family. Hope's parents had never been warm with her, but she'd known they cared about her. They were typical emotionally detached Asian parents—not big on touch, formal around her, gruff when they were proud of her. Not at all like the American families Hope saw on TV. Hope had been eight when Cassidy was born—an oops baby—and she'd sensed, even at that young age, the way her mother had dissociated from the child. As if she hadn't given birth to her, and didn't know what to do with this extra person who was suddenly in their lives. Hope had thought Cassidy looked like a doll. Her younger sister had been born with a headful of black hair sticking straight up, like Marge Simpson from *The Simpsons*. Cassidy was Hope's very own doll to play with and protect because her parents were too tired from their menial jobs to pay much attention to her.

"Ma . . . ," Hope started.

At the same time, her mom said, "Just like Cassy."

"What's just like Cassy?"

"He disappear. Just like Cassy," her mom replied. "I never understood her." And her mother heaved a big sigh.

It was true. Hope had been the one to mother Cassidy. Cassidy had been a handful right from the start, screaming all the time, crying and crying, never soothed.

"She nothing like you. You such good baby." The note of nostalgia in her mother's voice surprised Hope. It was true, though. Hope hadn't been fussy, obeyed her parents as she got older, always earned straight As, and didn't worry them. "Only you could get Cassy to stop screaming. Stop those tantrums."

"You never wanted her, did you?" The words blurted out of Hope's mouth before she could stop them. She sucked in a breath, horrified. She'd never been so blunt with her mother before. Avoidance and ignoring the problem had always been their way.

"I . . . ," her mother stammered. Hope could feel her shock emanating down the phone line.

"I know you and Ba hadn't wanted another child." Now that Hope had opened her mouth, the words poured out of her. She didn't have the bandwidth right now to pretend with her mother, not when Luca was missing and it was Hope's fault. "I saw the way you sighed and turned away when Cassy used to cry as a child and reach out for you. And the way Ba always pressed his lips together tightly and left the room, when Cassy asked for money to go to the movies with her friends."

Hope had become Cassidy's defender, trying to pick up the slack when their parents neglected her. But she was still a child herself, and there was only so much she could do for her baby sister. There was only so much she could do to bridge the gap between Cassidy and their parents.

"We . . . we struggled, Hope." Her mother's voice was resigned. "We never had money. We didn't fit in."

Life had beaten them down. Moving to the States hadn't been the American dream for them. Hope's father's business hadn't taken off, and her mother had had to waitress in a Japanese restaurant to make ends meet. They hadn't known anyone here in New York, and had endured more than their share of racist slurs and people telling them to go back to where they came from.

"But she was your daughter too," Hope said.

"She so much trouble. Not listen to us. Like she not our daughter."

Hope inhaled sharply. She couldn't believe her mother had said that. Cassidy had been a mistake, and Hope knew her mother hadn't spared Cassidy from knowing that. No wonder her poor sister had acted out in her teen years. Their parents hadn't known how to handle a teenage Cassidy. She'd started drinking and smoking at thirteen, and who knew when she'd lost her virginity. Hope, who'd already been in college by then, wasn't around anymore to cover for her younger sister. When Cassidy was arrested for stealing a car, Hope had answered a frantic phone call from their mother.

"*Aiya*, Hope, Cassy—she steal car. Why she do that? We have car. She in jail. What we do?"

Hope had rushed home from college to bail Cassidy out and take care of the legal issues.

When Cassidy hadn't come home one night, their mom had called Hope again. "She gone! Not come home! I know she dead." And her mother had muttered something that was the Mandarin equivalent of "good riddance" under her breath. Hope had once again rushed home to find her sister, knowing her parents wouldn't.

"They hate me," Cassidy had said, when Hope had finally found her hiding at her best friend Dan Stern's house.

"No, they don't." Hope reached out to brush Cassidy's hair off her face. "They were so worried. Mom was upset because she thought you were dead."

Cassidy snorted. "She was only upset because they don't have the money to pay for my funeral."

Hope wanted to protest, but there was truth in what Cassidy was saying. And so it went through the years: Hope always to the rescue because Cassidy baffled their parents. They didn't understand her and didn't know how to control her except to enforce more rules, which only made Cassidy rebel more. The only person she'd ever listened to was Hope. But Hope had been caught up in her own life, meeting Shaun, getting engaged, planning their wedding. And to be honest, she was sick of always cleaning up after her sister. It was *her* turn to live, damn it. She'd taken care of Cassidy's messes her whole life, and Hope was tired. She wanted to put herself first for the first time since Cassidy was born. She'd started to resent all the chaos Cassidy created and had vowed to focus on her own life for once. And because of her selfishness, Cassidy had disappeared.

"Hope-ah?"

Her mother's voice brought Hope back to the present. She waited a moment to see if her mother would say more, and when she didn't, Hope sighed. She'd never been able to relate to her parents; what had made her think this time would be different? She'd tried, but when her parents had moved to California after Cassidy left, the gulf between them had widened. Now it felt like talking to a stranger, the few times a year she spoke to them on the phone.

"I have to go," Hope finally said.

"Let us know if you find him." Her mother said this in Mandarin. Hope could hear her father in the background, asking something.

Hope waited, wishing her mother would say something comforting, or convey whatever her father was saying. She couldn't help but hope that maybe this time, things would be different. But her mother said nothing else.

"Bye." Hope hung up, staring at her phone for a moment. Her heart hurt, but she needed all her strength to focus on getting Luca back. She pushed her parents to the back of her mind and looked up to see Shaun studying her with a look of concern.

"Fun times with the maternal figure." Hope tried to joke, but the smile on her face was forced.

He walked over and sat down on the couch next to her. Putting an arm around her, he pulled her close, and she laid her head on his shoulder. Even after seventeen years together, fourteen of them married, she and Shaun were still very much in sync. When one hurt, the other felt it. Hope didn't have to say aloud that Luca's disappearance was bringing back all the old feelings of guilt and helplessness she'd gone through when Cassidy disappeared. When Cassidy had turned up dead, the guilt and self-blame Hope had heaped on herself were unbearable. Only the presence of Luca, who needed her now that his mother was gone, had kept Hope from being pulled down by the loss of her sister. And now her nephew had gone missing on her watch and Shaun knew she blamed herself.

"We need to look at this logically, step back. Not get emotional." Shaun's voice came out as a rumble, since Hope's ear was so near his chest. "Officer Harmon said if they have any evidence that points to an abduction, detectives would 'respond out,' take over. So far, there's nothing. No ransom note, or phone call with instructions. No signs of a struggle, and so far, no one has seen anything, like Luca getting into a car with someone."

"So, you're thinking he might have left." Hope picked her head up to look at her husband.

He gave her a gentle smile. "Let's just play devil's advocate. Take your feelings out of this. If he left, why? And where would he go? He doesn't have any money, and if he really was planning on running away, why wouldn't he have packed a bag or taken Mochi's harness? Why just disappear from the driveway?"

"And also, why leave so late in the day, when it's going to get dark soon?"

"Right. Unless he had someone or somewhere that he was going to. But that comes back to the fact that he hasn't made any friends or close connections except for the Caine boys. And they were with Jalissa after school." Shaun stroked a hand through Hope's hair.

"Maybe he had contact with someone that he knew from his life before." Hope sat still, soothed from the way Shaun was stroking her hair.

"We need to search his room."

"You're right." Hope nodded. "But let's also play the other side. If he didn't run away, who took him? It had to be someone he knew. I didn't hear anything—no shouts, or loud noises, no signs of a struggle. Mochi didn't bark."

"We already told the police about that racist neighbor, and you spoke to Tessa. They've questioned George and Mr. Alden. And Beth and John down the street. Who else knows him from around here?"

"What about Jalissa and Jack?" Hope felt better, being able to talk out her suspicions with Shaun. "You know those rumors about Jack." Jack was a good-looking man with blond hair and blue eyes, who had left a string of broken hearts behind him when he married Jalissa. "Maybe an ex is trying to get back at him or he got involved in something shady and . . ." She trailed off because it sounded ridiculous even to her own ears.

"We still haven't heard from the police about the bus driver, Mike." There was a frown on Shaun's face. "Officer Harmon said he wasn't home when they went by earlier."

"I think we also need to look at Mr. Alden closer." Hope's eyes shifted in the direction of their neighbor's house. "I realized earlier that we've never seen anyone go in or out of his house. He always parks in his garage. He only leaves to get groceries. What if he's got kids stashed in his basement? Why does he have no friends?" A thought occurred to Hope, and her gaze flew to Shaun's. "He asked if Luca wanted to watch *Jeopardy!* with him earlier. Maybe he likes little boys."

34

They stared at each other for a moment until Shaun blew out a breath. "I don't know. That seems really far-fetched. I can't imagine Mr. Alden . . ."

"We should tell the police. Just in case. Have them search his place. What if Luca is in there right now?" Hope stood, turning to look in the direction of Mr. Alden's house.

"The police can't just barge into Mr. Alden's house without a warrant." He dropped his hand by his side when Hope started to protest. "Okay, no, you're right. We need to eliminate every possibility. I'm sure Mr. Alden would cooperate. I'll go talk to Officer Harmon."

"I can't fail Cassidy again."

Shaun stood and went to her, and she wrapped her arms around his waist, putting her cheek against the hard ridges of his chest as he pulled her close. He rubbed a hand up and down her back but didn't say anything, just let her cling to him as she fought tears.

"We'll find him." Hope felt, rather than heard Shaun's words. He dropped a kiss on the top of her head as she pulled away.

"What if Luca took a bus or train or something?" Hope was back to the running-away scenario. Her mind couldn't decide which one was more likely.

"I'm sure the police are checking on that. But I'll ask."

"Okay. I'm going to search his room. See if I can find anything useful." She'd given it a cursory look earlier, not finding anything of significance. But now it was full dark out and there was still no sign of Luca. She would turn his room upside down if she needed to.

Shaun nodded at her and then went back out into the night.

5

Hope stood in the doorway of Luca's room, which was across the hall from theirs. She turned on the light and surveyed it, almost expecting to find him and Mochi in the full-size bed. Mochi had slept in Luca's bed with him ever since they'd adopted her. But it was empty, the navy-blue comforter bunched up at the foot, the pillows thrown around, the sheet pulled out and hanging to the floor next to Mochi's stuffed Lamb Chop toy. Hope picked it up and studied it. It had lost its squeaker as well as most of the stuffing. She smiled, and for a moment, she was glad Luca had Mochi, wherever they were. At least he wasn't alone. Mochi was so devoted to Luca that she'd protect the boy as best as she could.

Hope and Shaun had been fostering dogs for years, ever since the pandemic started. When Luca had come to live with them, he had bonded with a pair of dogs they were fostering at the time, a black one named Shadow and a white one named Buttercup. Luca had been so good with both of them, helping to take care of them, feed them, and even picking up their poop on walks and in the backyard. When Shadow had been adopted a month and a half ago, Luca had been inconsolable. He'd cried when the new owners came to get Shadow, and stayed in his room all night with Buttercup, not even wanting dinner. Hope had found Luca curled up around Buttercup that night in his bed. He wouldn't talk. She'd sat at his side, silent. But finally, he'd rolled over and said, "Don't let her leave too."

His voice had been so sad that Hope's heart had broken in two. She'd looked up at Shaun, who was standing in the doorway, and known they had to adopt Buttercup.

"She can stay," Hope had said, after a nod from Shaun.

"Really?" The look on Luca's face was everything to Hope. It was every missed chance she'd had with Cassidy, making up for every time she had felt that she'd failed her sister.

Hope had nodded, a small smile on her lips, even as her heart cracked a little bit more at the wonder in his voice. "She's yours, Luca."

He'd stared at them as if trying to decide if they were for real, then buried his face in the dog's side. "I'm going to name her Mochi. She looks like the mochi snack my mom bought for me when we were in LA, all white with a sweet bean center." He picked his head up and looked at them. "Can I call her Mochi?"

Mochi leaned over and licked him on the face, making them laugh. "I think she likes her new name," Hope had said.

And Mochi hadn't left Luca's side since, except when he was at school.

Hope let the dog toy drop to the floor and sat on the edge of the bed. She saw an old ratty brown bear partially under a pillow. She picked it up and studied it. The bear had been Cassidy's, the one that Hope had bought her when Cassidy managed to graduate from high school by the skin of her teeth. Hope had convinced Cassidy to go out to dinner with their parents to celebrate her graduation at the fancy Chinese restaurant the next town over. Cassidy had sat there, sullen, while their parents toasted her with hot oolong tea.

"Why do we always have to eat at Chinese restaurants?" Cassidy had grumbled to Hope under her breath. "Why can't we have Italian like normal people for once?"

Hope shushed Cassidy. "You know Ma and Ba—"

Cassidy cut her off. "They act like they still live in China or Taiwan. Don't they know we're in America?"

Hope had whacked Cassidy over the head with the teddy bear she'd bought her. Right after high school, Cassidy had moved out. She'd slept on friends' couches and wandered around the country, often out of touch for months. She didn't want to go to college, and never seemed to have a job.

Hope looked at the teddy bear in her hand. When Luca had come to live with them, she'd been surprised to see him clutching the old bear. It must have meant something to Cassidy if she'd kept it all these years and then given it to Luca. Perhaps Cassidy had loved her deep down after all and she'd thought of Hope these past years.

Hope placed the bear back on the bed and then looked around the room. Other than the bed, the rest of the room was neat. Books stacked by size on the bookshelf, his closet door closed, and his desk empty except for the cup holding his pens and pencils. Officer Harmon had explained to them that the police had done only a cursory search earlier, looking for the actual boy. They'd taken Luca's school iPad, which they'd found on his desk, in case there was something in it that would give them a clue. Any deeper searches would be conducted later if detectives responded out.

Where to start? Hope got off the bed and opened the desk drawers, rummaging around inside. They held the expected notebooks, folders, papers, and other school supplies. In the bottom drawer was a stack of Fishnacks bags, the dried fish-strip Taiwanese snacks that Luca loved so much. Cassidy had loved them too. She'd looked forward to the times when they went to the Asian grocery store and their father would buy them each a bag of the salty, chewy treat. Hope would usually eat only a few strips and then give Cassy the rest of hers. Luca had inherited Cassidy's love of them, and when Hope had found out, she'd bought him many bags the last time she'd gone to the Asian market.

She picked up the open packet on top and brought it to her face, the not-unpleasant fishy smell assaulting her senses. She was surprised when her nose prickled and tears stung in her eyes. Fishnacks always made her think of her sister. She set the bag back in the drawer and shut it quickly, looking around to see what else was in the room. She spied Luca's backpack on the floor next to the desk, and looked in it. But there was nothing of interest, only his school folder, a notebook, and the water bottle he hadn't unpacked yet. She placed the water bottle on his desk, intending to take it to the kitchen once she was done here.

Hope walked to the night table next to the bed and opened the top drawer. She found his key chain collection from around the United States and her heart constricted, thinking of the bubble tea one the police had found in the woods. Had Luca merely fallen, or had someone hurt him? Shaking the image aside, she lifted out a comic book, some odds and ends, and a box that held a collection of shells and rocks. She assumed Luca and Cassidy had collected them from their travels. She was about to shut the box when she noticed writing on some of the shells. Curious, she took one out and squinted at the tiny words.

CAPE COD, 5-23-16

Hope took out another one, a bigger rock so it was easier to read the writing on it.

SHELBY, SD, 3-1-18

She'd never even heard of Shelby, South Dakota. Hope sat on the bed and continued taking out shells and rocks, studying each one.

TAMPA, 12-25-15

SAN DIEGO, 6-4-21

TUCSON, 8-4-17

BAR HARBOR, ME, 7-15-22

AUSTIN, 7-23-21

EMMY'S FARM, 2-3-23

Hope picked up this last rock. Emmy. Luca had mentioned her. A woman they'd met camping out West somewhere, who had a goat and whom Luca stayed with sometimes when Cassidy had to go away. Hope couldn't remember Emmy's last name. Could Luca have gone back to her? But Emmy was on the other side of the country, and how would Hope even find her without a last name?

Hope dumped out the entire box of shells and rocks. Was this a map of where Cassidy and Luca had been ever since they'd left? If she put them in date order, would it show her the path they'd taken in the years they were away? Luca hadn't talked very much about his life with his mother. Hope knew he was grieving and probably in shock, so she hadn't pushed, thinking he'd talk about Cassidy when he was ready. When he trusted Hope. Had he gone back to one of these places because it meant something to them? But why would he have left suddenly like that? Why not pack a bag?

With a sigh, Hope replaced the shells and rocks and then put the box back in the top drawer. Leaning down, she opened the bottom drawer. A used tissue, one sock that appeared clean, a small stuffed monkey, and a large bulging manila envelope. Under it was another iPad, its dark-blue cover worn and stuck together in places by duct tape.

Hope hadn't known Luca had another iPad. Where had it come from? Had Cassidy given it to him? She turned it around, puzzling over this. She'd never seen Luca using anything except the one provided by the school. She opened it, but it was password protected. Putting it aside, Hope decided she would show Shaun when he came in.

Her attention returned to the manila envelope. She took it out of the drawer and looked at it. There was nothing written on the front. She opened the flap, reached in, and drew out a pile of paper—all small pieces, some ripped from a larger sheet of paper, some that appeared to be from a notepad. She immediately recognized Cassidy's handwriting. Her sister had always had very loopy writing, girlish with large embellishments.

Her heart quickening, Hope looked at the one at the top of the pile.

> Hi Monkey, I left your assignment for the day on the
> kitchen counter. I need to go see someone—should
> be back next week. Emmy said you can stay with her
> like always until I get back. Be a good boy and help
> take care of her goat, okay? You can also help Emmy
> with the other animals. Remember our assignment on
> farm animals? And if you figure out that bonus math
> problem, I'll bring you a surprise. Love you.

Hope swallowed. Here was Emmy again. Hope wondered where Cassidy had gone when she left Luca with Emmy. She knew Cassidy hadn't completely kicked her addictions, from the little that Luca had let slip. Had she trusted Emmy to watch Luca when she relapsed? Maybe somewhere in all these handwritten notes, she would find a clue as to Emmy's location or last name.

Luca had also told them Cassidy had been homeschooling him. This had surprised Hope, since Cassidy had hated school. They'd expected Luca to be behind when they enrolled him, but he'd soon proven that he was well within the third-grade level. Judging from this note, it seemed Cassidy really had kept Luca up to date on schoolwork. This was so unlike the sister Hope thought she knew.

Putting the note aside, Hope read the next one.

> Haha, very funny Monkey. You thought I wouldn't
> find the monkey stuffed into my shoe? Now you have
> to find him. I think it's going to take you a while . . .

Hope hadn't known that Cassidy had called Luca "Monkey." Luca had never mentioned it. She leaned over and took the small stuffed monkey out of the bottom drawer. Was this the monkey that they'd apparently taken turns hiding from each other? Her heart lifted to think that Cassidy and Luca had shared what appeared to have been a great bond. But then Hope's cheeks warmed. What did that say about her? That she'd always assumed Cassidy was a bad mother because she couldn't get herself together?

Looking at the next note only affirmed how wrong Hope was.

> You know it's wrong to steal something that's not yours right, Monkey? When I take perfectly good food that people leave behind at campsites, that's not stealing. But if you go into a store and take candy that you didn't pay for, that's stealing. We don't do that. We may not have much, but we won't resort to stealing. I know you're mad at me right now, but you can't play with the kids today.

And again, Hope flushed. She'd thought Cassidy would have resorted to stealing if she wasn't working. But it sounded like she'd instilled good values in Luca, which Hope had seen for herself in the two months Luca had been living with them. He was polite, neat, organized, and thoughtful. Hope bit her lips. She'd imagined the worst about her sister. A part of her felt wrong reading Cassidy's private notes to Luca, but at the same time, she knew nothing about their lives. And if she was going to find a clue as to what had happened to Luca, she needed to keep reading.

Even if a small part of her knew she was doing this for her own gratification, she yearned to know more about the sister who had disappeared from her life. A sister she really didn't know.

◆ ◆ ◆

Half an hour later, after reading through most of the pile of notes that Luca had evidently kept, Hope had a better idea of her sister as a mother. She'd been a great one. And she had worked, picking up shifts at grocery stores in whatever town they were in, waitressing or bartending if she could convince someone to hire her, and either brought Luca with her or found someone to watch him. If they could afford it, they rented a room or studio, and if not, Cassidy was somehow able to find someone willing to let them stay for a few weeks. Emmy was mentioned several times, but no last name, not even what state she lived in. When they couldn't find anywhere to crash, they slept at campgrounds in their car and used the showers and facilities.

Hope had been wrong to judge Cassidy. Maybe their nomadic lifestyle wasn't normal to most people, who needed a home and a steady job. But it sounded like they had been happy, as long as they'd had each other. They might not have had much, but Cassidy had kept Luca fed, clothed, and educated. A part of Hope had to admit that traveling around the US was a pretty good education in and of itself. Luca got to see places most children only read about. And while Hope had imagined that they never had enough to eat, from the notes Cassidy had left for Luca, it sounded like she was always able to feed him. Maybe they hadn't been the most inspiring meals, but he'd never gone without.

Picking up one of the last remaining notes in the envelope, Hope started reading. But then her whole body froze. This one had a different tone. The ink looked fresher, as if it were recent, and the paper was still bright white, not faded like some of the others.

> Monkey, promise me. If anything were to happen to me, go to your Aunt Hope. Your Ayi. You have her address and phone number. I gave it to you years ago, remember? I also saved it for you in Dan, along with other information you'll need if something happens to me. I don't want to scare you, but this is very important. I love you so much Monkey. I hope I'm wrong. But I need to keep you safe. Find Hope if you need to.

Hope read the note over and over again, trying to figure out what it meant. Had someone been after Cassidy? What had she been so scared of? Did Luca know? And what had Cassidy meant by "I also saved it for you in Dan"? Was she referring to her old best friend, Dan Stern? Luca had never once said a word to her about this.

Jumping off the bed with the note still clutched in her hand, Hope picked up the old iPad. She needed to show the note to Shaun and the police. She had a bad feeling about it.

6

The day of
10:05 p.m.

The police and the dogs had been out for hours, knocking on doors, searching the vast wooded areas in the neighborhood. It had been five hours since Luca and Mochi disappeared, and there was no trace of them, even with so many people looking on land and from above. There was no ransom note, no phone calls. Just a whole lot of nothing. But the police reassured them they would continue searching into the night.

Hope headed for the front door, intending to give the notes and the iPad to Officer Harmon. But for some reason, she paused with her hand on the front doorknob, and instead turned and went into her bedroom, slipping Luca's iPad into her night table drawer. She didn't know why, but the urge to see what was on it first was so strong that she couldn't fight it. She promised herself if she couldn't get into it by morning, she would turn it over to the police.

She found Shaun talking with a group of officers by a police car in front of their house. "Anything new?" she called out.

Her husband shook his head. "They bagged the key chain and just brought it over." He held out the plastic bag containing the bauble.

Hope took it from him and studied it. It was Luca's bubble tea key chain, purple to depict the taro flavor. She noticed that the actual ring of the key chain was no longer attached to the bubble tea.

She looked up. "This is Luca's." She took in a quick breath and then released it through her mouth. "What happened to him?"

Officer Harmon spoke up. "We don't know, but we're guessing he went down the hill through those woods. Maybe he fell and the key chain came undone. The dogs followed his scent down to the road and then nothing."

"I don't get it. Did he just disappear?" Hope looked around at all the faces surrounding her, lit by only the one streetlamp across the street and the flashing red and blue lights of the police car parked in front of their house.

An officer that Hope hadn't seen before spoke up. "Or someone picked him up in a car from the road down by the lake."

"Oh god. Who would have taken him?" Hope reached out to clutch Shaun's arm, dropping the envelope in her hand.

Shaun bent to retrieve it. "What's this?"

"I found it in Luca's drawer." Hope was still thinking of the horror of someone grabbing Luca and Mochi and stuffing them in a car before driving off. Her eyes stung as she tried to bring her focus back to the envelope and the last note clutched in her hand.

"What is it?" Officer Harmon asked, taking the envelope from Shaun.

"They're notes that my sister wrote to Luca over the years. Most are just little notes between them, but this one"—she waved the piece of paper in her hand—"this is the one that concerns me. I think my sister was afraid of someone. I don't know if it has anything to do with Luca's disappearance but . . ."

She held it out and Officer Harmon took it from her.

He scanned the handwriting and nodded. "Okay, we'll look into this." He stepped away and spoke into his radio.

The officer Hope didn't know spoke up. "I'm Officer Reilly. I was just coming over to say that we found footage of George Manning on the gym's security cameras. He was there at the time Luca disappeared. The front desk staff remembered him checking in."

Hope's shoulders slumped forward in defeat. Another dead end. "Then why was he at our house?"

"His fiancée recently broke up with him." Officer Reilly looked at Hope, abashed. "She's Japanese. I guess George transferred his feelings for her to you."

Hope's nose scrunched up, and she and Shaun shared a look. "One of those."

Officer Reilly looked confused. "One of what?"

"Guys with yellow fever, who have an Asian-girl fetish." Hope made a face. "It doesn't matter that I'm not Japanese. I'm Asian; therefore I'm lumped into the same category as his ex."

"Oh." Officer Reilly paused, then nodded. "Sounds about right. But anyways, unless he was working with someone, he couldn't have taken Luca. We did advise him to stop following you and to leave you alone."

"Thanks." Hope looked at the officers standing with them. "What happens now? It's so late. Are you going to call off the search?"

"No. We'll keep searching, into the night." Officer Harmon came back and gave them a reassuring look. "You should try to get some rest. Just keep your phone on you at all times, in case Luca or someone else calls you."

Hope covered her mouth with one hand, biting her lips to keep from crying out. At this point, she didn't know whether to hope for a phone call or not. Not knowing what had happened to Luca was excruciating, but at the same time, if they got a call, how could she bear knowing someone had taken her nephew and done who knew what to him? Which was worse?

Her ears buzzed and she tuned out, looking down the dark street in vain, wishing Luca and Mochi would appear and end this nightmare. But nothing happened. She allowed Shaun to guide her back into their house once they were done with the police.

"Why don't you take a bath, relax?" Shaun suggested as they walked into their bedroom. "The police are right. They'll keep searching, and we can do more tomorrow with a clearer head." They'd both taken the next day off from work.

Hope's eyes zoomed over to where she'd hidden Luca's iPad. She was itching to try to open it. She didn't want to tell Shaun about it yet—she knew he'd tell her to hand it over to the police right away. "You can take a shower first."

"Okay." He came over and looked her in the eyes. "Are you okay?"

"No," she answered honestly. "But I'm not going to fall apart, if that's what you're asking." She wasn't. She would do whatever she could to find Luca and hold it together until he came home.

As soon as Shaun closed the bathroom door, Hope took Luca's iPad out of the night table and stared at it. A sudden memory came over her. Cassidy, at about five, trying to say the Mandarin word for computer, *dian nao*. Hope spoke some Mandarin with her parents, but Cassidy had never picked it up. Her pronunciation was atrocious, according to their parents, and it came out sounding more like *dan now*. Cassidy had called computers Dan from then on.

What had that last note from Cassidy said? Hope tapped her iPhone to bring it to life. She'd taken a picture of it before giving it to the police. "I saved it for you in Dan." Had she meant Luca's iPad, the one Hope held now, and not Dan Stern, her best friend? Was there information in here that would help Hope figure out what or who Cassidy was afraid of?

Taking in a breath, Hope was more grateful now that she hadn't immediately turned the iPad over to the police. She needed to see what Cassidy had put on here for Luca. Knowing she had only six attempts

48

before the iPad locked her out, she had to be careful about what numbers she tried. The first part was easy: 4482 had always been Cassidy's go-to whenever she needed a passcode—44 because in Mandarin, the number four sounded like the word for "death," and most Chinese people avoided it. But Cassidy, rebel that she was, had delighted in saying her favorite number was four, making their parents cringe. And she always used two fours because what was better than two deaths? The 82 was for her birthday, August second.

But what would she have used for the other two digits? Hope racked her memory. She knew Cassidy had used a six-digit passcode before. It had something to do with Dan Stern. And then it came to her. Dan had played football for one year in high school, and his jersey number had been . . . Shit, what was it? Something that ended with a seven. Thirty-seven? Twenty-seven? Holding her breath, Hope tried 37 first, but it was wrong. She tried it with 27. Still no luck.

Shit. Two down, four more to go before the iPad locked her out. Hope had thought it most likely that Cassidy would have put the 4482 first. At least, the old Cassidy would have done this. She wasn't sure what the Cassidy of the past nine years would have done. Maybe she'd flipped them? She tried it with the 37 first, but again, it failed to open.

She heard the shower turn off and tried it again, but starting with the 27. Nope. Not it either. And now she had only two attempts left. Hope tried to think like Cassidy. But the problem was, too many years had gone by and she had no idea who Cassidy was anymore. Since it was Luca's iPad, maybe she would have put his birth date? Hope punched in the 4482 first and then Luca's birthday and . . .

Nothing.

She had only one more attempt left. She could hear Shaun brushing his teeth and knew he'd be out any minute. Closing the iPad, she put it back into her night table. Maybe something would come to her overnight. She knew there was no way she could sleep. Her mind was going a million miles per hour, spinning from one theory to another, trying to find something, anything she had missed that might tell them why Luca was gone. Even though he'd taken Mochi, Hope didn't believe in her gut that Luca had run away. He had been starting to come out of his shell and talking to them more, even requesting the mapo tofu for dinner. She'd overheard him talking to Mochi recently, when he hadn't known Hope was in hearing distance. He'd told Mochi how glad he was to have her as his dog, and to have his ayi and uncle and Toby. He was looking forward to basketball camp. He'd made friends with Andrew Caine across the street, and they were going to go to the beach every day they weren't at basketball camp.

These were not the actions of a boy planning to run away. But if he hadn't left by himself, then who would have taken him?

7

Hope had been sure she'd never fall asleep, but somehow, it was the next morning and the sun shone through the curtains where she hadn't closed them all the way. She remembered that Luca was gone the minute her eyes opened. There was no haziness, or moment of blissful unawareness when her mind hadn't quite caught up to reality.

She blinked in the morning light and rubbed a hand over her eyes. Picking her phone off the night table, she checked to see if she'd gotten a message from the police. Nothing. Hope blew out a shaky breath. After slipping out of bed quietly so she wouldn't disturb Shaun, she walked to the bedroom door, Toby following her from his dog bed, where he had been curled up all night.

Hope paused in Luca's doorway, wishing more than anything she'd find him in bed and that last night had just been a bad dream. But his room was empty. No Luca, no Mochi. Her heart ached and she blinked rapidly. She couldn't give in to the tears. She needed to stay clearheaded. She needed to figure this out.

After turning on the pot of coffee that she'd prepared the night before, she let Toby out into the fenced-in yard. She watched him from the back door and rubbed her forehead, where a headache was starting to bloom. When the coffee was ready, Hope made herself a mugful doctored with milk and sugar, and took it out onto the back patio. She sat down and inhaled the fragrant aroma before taking her first life-affirming sip. Letting out a sigh, she settled back in her chair, her mind drifting back to Cassidy and when she'd first told Hope she was pregnant with Luca.

The sound of the door opening startled her, and she turned to see Shaun coming onto the deck.

"You look deep in thought." He walked to her side.

Hope gave a little shrug. "Just thinking of Cassidy. I wish she'd stayed with us when she was pregnant. Let us help her. Maybe she'd still be alive."

Shaun placed a hand on Hope's shoulder, and the weight of it reassured her. "There's only so much you can do to help someone. They have to be willing to change."

"I know." Hope's voice was low. Shaun had said this to her over the years whenever Hope had beaten herself up for not helping her sister more. He had seen Cassidy at her worst more than a few times. Eyes bloodshot and puffy, darting around as if searching for something. Twitchy, shifting from one foot to the other, her face dirty and marked with acne, bruises on her arms, and her speech slurred. "But she told me she could stay clean. For Luca."

When Cassidy had realized she was pregnant, she'd called to tell Hope. Hope had begged her sister to come stay with them so that they could help her with the baby. But Cassidy had refused. Hope remembered the fire in her sister's voice when Cassidy had told her she was keeping the baby, that she could stay clean. For a few seconds, the old Cassidy, the little girl who had begged for piggyback rides, who had followed Hope around everywhere, asking questions, was back.

Cassy had said to Hope, "There's something I can take to help with cravings. Bu . . . bubreno . . . something."

"You don't have health insurance." Their parents had taken Cassidy off their plan when she refused to go to college. Hope had argued with them, but they said only they couldn't afford it.

"There are clinics I can go to . . . or I can get them some other way." Cassidy's voice was determined. "I can do it. I can stay clean. I want this baby."

Shaun's voice brought Hope back to the present. "She never told you who the father was?" There were things that Hope hadn't shared with him about Cassidy. It hurt too much to think about her sister sometimes.

Hope sighed and pulled away from Shaun to look up at him. "She either didn't know, or wouldn't tell me. I always hoped Dan is Luca's father."

"He's a good guy." Shaun pulled out a chair and sat down.

Cassidy and Dan had never dated, but Hope knew Dan would have leaped at the opportunity if Cassidy had given him half a chance. Hope had thought they'd get together back in high school. Dan was steady, the exact opposite of Cassidy, and a good balance for her sister. But Cassidy had only ever seen him as a friend.

"He is." Hope nodded in agreement. "He talked Cassy out of more than one crazy scheme and always watched out for her."

"Where's he now?"

"I can't remember. Somewhere out West." Hope took a sip of her coffee and then let out a grunt of frustration. "Why couldn't she have just accepted our offer to help?"

"You can't change the past. And besides, she didn't want to crash our honeymoon pad." There was a hint of laughter in Shaun's voice. But he was right. They'd only recently moved to this house back then and were still unpacking.

"I'm going to get some coffee." Shaun stood. "Want a refill?"

Hope drained her mug. "I'll come in with you." She called to Toby, and they followed Shaun into the kitchen. While he refilled her mug and got himself one, she wandered over to the window by the front door.

Pushing the curtain aside, she noted that no one was stationed at the corner. It was probably too early for the news crew. Her eyes scanned the surroundings and went to the three mailboxes across the street: theirs, Mr. Alden's, and one for the empty house across from them. The Caines' mailbox was right in front of their house. All the mailboxes were on that side, making it easier for the carrier to deliver their mail. The door to theirs was open, and Hope realized they hadn't checked their box in a few days.

"I'm going to get the mail," she called out to Shaun. "Before the news crews show up again."

"Good idea," he replied.

Slipping on her flip-flops, Hope unlocked the front door and ran across the street to their mailbox. She pulled out the pile, slammed the door shut, and looked around. There was a police car parked on the corner, and she could hear activity down by the beach. It reassured her that they were still searching for Luca. She crossed the street back to their house and closed the door firmly behind her.

With a sigh, she glanced at the bundle of mail in her hands. The top envelope caught her attention. It was hand addressed to her, and Hope's breath hitched. She'd recognize the handwriting anywhere. It was Cassidy's, an exact match for the handwriting in the notes to Luca that Hope had found yesterday.

The world spun for a moment as Hope rubbed her eyes, not quite believing what she was seeing. Where had this letter come from? Studying it more closely, she realized there was no stamp on it. It had been personally delivered to their mailbox.

The hair on her arms suddenly stood up, and Hope whirled around, her eyes scanning the street through the window. Was Cassidy here? Had she taken her son? But in the next instance, Hope knew that was ridiculous. Cassidy was dead. Hope had ID'd her sister's body, seen with her own eyes the lifeless form that used to be Cassidy. Even though it'd been more than nine years since she'd seen her, Hope had recognized her right away.

So where had this letter come from? Who had stuck it into their mailbox? She put the rest of the mail on the bench by the door and sank down on it. Her ears buzzing, she tore into the envelope and took out a sheet of cream stationery filled front and back in Cassidy's loopy, elaborate handwriting. Hope saw that it was dated a month after the last time she had seen Cassidy and Luca.

Dear Hope,

I've started writing to you so many times. I don't even know if I will send this to you. I don't know if it's safe. I guess I'm writing this for me, since you'll probably not see this ever.

I never thought I'd want to be a mom, but Luca has changed my life. I find myself fiercely protective of him. It's why we had to go. For a week or so there, I thought we could live with you and Shaun and I could give Luca a better life. But I was stupid to think that I could have the kind of life that you were building for yourself. A husband, a new house in a lake community, a steady job. But that was never me, right? You know I can't stay still in one place long. It's like an itch, the need to move and see places and try new things. For Luca though, I thought I could stay with you for a while before finding an apartment for the two of us.

But just as I was starting to envision a new life and a home of our own without drugs or alcohol, my past caught up with me. I was stupid to think it wouldn't. I couldn't tell you about it because they threatened me. Said if I told anyone, that they would hurt Luca. I had to go away, and stay far away. Or they'd take Luca from me.

So I left. They sent me money through MoneyGram and said they would every month, as long as I stayed away. If I came back, the money would stop and they would take Luca. I wanted to say good-bye to you, but I couldn't. I'm sorry, Hope. I know I'm your flighty little sister who always caused problems but I always knew I could come to you when I needed. But now, for the first time in our lives, I can't. I can't tell you why I left if it will put Luca in danger. I'm sorry for everything. But I'll figure it out and hope-fully, we can come home soon.

Love,

Cassy

Hope looked up, her face a mass of confusion as her mind spun. Was Cassidy still alive?

"Shaun!" Hope yelled for her husband. He wasn't in the kitchen anymore. She looked around, and saw that he and Toby had gone back out on the deck. She ran to the kitchen door and pulled it open. "Shaun, you have to see this."

Shaun's head whipped over to hers, his eyes widening in alarm at her tone. "What's the matter? Is it Luca?"

"No." Hope held out the letter in her hand. "I found this in our mailbox just now. A letter. From Cassidy."

"What?" Shaun's face was scrunched up. He scrubbed a hand down his cheek. "What do you mean?"

"This letter. It's from Cassidy." Hope's voice rose. "It's her handwriting."

Shaun took it from her and read it, then looked at Hope, his forehead furrowed. "What's going on? How did this get in our mailbox?"

"I don't know. It's dated about a month after we last saw them." Hope paced in front of Shaun, thinking back in time.

Cassy had shown up at their doorstep a few months after Luca was born. She looked good. She told Hope that she'd been clean since she found out she was pregnant. Cassidy's eyes were clear, her skin glowing, and Luca was well cared for and happy. Hope wanted them to move into their house, but Cassy wouldn't make any promises. She stayed for two weeks, and for the first time in their lives, they existed as equals.

Gone was the flighty, irresponsible girl Cassidy had been ever since her teenage years. She even made breakfast for Hope and Shaun since she was up with the baby. They fell into a routine, an easy truce between the sisters. Hope had thought her sister would finally stay put this time. For Luca.

But then, toward the end of those two weeks, Cassidy had gotten a series of phone calls that put her on edge. Hope had come across her after one of them, muttering to herself and pacing the guest room.

"Cassy, what's wrong?"

Cassidy just shook her head. "Nothing. I've got it under control. I can take care of it."

Hope had let it go, not wanting to pressure Cassidy. But then Cassidy and Luca had disappeared later that same night. Hope still remembered the bitter disappointment that had washed through her when she'd woken up to find them gone, along with the emergency money Cassidy knew Hope kept in a kitchen cabinet. There had been almost a thousand dollars in there, but it wasn't about the money. Hope would have gladly given it to Cassidy if she'd asked. It was the betrayal that had wounded Hope the most. She'd thought Cassidy had finally grown up, that they could finally have a real relationship. She should have known Cassidy would leave again, stealing from her in the process.

She didn't know it then, but that was the last time she'd see her sister alive. She'd been so mad at Cassidy that she hadn't bothered looking for her for the longest time. But later, how Hope had regretted not pressing Cassidy to tell her what was wrong. If Cassidy had only let her, Hope would have done anything to help her. The anger had carried her for many months, and she refused to speak of her sister to anyone. When her parents called to ask if she'd heard from Cassidy, Hope had been brusque and told them she hadn't and didn't care.

Now Hope stared at Shaun, guilt washing over her. Something *had* been wrong. Her sister had been scared of someone, and Hope hadn't helped her.

"What's going on, Shaun?" Hope's legs felt like they were going to collapse, and she sank onto a chair. "What does this mean? Why are we just getting this now, the day after Luca disappeared?"

"We need to tell the police." Shaun gave the letter back to Hope and stood.

"Do you think Cassidy is alive?" Hope asked, her voice trembling. Shaun turned to look at her. "You ID'd her body."

"I know but . . ." She rubbed her head. "I don't understand what's going on." It was as if she'd been given a puzzle but didn't have the first clue how to begin to piece it together. Hope turned the envelope around, hoping to find something, but besides her name and address, there was nothing else on it. No return address, no postmark stamp, nothing to indicate how the letter had ended up in their mailbox.

Maybe whoever had put it in the mailbox had taken Luca. Maybe it was the same people who had scared Cassidy all those years ago. All Hope knew was that she would keep digging until she figured out what had made Cassidy leave her back then.

8

An hour later, Hope was alone in the house. They'd made a copy of the letter and given the original to the officer who had shown up at their door after they called. Officer Harmon had contacted them soon after that, and told them to expect detectives soon, who would be taking over. Shaun had to stop by the hospital to find paperwork that someone was looking for and to delegate other stuff so he could take off as long as needed. Hopefully, they would find Luca soon and this would be the only day he missed. Hope couldn't imagine what she would do if Luca didn't come home today.

Hope herself had sent an email last night to her boss that she wouldn't be back until Luca was found safe and sound. The yoga manager could take over her duties for a few days; they often covered for each other. Hope did the scheduling for the group-fitness classes at the gym, was the point of contact for her instructors, and ran interference with unhappy members who often had self-serving complaints. Faced with Luca's disappearance, Hope knew the disgruntled comments from members who wanted a Zumba class at a certain time and couldn't understand why she couldn't schedule it would be far from her mind. She had more important things to think about right now. Luca and Mochi had now been missing for more than twelve hours. They *had* to find them soon.

Hope sat at the breakfast bar and reread Cassidy's letter, wishing with all her might that her sister really was alive. What she wouldn't give to see her again, hold her in her arms, and tell her she was sorry that she hadn't done more to find her. Hope had hired a private investigator after almost a year of no contact from Cassidy, even though she couldn't really afford it. Worry and guilt about her sister and the baby had finally taken over. What if something had happened to them? Cassidy had never gone that long without at least texting Hope to let her know she was alive. The initial anger had turned to fear, and she'd tried to find her sister by herself but had come up empty.

A year after Cassy's disappearance, the investigator, Mel, had tracked her to Miami. Mel even managed to speak to Cassidy, who was working behind the counter of a deli. Mel had urged Cassidy to call her sister. There'd been no sign of Luca, and when Mel had asked about the child, Cassidy had flung off the apron around her waist and run out the back door. Mel had followed Cassidy to a campsite and contacted Hope, asking what she wanted her to do.

Hope sighed now, remembering the relief, like a shower of cold water, when she learned her sister was alive. But then that anger had come back because here she was, worried sick about Cassidy, and she was fine, probably living it up on the beaches of Miami. She'd been about to tell Mel to approach Cassy again and convince her to speak to Hope when her phone had dinged with an incoming text from an unfamiliar number. But the message was clear.

Stop wasting your money. Leave me and Luca alone. I mean it. Or else you'll never see us again.

The white-hot rage had erupted into something bigger, and for a moment, Hope actually hated her sister. How selfish Cassidy was, disappearing like that and now threatening Hope, who had only ever tried to help her. In a fit of anger, Hope had called off the PI. She knew her sister well enough to know she meant it. There was no point in tracing the number—Cassidy had most likely borrowed a phone from someone. And she'd be gone by the next day. At least she'd said "me and Luca," so Hope knew her nephew was fine. She'd let them go, washing her hands figuratively of her sister, and told Shaun she was glad not to have that burden in her life. She was sure Cassidy would come crawling back to her once she needed money.

But she never heard another word about her sister again. Until the day the police came to tell her that Cassidy had overdosed in her car, just a town over, and that Luca had been with her. Hope would never forget how the world had tilted for her that day. The news had stolen the breath from her body. She hadn't even known Cassidy and Luca were back in the area.

Looking down at the copy of the letter in her hand, Hope shivered. Was Cassidy alive? Could the woman Hope had ID'd a couple of months ago not have been her sister? As Hope stared at the letter, her mind suddenly latched on to something in her subconscious. Cassidy had said in the letter that she'd wanted to confide in Hope back then. If she'd been a better sister, would Cassidy have told her what was happening or, at the very least, not disappeared without a word? But Cassidy had told Luca to find Hope if anything happened to her. She'd put Hope's info in Luca's iPad. And she'd written this letter to her, even if Hope hadn't gotten it until now.

Hope put the letter down and went into her bedroom, retrieving Luca's iPad from her nightstand. Walking back to the kitchen, she punched in her own birthday, 090483. Just like that, the iPad opened. Hope blinked, not quite believing that she'd figured out the password. Sinking back onto the stool, she took a breath and let her eyes roam over the home page, looking at the icons.

She clicked on a few: games, apps, music, and photos. She paused, looking through them. The most recent ones were of the dogs, including Mochi with Shadow before Shadow was adopted. Then they were mostly of Luca with Cassidy.

She traced a finger over a picture of Cassidy. Her sister was smiling, her eyes nearly shut with glee. Cassidy had always hated that about her eyes. Hated that when she smiled too widely, her eyes went nearly into slits, causing kids to make fun of her when she was younger. Her sister had complained she was basically a walking stereotype of an Asian person. She'd lamented that she hadn't gotten the double-lidded eyes only Hope had inherited from their mother. Hope smiled, thinking of how Cassidy used to try to draw in an extra eyelid with eyeliner to make her eyes appear larger.

She clicked out of the photos and looked at the icons again. The most logical place that Cassidy would store Hope's info would be in the contacts. She tapped on the icon, and when the app opened, she saw it had only two names, Cassidy's and Hope's. She went to her own name, and when she opened it, she saw her cell number, address, and birthday, but that was it. Where was the "info" that Cassidy had alluded to in her note to Luca? Why was there only her and Cassidy's contact info in here? Where was their parents' information? And what about Emmy, whom Luca had told her about? Thinking of Emmy, Hope wondered if she knew Cassidy had died.

Hope shook her head in frustration. Somewhere on this iPad was a clue as to what Cassidy and Luca's life had been like. Hope was sure of this. She was starting to think that Cassidy and Luca's disappearance all those years ago had something to do with Luca's disappearance now. It was just a feeling, a niggling in her gut, but it was growing stronger by the minute. If she could only figure out what Cassidy had been afraid of, so afraid she'd taken her son and run from her only family, maybe she could figure out what had happened to her nephew.

Letting out a huff of exasperation, she was about to click open every app on the iPad when the doorbell rang. Putting the iPad aside, Hope ran to the door, hoping it was Luca. But she found two strange men on the doorstep.

"Mrs. Chen? I'm Detective Hanson, and this is Detective Regel." The tall, burly man with a mustache, who appeared to be in his fifties, held out his badge. His partner, a younger man with sandy hair, gave her a nod.

"Oh yes. Officer Harmon said to expect you." Hope was grateful to see the detectives, yet at the same time, something sank in her stomach. Detectives meant they were taking Luca's disappearance more seriously, that they no longer believed he'd run away.

"Can we come in?" Detective Hanson asked. "We need to ask you some questions."

"Yes." Hope stepped back to allow them to enter.

After some preliminary questions, Detective Regel got down to business. "I understand you want us to look into your neighbors more closely. You had some concerns about them?"

Hope nodded, feeling as if she were ratting them out. But they had to be sure, to be able to eliminate them and move on to other suspects.

"I feel like Mr. Alden is hiding something. I feel bad saying this but . . ." Hope trailed off, twisting her hands together in her lap. What was she doing, throwing her neighbors under the bus? Was she just being paranoid?

"It's okay, go on," Detective Hanson said.

"I don't know. I guess I'd just feel better if you spoke to him again. Make sure he's not keeping Luca in his basement or something." Hope laughed, but it wasn't a joyful sound.

"And the Caines?" Detective Regel asked.

"I know them well." Hope looked away, uncomfortable with bringing up her friends. "Luca is good friends with Andrew Caine. They're in the same grade at school. Maybe Luca said something to him that he didn't want to say to us?"

"Mrs. Chen. We did question all the Caine boys with their mother last night, but we'll go back and question Andrew again. Maybe Luca had said something that he didn't think was important but might give us a clue as to what was going on in his mind." Detective Hanson waited until Hope met his eyes. "Also, Jack Caine didn't want to give us his front-door camera footage at first. In fact, he outright refused, until we told him that we'd still get it, even if we had to get a warrant."

"What?" Hope's forehead creased. "Why?"

"Is there anything about the Caines that has raised your radar in the past?"

Hope looked at the detectives, trying to read their minds. What were they getting at?

"I mean, they went through a hard time a few years ago, before their youngest was born. I used to hear them shouting and fighting a lot. I don't listen to the local gossip, especially because I consider Jalissa a friend, but there were rumors about Jack gambling or investing in something shady." She shrugged. "I don't really know."

The detectives exchanged a glance, making Hope wonder what they knew.

"Do you mind if we search Luca's room? And any other areas of the house where he might keep stuff?" Detective Hanson asked. "I know you've given us the notes from his mother, but maybe we'll find something else that would be helpful in trying to get an idea of his state of mind."

"Yes, go ahead." Hope and Shaun had talked about this before he left, and they both agreed they had nothing to hide.

She pointed in the direction of Luca's room, and as the detectives walked back to it, Hope's glance fell on Luca's iPad that she'd left on the breakfast bar. She opened her mouth to tell them about it, but then snapped it shut again. She wanted to see what was on it before turning it over to the police. She would look through it again while the detectives searched Luca's room and give it to them when they were done.

9

Glancing over her shoulder to make sure the detectives were in Luca's room, Hope picked up Luca's iPad. She felt like a thief. Pursing her lips, she searched the icons on the home page again, thinking maybe Cassidy had downloaded a passcode app or something like that, but there was nothing. And then her eyes caught on the Notes app. She often saved bits of information in her own Notes. Maybe Cassidy had done the same?

She opened it, and bingo. She scanned the list and saw headings like "Bank Info," "Savings," "Passwords." Luca had given her the banking information and most of the other things in the Notes when he first came to them. But then she saw some other random Notes without headings. After clicking on one dated about a month ago, Hope started reading and then sucked in a breath. She reread the short passage and then looked up, her eyes glazing over. Cassidy hadn't written this. She had already been dead a month ago. Luca had written this. Blowing out her breath, she blinked to clear her vision and then looked back down.

People used to ignore me. When I lived with Mom. But now they don't and I have a dog. Mom said we couldn't get one. I don't know why. We traveled a lot, but a small dog would be good. But she said no.

Now I have Mochi and the boys across the street. Andrew Caine is in my grade and we have lunch together. I sit with him and his friends. It's good.

I miss Mom. I miss her notes. I wish there was more. I wish we'd never come back here. She said it was safe, but then she went and died. Right in our car. And now she's gone and I'm here. People don't ignore me now. If I can't live with Mom, then I'm glad I have Ayi and Uncle Shaun. But I'd rather have Mom back.

Hope looked up from the iPad. Here was proof that he hadn't run away. *He was glad to have her and Shaun.* Emotions clogged her throat and she blinked rapidly. There was so much she didn't know about her nephew. This little snippet was a glimpse into his mind. She looked down the list and clicked on a few, noting that there were two others that Luca had written. She sank onto a stool at the breakfast bar, her fingers already clicking on another entry. It was from two weeks ago.

I'm glad Shadow is happy in his new home. Ayi told me Shadow is some sort of Labrador Pitbull mix. He's about a year old and he's a good boy. He doesn't chew shoes like other puppies Ayi and Uncle Shaun fostered. He listened to me and followed me everywhere when he lived with us. I'm glad he found a home but I miss him. Mochi misses him too.

She skimmed through the rest of it, her eyes darting over the words. It was mostly about the sports camp he would be going to, and playing basketball with the Caine boys. The only mention of Cassidy was that he still missed his mother.

Hope clicked out of that entry and onto the last one, noting it was from a few days after Luca came to live with them.

Mom is gone. It's not like the times when she was sick and would take me to Emmy's. I hated it when Mom was out of it. It made my stomach hurt and she always said sorry. I'm sorry, Monkey. We were supposed to go see Aunt Hope. Mom said we needed her help. She didn't want to be sick anymore. She wanted to get better. But she took drugs that day. She promised she wouldn't anymore. I got to the car and she was out of it. Sick. I was so scared. She wasn't breathing. I couldn't find her phone. I started screaming. I held her hand because I didn't know what else to do. I stayed with her until the police came.

Hope felt tears prickle her eyes and swiped a hand over them. She'd been told he was in the car with Cassidy, but he'd never talked about it, and reading his words now, her heart seized with grief for him and for her sister. How scared he must have been to see his mother like that. And how brave of him to hold her hand. She'd been told that he'd screamed for help, and a bystander had called 911.

Luca hadn't told them that Cassidy had been trying to get back to Hope. It broke her heart, not knowing Cassidy had needed her help.

How she wished Cassidy had made it to her before she overdosed. Hope would have taken care of things. She would have gotten her sister into a program and taken care of Luca. But now it was too late and Cassidy was dead and Luca was gone.

Hope stared off into space. She'd never thought she'd be in the position of having to report a missing child. She and Shaun hadn't wanted children. Maybe it was having to bail Cassidy out all those times when she was younger, or the pained ways her parents had seemed around her and Cassidy. Almost as if it were a duty to take care of them, and not much more. And Shaun's parents' bitter divorce had soured him to any thoughts of children. His mother had been born and raised in France, and his father was the only child of Taiwanese immigrants. His mother had gone back to France when Shaun was three, and his father hadn't been able to handle the responsibility of a child. He'd left Shaun with his Taiwanese grandparents, who'd felt that they were too old to raise a child. They'd done the best they could, but Shaun had always felt like a burden to everyone in his life.

Neither she nor Shaun saw any reason to bring more children into this fucked-up world. They weren't equipped to mold young minds. And now with Luca missing, it just proved their theory correct. They'd had a child for only two months and already lost him.

"Where else does Luca keep his things?" Detective Hanson's voice made Hope jump. She slid off the stool and turned to them.

"He keeps his sports equipment and toys and balls for the dogs in the garage." She picked up the iPad and held it out. "This is Luca's. It was here in the kitchen."

Detective Regel walked to her side and took it from her. Hope held her breath, wondering if he was going to ask why she had withheld it from them but all he said was, "Do you have the passcode?"

"Yes." Hope gave it to him and then said, "It was on the breakfast bar." Technically, that wasn't a lie, right? "I found some notes that Luca had written. He said he was glad to be living here. I don't think he ran away."

She could tell by the look they exchanged that they too were becoming more convinced that Luca hadn't run away.

"If you find anything else of his that might be helpful, anything at all, let us know."

She nodded, and they went outside to search the garage. Hope was alone again. The walls suddenly started to close in on her. She couldn't sit here doing nothing. She needed to get out, do something. She opened the front door and stepped out onto the porch. A few newspeople were already on the corner, and she turned her back to them. Her eyes skimmed over to Mr. Alden's house, and she focused on his small cottage. She couldn't forget that Luca's key chain—and possibly his blood—had been found in the woods on the other side of Mr. Alden's house. Hope suddenly wanted to check the spot herself. Maybe she'd see something that the searchers had missed, because she knew Luca better than they did. But would it be cordoned off? There was only one way to find out.

She jogged to the street and ran the short distance until she was in the woods, well away from the road and shielded by all the trees. Only then did she stop to catch her breath. There was something peaceful about being in here, as if the tall trees all around her created a safe haven against the bad things happening outside. The leaves blocked out the sun, making it cool, and a breeze whispered along Hope's neck. She breathed in the scent of the loamy earth and listened to the caws of birds, the buzzes of bees and insects, and the chirps of crickets hidden in the vegetation.

But then her eyes caught on the yellow police tape about halfway down the path that led to the lake. That must have been where they'd found Luca's key chain. Stepping carefully, she made her way to the spot and looked around. There wasn't much to see. The police had apparently collected whatever evidence they'd found.

Hope looked up and, without realizing it, started walking deeper into the trees, off the path and closer to Mr. Alden's house. She stepped over fallen branches and waded through weeds. Too late, she realized she hadn't put on bug spray. She'd probably be covered in ticks, and even as she thought that, gnats swarmed around her head. She swatted at them with one hand. She'd told Luca never to go into the woods without tick and bug spray, and here she was in the thick of it, getting eaten alive. She should turn back. But something about Mr. Alden's house beckoned to her, like an itch she couldn't ignore, and she was helpless to stop it. She kept going until she was at the six-foot wooden fence that separated his backyard from the woods on this side.

As she contemplated the weathered wood, which had turned green in places, she could hear someone from the news crew shouting out a question. The low murmur of an answer told her Shaun was home from the hospital. He'd be wondering where she had gone. She suddenly felt foolish, standing deep in the woods, trying to spy on her neighbor. She was about to turn back, but then she heard Mr. Alden's voice on the other side of the fence.

"Now don't you look pretty in the sunlight?" His voice was light, and his tone sounded as if he were talking to an animal or a small child.

Who was he talking to? Placing a hand on the fence, she looked for breaks in the wood so she could peer into her neighbor's yard. A part of her couldn't believe she was skulking around like this, as if she were playing Nancy Drew, girl detective. She was a grown woman, for heaven's sake. What was she doing, frolicking in here, being eaten alive by bugs? Yellow jackets buzzed around her, and then she saw a spot where the wood had separated. Putting an eye to the space, she stared into Mr. Alden's yard.

It took her a moment to figure out what she was looking at. But then she saw Mr. Alden's form hunched over something on the ground of the small concrete patio. His back was to her, and she strained forward, trying to see what it was. She lost her balance and fell against the fence heavily, causing a thump.

Shit.

Hope froze, sure that Mr. Alden had heard and was now on his way to investigate. But when she pressed her eye to the opening again, she saw that he was still talking to whatever was on the ground and didn't appear to have heard anything. For once, she was thankful for the fact that he was slightly deaf and hadn't realized she was lurking on the other side of his privacy fence.

It was almost enough to make her turn around and go back to her house. But she couldn't. She had to make sure Mr. Alden didn't have Luca. Once she saw with her own eyes, then she could apologize to him for suspecting him. Better to eat humble pie than to ignore her instincts and be sorry later.

Peering through the small opening, she watched as Mr. Alden picked up whatever it was. His back was still to her, so she couldn't see what he was doing, but whatever he was holding wasn't very big. Too small to be a child. Just when Hope was admonishing herself for being suspicious of their kindly neighbor, Mr. Alden suddenly lifted his head and froze, one ear cocked as if he'd heard something.

Hope's cell phone was ringing in the back pocket of her shorts. The ringer was on low, so the chiming notes of the ringtone she'd assigned to Shaun were no more than the tinkle from a music box. But in that instant, it seemed like every creature in the woods had gone silent and every living thing was focused on the ringing coming out of Hope's rear end. Mr. Alden turned his head in her direction, and her breath caught in her chest.

Pushing herself away from the fence, she backed out of the vegetation slowly. But her foot got tangled in a thicket of weeds as her body kept going, and then she was falling. She could see it happening in slow motion, and in her head, she was screaming the word "no." Her arms windmilled as she tried to right herself. But in the next instant, she crashed into a bush next to the fence with as much grace as a buffalo, twigs snapping under her weight and leaves rustling as she landed with a thud.

She lay still for a moment, the breath knocked out of her. Then she heard Mr. Alden getting closer to the fence on his side.

"Hello?" he called out. "Who's there?"

Hope contemplated not answering, but in the next moment, the top of Mr. Alden's head peered over the fence and his eyes took in her sprawled form. He was tall and thin, around six feet, and could see over the fence easily. Hope cursed under her breath, wishing their neighbor were more height challenged.

"Hope?" There was confusion and concern in her neighbor's voice. She lifted a hand feebly and then focused on untangling her feet and standing up. She brushed herself off before speaking. "I, um. The police found a key chain of Luca's here. I was just searching to see if I could, um, find anything else."

When she finally looked up, Mr. Alden was nodding sympathetically. "That nice fellow told me. I'm sorry about Luca."

Hope met his eyes. "Did you hear anything yesterday?" She spoke clearly so that she wouldn't have to repeat herself. "If Luca was here, did you hear him talking with anyone?"

She could see only part of his face, but she recognized the mournful look in his eyes as he shook his head.

"My hearing isn't like it used to be. An elephant could be thrashing around out there and I probably wouldn't hear."

Hope nodded, even though he'd sure as hell heard when *she'd* crashed just now. She began to pick her way out of the vegetation. "Sorry to disturb you." She suddenly needed to get out of there as a shiver ran down her spine.

She could hear Mr. Alden saying something, but she didn't look back. She needed to get out of the woods. She needed sunshine. The dark coolness that had been soothing before had suddenly turned ominous. Once on the path, she ran the rest of the way out and burst onto the street in time to see every person staked out on the corner turn in her direction.

10

Day two
10:00 a.m.

"What happened to you?"

Shaun looked up when Hope walked into the kitchen. He was sitting at the dining room table, papers spread out before him. Hope had looked in the mirror hanging in the foyer when she came in and knew she looked like a mess. Her chin-length hair was all over the place, and she had scratches on her arms and legs from where she'd fallen into the bush. There were pieces of dried leaves stuck to her clothing, and she was sweaty and out of breath.

"I wanted to see if I could find anything in the woods, but I tripped and fell." Hope was too embarrassed to tell Shaun she'd been spying on their neighbor.

Shaun lifted his eyebrows but didn't comment. After a moment, he said, "I ran into the detectives when I got home. They were just leaving. They didn't find anything that could be helpful, except for the iPad."

Hope pulled out a chair across from Shaun. "Did you know Luca had that iPad? I've never seen it before."

Shaun shook his head. "Where did you find it?"

Hope looked down. "At the bottom of one of the drawers in Luca's night table last night. I wanted to see if I could get into it before giving it to the police."

"You found it yesterday?"

"Yeah. I thought maybe Cassidy had left a message in there or something." She bit her bottom lip. "I should have told you."

Shaun was looking at her with a thoughtful expression on his face. "You know I'm on your side, right?"

"I know." Hope's shoulders lifted and then fell. "I just . . . I feel so guilty, and I don't know . . ."

"It's okay. I'm here for you." Shaun got up and came around the table to her side. He leaned down and gave her a kiss. "Luca means just as much to me as he does to you."

"I know." She closed her eyes, wishing Luca were back and their biggest problem was having him walk in on them kissing.

"You don't have to do everything yourself." He squeezed her shoulder. "You don't have to carry the burden by yourself."

She nodded, not trusting herself to speak.

"And two heads are better than one."

She gave a tremulous smile. "You're right."

Shaun held up one of her arms, looking at all the scratches. "We need to clean you up."

She followed him into the bathroom and sat on the toilet seat. He wet a washcloth and started to clean up the thin trickles of blood on her arms and legs.

"I've been thinking." Hope winced as a deeper scratch on her leg stung when Shaun cleaned it. "If someone was threatening Cassidy back then, would she have confided in anyone? Like Dan?"

"But you said they'd drifted apart before Cassidy disappeared?" Shaun rinsed the washcloth off and opened the medicine cabinet. He took out a tube of antibiotic ointment. "What about her other friends?"

Hope made a face. "You know Cassy. She didn't have a lot of close friends. She always preferred to go her own way, and friends drifted in and out of her life. Dan was the only one who stayed a constant."

"Was he still living in this neighborhood back then?" Shaun carefully applied the ointment to Hope's scratches.

"I know he lived with his parents for a few years after high school. But I can't remember when he moved away." Hope's forehead furrowed. Dan's parents had moved to this lake community when he was in middle school, from the town where Hope and Cassidy had grown up, about half an hour south of the lake. He and Cassidy had remained fast friends, even though they were no longer at the same school. In fact, he was the reason that Hope and Shaun had bought a house here at the lake. She'd picked Cassidy up a few times from Dan's parents' house, and fallen in love with the neighborhood.

"Was it before or after Luca was born?" Shaun replaced the cap on the tube and put it away.

Hope thought back. Like Cassidy, Dan hadn't gone to college. She knew he'd moved out West somewhere, because his parents had told her.

"I think it must have been before Luca was born, because I remember asking Cassidy if Dan knew about the baby." Hope looked at Shaun. "I thought it was strange that she hadn't told her best friend she was pregnant. She said they lost touch."

Now Hope wondered. What had happened to break up their friendship? Dan had always been around, in and out of their home with Cassidy as if he lived there. Their parents hadn't approved, muttering under their breath in Mandarin that Cassy shouldn't be running around with boys. Especially not white boys. But Cassidy had ignored them. She was loyal to Dan and always stood up for him when their parents started muttering about the *waiguoren* in their house. So what had happened to their friendship?

"We need to talk to Dan." Hope stood up.

"You're right. Maybe he knows something." Shaun followed her out of the bathroom and back to the dining room, where she'd left her cell. "Do you have his number?"

"I don't know." She picked up her phone and scrolled through the contacts, searching for Dan Stern. "Shit. It's not here. I used to have it, but I've switched phones a few times." Hope gave a grunt of frustration. What if Cassidy and Dan had been in touch in recent years? She needed to get hold of him.

"What about his parents?" Shaun asked.

"His father passed away a few years ago. I remember an email the lake association sent out about it. And I heard his mother sold the house and moved to wherever Dan's sister lives."

"We could look him up, but with a name like Dan Stern, it'd be pretty hard to find him that way." Shaun paced behind Hope. "Who else knew him around here?"

As Hope drummed her hand on her thigh, her forehead wrinkled—and then she remembered. "Mr. Alden. Dan used to cut his grass and help him with repairs around the house."

"You're right." Shaun's eyes lit up. "I bet he'd have Dan's number, or at least his mom's."

"I'm going to ask him." Hope would ask Mr. Alden for Dan's number, *and* it would give her a legitimate reason to get into his house and find out if he was hiding anything.

"I'll come with you," Shaun said.

But just then, Shaun's cell rang. Hope's heart raced, hoping it was Luca. But when it became clear it was a work-related call, she blew out a breath. Pointing next door, she let Shaun know she was going to Mr. Alden's. He nodded and she headed for the door, Toby following her.

"You can't come with me, Toby." She opened the door a crack and slipped through, so that the little dog couldn't get out. She ducked her head to avoid eye contact with anyone on the corner and cut through the lawn onto Mr. Alden's property. She ignored the questions being aimed at her and put a hand up to shield her face from the sun and cameras.

She rang Mr. Alden's bell and tapped her toes on the ground when her neighbor didn't answer right away. What was he doing? She knew he was in there. He rarely went out, and his car was in the driveway. She rang the bell again, this time leaving her finger on it a few seconds more than necessary. Maybe he hadn't heard the bell the first time. She waited a few more moments and was about to ring again when she finally heard the sound of someone walking toward the door.

Seconds later, Mr. Alden opened it, and Hope dropped her arms by her sides.

"Oh, hi, Hope. Did you hurt yourself earlier?" He squinted at her while holding his hands away from his body.

"Just a few scratches." Hope's eyes went to her neighbor's hands, and she noticed flecks of something white clinging to his forearms and some of his fingers. What was it? "I need your help. Can I come in?" She gestured behind her, indicating the newspeople, who had followed her down the street and were now clicking their cameras at them.

Mr. Alden looked over her shoulder and then back at Hope. His body language told her he didn't want to let her in, but at the same time, he didn't like to be stared at any more than she did. He regarded her for a moment but then finally gestured with a hand. "Come in. I'm sorry it's a big mess."

He stepped back to allow Hope to enter, right into the kitchen. Mr. Alden's house was tiny, only a one-story cottage. The kitchen was small, and Hope stood there awkwardly for a moment before Mr. Alden pointed to a chair at the table.

"Sit, dear. Let me wash my hands." He turned his back and went to the sink to the left of the front door, and Hope crossed to the chair, sinking down even as her eyes took in his kitchen.

She'd been here once before, when she'd brought over a lasagna that she'd made when he was sick with the flu a few years ago. But she'd never gone past the small square of the kitchen. It was crammed full of stuff: boxes and papers on top of the side counter, books on the dining table, and all sorts of knickknacks on the shelves surrounding the sink. She could see the remnants of breakfast still out: a greasy pan on the stove, a bowl that he must have used to whisk eggs in, and dishes and cups piled in the sink. There wasn't a dishwasher, so she assumed he washed his own dishes.

As Mr. Alden scrubbed his hands, Hope's eyes found a door, slightly open, just past the doorway to the living room. Maybe it led to the basement? Most of the houses in this community had a basement. She wondered if it was finished like theirs. What did Mr. Alden keep down there?

When Mr. Alden turned around again, drying his hands on a dish towel, Hope spoke. "Do you have Dan Stern's cell number?"

Mr. Alden cocked his head to the side. "What's that, dear? Dan Burns?"

"No. Dan Stern." She raised her voice and enunciated each word clearly.

"Oh, Dan. Yes, what a nice young man. He used to cut the grass for me." Mr. Alden smiled at her.

"Yes, very nice. Do you have his phone number?" Hope spoke loudly and clearly.

Mr. Alden pressed his lips together and thought for a moment. "I might have it somewhere." He waved a hand toward a pile of papers and books on the sideboard.

"Can you please look for it? It's really important." When Mr. Alden only stared at her, an odd little shiver ran down Hope's spine. Why was she getting the vibe that Mr. Alden didn't want her here? Was there something sinister under the kindly neighbor she'd always assumed he was? She wrapped her arms around her middle, struggling to get herself under control. The urge to push past Mr. Alden and search his house was so overpowering that she had to physically restrain herself.

"Are you okay?" Mr. Alden took a step toward her. In concern? Or to intimidate?

She shook her head, trying to rid her mind of these wild thoughts. This was Mr. Alden, who wouldn't harm a fly, not a secret serial killer hiding secrets in his house.

"Dear?"

Mr. Alden's question made her realize she'd never answered him. "Until Luca comes back, I'm not going to be okay."

"I'm so sorry. I wish there was something I could do to help."

Hope's eyes went to the door, and she pointed at it. "Where does that go? The basement?"

"What?" He followed her finger to the partially open door in the hallway.

Was it her imagination, or did his face flush? His eyes darted to hers before he stepped in front of her chair, blocking her view of the door. Something flashed across his face.

"It's um . . . yes. I have a . . . kind of workshop down there." He looked everywhere but at Hope.

Hope stared at him and could have sworn something crackled in the air between them. The hair on the back of her neck stood up. She knew without a doubt that he was hiding something. Her breath quickened and she stood, taking a step toward him, hoping he'd back away. But he stood firm. They had a stare-off for a few moments before he whirled and, with surprising speed and grace, walked to the door and shut it firmly. He turned back to Hope.

"Dan Stern. Let me look for his number." He brushed by her, and Hope froze in place. What had just happened? Why had he slammed the door like that? As ridiculous as it was for her to think that Luca was down there, Mr. Alden's behavior was scaring her.

She had to be sure. "Luca," she screamed. "Luca, are you here?"

No answer. He either wasn't here or Mr. Alden had gagged him and he couldn't answer.

When she turned, Mr. Alden was staring at her, his mouth open in surprise. "Hope? What are . . ." He broke off, seemingly at a loss for words.

"Sorry, I . . ." She trailed off too, since she had no explanation.

He didn't speak, and the silence was thick between them. Her face crumpled. "I'm sorry," she whispered. "I just can't believe he's gone."

"I understand, dear. There's no worse nightmare than losing a child." Mr. Alden's voice was low, but Hope heard the hardness in his words. "They'll find him."

He turned away and went to the sideboard with a hutch on top that was situated next to the dining table. The surface was piled with papers, magazines, mail, and odds and ends. He picked through the pile and plucked a black address book from the bottom. Hope stood still, her mind whirling, not sure if she could trust her neighbor. How well did they really know him? What did he do with his days, with no friends or visitors, and rarely leaving the house?

She watched as he took a pair of reading glasses from his shirt pocket. He put them on and flipped through the address book. Going to the *S* section, Mr. Alden ran a finger down the entries until he stopped at one.

"Here it is. Daniel Stern. This is the last number I had for him." He looked up at Hope. "But I haven't talked to him for years now, since he moved to Colorado."

Colorado—that's where he'd gone. Hope pulled out her cell. "Hopefully he still has the same number."

Mr. Alden read it out loud, and Hope inputted it into her phone. She tapped on the "Save" button and then looked at her neighbor. Silence hung between them, heavy and stifling.

Hope finally spoke, because she had to know. "Do you know where Luca is?"

Something flickered in Mr. Alden's eyes before he blinked and then shook his head. "No," he said. "I'm sorry."

Was he telling the truth? Hope narrowed her eyes. Or was he lying, and apologizing for lying? They stared at each other for a few more seconds, and then his gaze shifted. She didn't miss the quick glance he threw at the basement door before his eyes slid away.

Hope's entire body tensed, and her hands fisted by her side as her imagination ran wild. Had Mr. Alden threatened Cassidy back then, making her run? Was he now holding her son hostage? She needed to see the basement for herself. The only problem was, Mr. Alden almost never left the house. And now, with her yelling for Luca like that, Mr. Alden was going to be even more on alert. How was she going to get in there? No matter how far-fetched the idea was to the police and Shaun, Hope knew she needed to check for herself that Luca wasn't down there. Because if he was and she hadn't checked, she'd never forgive herself.

11

Hope called Dan Stern as soon as she got back to her house, still spooked from her visit with Mr. Alden. It went straight to voice mail, and she shot Shaun a look of frustration. She never left voice mails, but after all these years, it didn't feel right to send a text. She took a breath.

"Um, hi, Dan. It's Hope Chen. Cassidy's sister. Um, I know it's been a long time, but I need to speak to you. I don't know if you heard that Cassidy's son, Luca, came to live with me after she passed away. Luca is missing. I thought maybe Cassidy might have said something back when she first disappeared . . . I know I'm not making sense, but can you please call me as soon as you get this?" She left her cell number and then hung up.

She looked at Shaun. "I hope he calls back soon."

"Me too."

Hope's cell rang just then, and they both jumped. Looking at it, she said, "It's Jalissa." She didn't miss the way Shaun's body had tensed when the phone rang, just like hers did. They would never be able to hear a phone ring again without their bodies reacting physically.

Hope picked up the call and Jalissa said, "Hi, Hope. The board is calling an emergency meeting at noon. Anyone who's not working is asked to come. I told them I'd let you know."

"Is it about Luca?" Hope asked.

"Yes. The board is concerned that something bad is going on in this neighborhood. You'll come?" Hope knew Jalissa was referring to the teenage girl who had died in the woods next to the beach last summer.

"Yes. Shaun and I will both be there."

"Okay, see you soon."

Less than an hour later, they sat on folding chairs in the main room at the clubhouse upstairs, along with a sizable group of their neighbors. Many of them were still working from home since the pandemic, and it seemed Luca's disappearance was alarming enough for them to take time out of their workday to come to the meeting. Most had offered their condolences when Hope and Shaun first came in, while others had nodded at them from across the room. Now they were respecting their privacy and leaving Hope and Shaun alone. Jalissa sat next to Hope, and her presence was calming.

As conversation buzzed around her, Hope tuned them out, her attention on her phone, willing it to ring with a call from either Luca or Dan Stern. She also needed to figure out how to get into Mr. Alden's basement. She knew Shaun wouldn't approve, so she hadn't said anything to him about her plans to spy on their neighbor.

Nancy Meza, the president, rapped her knuckles on the table she sat behind at the front of the room, and people started drifting into chairs. Once everyone was seated, Nancy cleared her throat.

"As you all know, Luca Wen disappeared from the Chens' driveway at approximately five fifteen last night." She paused and gestured to Hope and Shaun, giving them a nod of acknowledgment. "And given Lindsay Miller's death less than a year ago, even though it was deemed an accident, this is cause for concern for our community." She paused for a moment and looked around. She was a tall woman in her forties with dark-brown hair, a stay-at-home mom who used to be an attorney in Manhattan before the pandemic hit. She ruled the neighborhood like she would a courtroom, but she got things done, and when she spoke, people listened.

"Ours has always been a safe neighborhood. A place where our children can play outside by themselves, ride their bikes around the lake, and we feel safe leaving our doors unlocked. But given what has happened to two children in our community, the board is very concerned." She gestured to the police officer, a stocky man in his sixties, on her right. "Officer Dillon is here to update us on the search for Luca. If any of you have seen anything, heard anything about Luca, please come forward, even if you think it's minor. The police are asking for any information you may have." She made eye contact around the room. "We also have to figure out if someone in the neighborhood is targeting our children. Is it a stranger? What can we do about it?"

As Nancy continued to speak, a movement at the entrance drew Hope's attention. It was Mr. Alden, slipping into an empty chair by the door, his gaze on Nancy. Hope sat up straighter. She had never seen Mr. Alden at a lake meeting before.

She nudged Shaun with her elbow. "Look who's here," she whispered in his ear.

Shaun peered around Hope at their neighbor, then looked back at Hope, a question in his eyes.

"He's never been to a meeting before. Why's he here now?"

Shaun shrugged and whispered back, "Maybe he's concerned and wants to find out what the board has planned."

Hope considered that, but then her forehead crinkled. Mr. Alden had no kids. He didn't have grandkids either, as far as they knew. He'd never once attended a board meeting, or any of the other meetings over the years. Not when they'd discussed a fundraiser to raise money to repair the dam. Not when the neighborhood was on opposing sides about whether to put in a sewer system around the lake, instead of relying on the septic systems that the community still used. And yet, suddenly, here he was?

Nancy was now taking questions, and their attention was diverted by a neighbor asking, "Is this going to decrease our property value? If it gets out that kids disappear and die in our neighborhood, that doesn't look good."

An older woman in her early eighties, tiny and white haired, stood and glared at the man who had asked that question. "Burt Whitman, hush your mouth. We're talking about missing and dead children here. What's more important?"

Burt crossed his arms over his burly chest and opened his mouth. "But Mae . . ."

Mae waved her arms, her eyes shooting daggers at Burt. "This isn't the time. Sit down. Now."

If Hope hadn't been so distracted by Mr. Alden's appearance, she would have laughed at the cowed expression on Burt's face. He relaxed his arms and muttered, "Yes, ma'am."

Once he was seated, Mae turned to Nancy. "You may proceed, Madam President."

A few neighbors chuckled, and Nancy waited until they settled down before speaking again.

"We need to establish a neighborhood watch, to keep our eyes open and report any suspicious persons or activity. We're also encouraging our neighbors to install video cameras at their front door if possible. Ann Roberts, our treasurer, who you all know is a whiz at technology, is creating an app just for our lake community. Ann, tell us more about it."

Nancy gestured to a redheaded woman in her fifties, who stood and took over the floor. As she spoke, Hope turned to study Mr. Alden. He appeared to be listening intently, but Ann had a soft voice, and Hope wondered how much of what she was saying he actually heard.

Hope shifted in her seat, and Jalissa gave her a sympathetic look. The hard surface was uncomfortable. She didn't want to be here. She wanted Luca back, and she didn't want to be talking about how to take precautions to keep the children of the neighborhood safe. She'd already lost the one in her charge. She needed to do something, to move, to search for Luca. Not sit here in this room, which was growing warmer with each minute.

Her eyes landed on Mr. Alden again, and suddenly, something occurred to her. If he was here, then his house was empty. This would be the perfect time to try and see what he was hiding in his basement. Her heart rate picked up as she glanced at Shaun, seeing he was engrossed in whatever Ann was saying about this app. Now was her chance to find out once and for all what was in the basement.

She leaned over and whispered in Shaun's ear, "I have to go to the bathroom. Bad." She gave him a grimace when he turned to look at her and then held a hand over her stomach.

His eyebrows lifted, and he nodded in sympathy.

"I'm going home. Don't want to use the clubhouse bathroom." She kept her voice low, then leaned down to pick up the purse she'd dropped on the floor.

"You want me to come with you?" Shaun put a hand on her arm.

"No!" The word came out louder than she intended, and the people closest to them turned to look at her. Jalissa gave her a concerned look. Hope lowered her voice. "You don't want to be there. Stay here. Tell me what happens. I'll be back soon."

Shaun nodded, and Hope rose, flashing a smile at Jalissa as she slipped past her. She was glad they were at the end of a row so that she didn't have to make people get up to let her out. Giving an apologetic nod to Nancy and Ann, she walked to the door, passing behind Mr. Alden on her way out. He didn't turn his head in her direction. His attention was still on Ann, who was now showing them on her phone how the app worked so that everyone who used it would be updated whenever something happened.

Slipping out of the room, Hope ran down the six stairs that led to the front door of the clubhouse, then burst out into the sunshine. She stopped for a moment, appreciating again the beauty of their neighborhood, and the way the sun shone off the lake, making it sparkle. As Nancy said, this used to be a safe neighborhood, the perfect place to raise children. Whether Lindsay's and Luca's cases were linked or not, something or someone was bringing harm to their children. And Hope was going to figure out who, if she had to eliminate suspects one by one. Starting with Mr. Alden.

With her back stiff and resolve hardened, she started down the street, heading up the hill back to their and Mr. Alden's houses.

12

Day two
12:15 p.m.

Hope stood on their back deck, looking over at the privacy fence that separated their yard from Mr. Alden's. Even though his property was fenced
in on both sides, the back of his yard, which ended in dense woods, wasn't
fenced like theirs. The best way to get into his yard was from there.

She walked across the flat, manicured lawn of their backyard. When
she got to the gate that led out of their fenced-in yard and into the
wooded area behind their property, she stopped for a moment, looking
down the hill. She could see part of the lake and the front door of the
clubhouse from here. In the winter, when the trees were bare, they could
see the entire lake from their deck and yard, and the sight of water
always soothed her. She took a breath and walked out of their yard.
She'd made sure to coat herself with bug spray this time.

Closing the gate firmly behind her, she walked along the fence line
toward Mr. Alden's property. Keeping an eye out for poison ivy, which grew
rampant in these woods, she picked her way through the tall weeds until she
stood at the edge of Mr. Alden's property. There were more bushes and vegetation here than she'd realized from their property. Taking a deep breath, she
parted the branches and wiggled her way through a hedge into his property.

Something scraped her leg as she pulled it through. Looking down, she saw a thin scratch, and as she watched, it beaded with blood. More cuts. Grimacing, she looked away and turned to study Mr. Alden's house. It was barely visible from where she stood, since his yard was covered in wild vegetation and sloped up to his house. Hope had often wondered why their backyard was so flat, yet Mr. Alden's was steep enough that a child could enjoy sledding down it in the winter. Had he purposely let the weeds and wildflowers grow so tall, taller than she was, to keep out prying eyes? Or was it because he had no one to take care of it, like Dan Stern used to do?

Taking another breath, she started across his yard, using her hands to push aside the tall weeds that tangled and brushed against her, releasing a swarm of insects that flew at her face. Swatting them with one hand, she used the other to cut a path through the thick undergrowth, mosquitoes whining in her ear and the buzz of yellow jackets and wasps following in her wake. She hoped she didn't step on a nest. Maybe this had been a mistake. She wasn't prepared to fight her way through a jungle.

Just as she was about to give up, she suddenly came upon an area that had been cleared. She could finally see the back of Mr. Alden's house. She stood in front of a small expanse of grass, only about a yard wide, that led to the concrete patio outside his basement door. There was a table with only one chair on the patio, aimed so that whoever sat there could look out into the woods and down to the lake. Potted herbs lined the patio. Hope recognized basil, rosemary, thyme, and parsley.

She crossed the grassy area and stepped onto the patio, turning to look behind her. She couldn't see the clubhouse from here because of all the vegetation. Mr. Alden had a better view of the lake, though, and she could see parts of it sparkling in the sunshine in between the trees. It was peaceful, and she took a moment to appreciate it. As wild as the vegetation was, it created an insular little bubble of nature, and the six-foot fence on either side gave Mr. Alden even more privacy. A sense of calm washed over her, something she hadn't felt since realizing she couldn't hear the thump of Luca's basketball in their driveway.

She gave an impatient shake of her head. She wasn't here for healing peace. She was here to see if Luca was in the basement. And she didn't know how much time she had. Mr. Alden could come back at any moment. She needed to do her snooping, fast.

She surveyed the back of the house and noticed there was only one window, to the left of the door. Knowing it was too much to ask that the door would be unlocked, she walked to it anyway and turned the knob. Locked. Damn.

She walked to the window and tried to look in, but the shades were drawn all the way down, not even a crack at the bottom to peek through. Hope let out a sigh of frustration. She hadn't come prepared to pick the lock or break in through the window. For some reason, she'd just thought she'd be able to get in, since they rarely locked their back door, even when they weren't home. But apparently, Mr. Alden was more cautious, giving her more cause to think that he was hiding something. Because as Nancy said, most people didn't bother locking their doors around here.

Hope decided to check whether there were windows on the side of the house that faced the woods where the police had found Luca's bubble tea key chain. She walked around the house and breathed a sigh of relief when she saw a window. But it was behind a tall hedge, some sort of evergreen bush about two stories high. There were no shades on this window. Walking to the hedge, she studied it and saw there was a small space between it and the house. She wasn't very big, and wondered if she would fit. Only one way to find out.

Taking a breath and holding it, Hope wedged herself in. Branches and leaves scratched against her, but she ignored it. Wiggling slightly, she got more of her body in the space, and inch by inch, she made her way through the tight tunnel until she could almost see into the window. But then her progress was impeded. She couldn't go farther, because here, the hedge grew right up against the house and a sturdy branch blocked her way. She pushed on it and it gave way a bit, but not enough for her to get past. Squirming to get into a better position, she suddenly realized she was stuck. Branches had snagged on her shirt and shorts, and the harder she tried to dislodge herself, the more they clung to her. Sweat broke out along her forehead, and the cut on her leg started to throb. Her heart rate quickened, and all she could think of was how Shaun would laugh if they found her wedged here and had to call someone to extricate her.

This had obviously been a very stupid idea. What had she been thinking, suspecting kindly old Mr. Alden? He'd never given her any reason to think he could have done anything to Luca. She was really losing it. And now she was stuck in a bush, skewered like a piece of meat ready for the barbecue. She wiggled her body again, sweat now pouring down her back. She had to get out of here before Mr. Alden returned and found her like this, stuck to the side of his house.

She wrenched her body forward to try to free a leg, and the branch in front of her suddenly gave way, slamming her entire body into the side of the house. Wincing at the throbbing pain in her head and doing a mental check of the rest of her body, Hope slumped against the wall. It took a few moments for her to catch her breath, and then she felt even stupider. She *could not* be caught like this. She needed to get the hell out of here.

But when she could finally breathe normally again, she realized the fall had thrown her right up to the window. There was a glare on the pane from the bright sunshine. Putting her hands up to keep out the sun, she pressed her nose against the pane. Her eyes searched the inside until she could make out shapes. And sighed in relief when all she saw was a large table with tools lying on top. Mr. Alden really had a workshop in his basement. She could make out paintbrushes of all sizes, from the finest tips to big bushy ones. There were pots of paints scattered across the worktable, along with scissors of all sizes, other tools that she couldn't identify, and what looked like zip ties or string.

Hope squinted, angling her head for a better look, and saw bins lined up next to the table holding what she assumed were more supplies. She wondered what it was Mr. Alden created down in his basement. Paintings? Maybe some sort of sculptures, since that fit with the tools scattered on the table? Remembering the white substance that had clung to his arms and hands when he answered the door for her earlier, she now wondered if he worked with clay. She'd have to be sure to ask him about his hobby, as a silent apology for having suspected him. He was just a nice man who must be lonely, living all by himself. His hobby probably kept him busy and engaged enough that he didn't seek out human companionship.

With a sigh, Hope started to turn away and figure out how to get herself out from this bush with as little injury as possible. But something on the other side of the basement caught her eyes. Turning back to the window, she focused on the forms lined up against the far wall. At first, she saw only shapes, lumps really, some leaning against the wall, some lying on some sort of platform on the floor. She narrowed her eyes, trying to make out what they were. And then she gasped when she realized a face was staring back at her. A child's face, her mouth puckered, hair done in two braids on either side of her face. Her palms were turned toward Hope as if asking for help.

With her nose completely pressed on the glass now, Hope's eyes scanned the rest of the shapes frantically, and she realized she was staring at the inert forms of children. They were slumped against each other, and before her brain could reassure her that they were just dolls, one of the figures moved. Hope's mouth opened in horror, and she found herself staring into the eyes of a little boy. This was no doll. This was a real human child, imprisoned in Mr. Alden's basement. A scream tore from her throat as she fell back into the hedge. Her breath came out in harsh gasps, and when her brain finally caught up to the rest of her body, she screamed again. With one giant heave, she threw herself toward the opening, ripping her shirt, shorts, and pieces of her skin in the process. But she didn't take any notice of the sting or of the blood seeping from the many cuts on her body. She burst out of the little prison she'd been in, ran around Mr. Alden's house to the front, and tore past her own house and to the corner, where the newspeople turned to stare at her. Hope sped up and pumped her arms, almost tripping as she ran down the hill to the lake. She screamed the whole way for Shaun and the police at the top of her lungs.

13

Out of the corner of her eye, she saw the newspeople following and yelling out to her. Cameras tracked her every move, but she ignored them. She was focused on only one thing: getting to Mr. Alden and confronting him. She hoped the police officer who had been at the meeting was still there. He could arrest Mr. Alden right away, and then they could rescue Luca and whoever else was in the basement. This nightmare would finally be over.

As if she'd conjured him up, Hope saw Mr. Alden walking out the front door of the clubhouse just as she rounded the corner and turned onto Lake Circle, the street the beach and clubhouse were on.

"You kidnapper," Hope screamed at him, as she closed the distance between them. She was still about three houses away from him and saw the look of shock on his face as he halted in place.

"You took Luca, didn't you, you dirty old man?" Rage spewed up in her chest, and she wanted nothing more than to rip him to pieces with her bare hands. "Who are all those other children in your basement? What have you done to them?"

She was almost there, close enough now to see the alarm in her neighbor's eyes as she barreled at him. He held up his hands as if to ward her off even as she advanced on him.

"Hope, what are you talking about?" Mr. Alden appeared genuinely confused, his eyebrows drawn together. "I don't have Luca. I swear." The contrite look on his face and his words almost stopped Hope. But then she remembered the resigned look in the eyes of the children she'd seen in his basement, and rage ripped through her again.

"You're a kidnapper. Maybe a murderer." She struck out with a fist and hit him hard enough in the chest that he stumbled back. "Is that why you never have anyone over at your house? Why you live alone? How long have you been doing this? How could you?" The last sentence came out in a hoarse whisper.

Adrenaline coursed through her, and she would have hit him again, old man be damned, if he hadn't raised both hands in surrender. "It's not what you think, Hope. I would never—"

"What I think?" Hope screamed, cutting him off. "I *saw* with my own two eyes. You can't get away with it. I saw." She heard shouting behind her and knew people were filming them, but she didn't care. She had to find out what Mr. Alden had done to the children in his basement.

Her neighbor's face crumpled, and he reached a hand out to Hope. "No, you have it all wrong. I can explain—" He cut himself off as he stared at her. "What happened to you? Why are you all bloody?"

"No," Hope shouted. "Don't change the subject." She was numb to her many cuts, focused only on getting Mr. Alden to confess. "How do you explain keeping children against their will in your basement?" She raised a hand, intending to strike him again, and this time, Mr. Alden stopped her by grabbing her arm. She winced, the pain from a scratch on her arm finally penetrating her angry haze. But then fury overtook her again, and she started pounding on his chest with her free fist.

He fought to stop her, trying to still her hands, all the while denying what she accused him of. "I swear I'm not . . ."

"Shaun!" Hope bellowed at the top of her voice. "Help me!"

"I'll take you down to the basement." Mr. Alden ducked his head in time to avoid the fist that Hope aimed at his face. "Stop. I'll show you . . . it's not what you think. Hope, stop."

But she was beyond reasoning, wanting to hurt this man who had them all fooled. He wasn't a nice old man. He was a pedophile or worse. It made her physically ill to think of what he'd done to those children locked up in his basement. Those poor, helpless kids.

She was dimly aware of the crowd of newspeople jostling behind her, shouting questions. Just then, Shaun ran out of the clubhouse. His eyes widened at the sight, and then he stepped forward, catching Hope's fists before she could strike Mr. Alden again.

Hope struggled against her husband. "You don't know, Shaun. He's a monster! He's got kids stashed in the basement, and God knows what he's done to them. There were so many of them." Hope tried to shake Shaun off, to claw at Mr. Alden, who'd now shrunk back against a post, but Shaun held her away. "He's got Luca. I know he's down there. We have to get the police."

Hope was aware of cameras pointed at them, and curious neighbors spilling out of the clubhouse or peering from the doorway, drawn outside by her yelling. *Good—let them all come, keep Mr. Alden from getting away.* They all needed to know that a monster lived among them, was collecting children in his basement.

Just then, Officer Dillon burst from the door. "What's going on?" he asked, as he approached, his eyes swiveling between Hope and Mr. Alden as he assessed the situation.

Hope explained, in jumbled words and lots of arm gestures while Mr. Alden just stood there, a defeated look on his face.

"He probably killed Lindsay too." Hope shot Mr. Alden a venomous look.

The officer turned to Mr. Alden. "Is everything she's saying true, Herbert?"

Herbert? Through her haze of anger, the name penetrated Hope's thoughts. How was it that in all the years they'd been neighbors, she'd never once known his first name? He'd always been referred to as Mr. Alden in the neighborhood. Hope stared in shock, wondering what else she didn't know about their neighbor.

Mr. Alden leaned in and whispered something in the police officer's ear. They held a hushed conversation while everyone gawked, and then the officer turned to Hope and Shaun. "I'm calling for backup. Mr. Alden wants to show me something. I'll escort him back to his house."

Officer Dillon turned to Nancy Meza, who hovered at the edge of the crowd. "Can you get everyone back inside?"

She nodded and started herding their neighbors, shooting Hope a sympathetic look.

"I'm coming with you," Hope said, breaking out of Shaun's hold. "I'll show you exactly what I saw."

The officer held up a hand. "No. Please go back to your house. Or back to the meeting. Someone will be over as soon as we can to update you. Let us handle this."

"But—" Hope started to say before Shaun cut in.

"That's fine." He put an arm around Hope's waist and gave it a slight squeeze. "Let us know what's going on as soon as you can."

"Please find Luca." Hope's voice broke at his name. "Bring him back to us."

The officer looked at her with pity or sympathy—she couldn't tell which—and then turned away to lead Mr. Alden to his police car. The crowd watched as they got in and the officer drove off.

Murmurs rippled through the neighbors gathered around as the news crews came forward, wanting to find out what had happened. Hope turned her face away. She didn't want to talk to anyone. She needed to know if Luca was in that basement and if he was okay. With a desperate look at Shaun, she pulled away from the crowd gathered around them and he followed, asking everyone to please let them through and leave them alone.

Hope all but ran down Lake Circle until she got to Peony Street, which led up the hill back to their street. She could hear Shaun behind her, but she didn't slow her pace. She was going to camp herself on the upstairs balcony and monitor Mr. Alden's house, praying that Luca was safe and that they'd bring him to them soon. He had to be okay. He had to.

14

Day two
3:05 p.m.

"What's taking so long?" Hope paced from one end of their living room to the other, too agitated to sit or do anything else. Shaun had cleaned her cuts (again) when they got home, and she now had bandages on the worst of them.

Officer Harmon had come to their house more than an hour ago to say that Luca wasn't in Mr. Alden's basement. He said Mr. Alden had given them permission to search his whole house and that someone would be back as soon as they had an update. He didn't say anything else, and when Hope had asked about the children she'd seen, Officer Harmon had said they were dolls.

"No!" Hope shook her head vehemently. "I saw a boy move. I swear." But then she paused. Had she really seen movement? Or was her mind conjuring up what she wanted to see? "I don't understand." She turned to Shaun. "If they were dolls, why does he have so many of them down there? What's he hiding?"

Officer Harmon hadn't had any answers yet. But he did have an update on Luca's bus driver, Mike, who'd been out late the night before at a birthday dinner for his brother at his brother's house in Danbury.

Mike had been forthcoming with the police, inviting them into his home this morning, letting them take a look around. He told the police that he felt a kinship to Luca because his own mother had died of a drug overdose, so he understood how Luca felt. He'd been keeping an eye out for Luca on the bus, not wanting him to be picked on by the other kids but, other than that, had no underlying interest in Luca.

"Do you really think it was a doll? Or do you think they found something else and that's why we haven't heard anything yet?" Hope asked now when Shaun didn't answer.

"I don't know." Shaun sounded as frustrated as Hope felt.

"I think Mr. Alden has Luca. That's why they haven't been back to update us yet. They must have found something." Hope dropped into a chair, suddenly too tired to keep pacing. Her entire body felt like it'd been wound up as tight as a wire and any sudden movement or thought could send her ricocheting through space. She couldn't stop her mind from imagining the worst of what Luca was going through right this minute as they sat safe and sound in their dining room.

"I'm sure they'll be here soon." Shaun drummed his fingers on the table, and Hope tensed at the sound. She wanted this nightmare to be over.

The doorbell rang, and both Hope and Shaun bolted up from the table. Exchanging a look, they rushed to the front door and Shaun yanked it open, revealing Officer Harmon standing on their porch. Toby came barking out of their bedroom, racing to the front door.

"Did you find him?" Hope blurted before the officer could speak, just as her cell rang, back in the kitchen. She looked over her shoulder, kicking herself for not having the phone on her. She needed to answer it. What if it was Luca? Or Dan Stern? But she needed to hear what the officer had to tell them just as badly.

Officer Harmon shook his head, and Hope's stomach plummeted as disappointment surged through her.

Shaun stepped back to allow the man to enter their home as Hope turned and ran for her cell phone. But it stopped ringing right as she picked it up and checked the screen. Damn, it had been Dan. Torn between wanting to call him right back and hearing what the police had found at Mr. Alden's, she hesitated beside the dining table. She looked toward the foyer, where Shaun and Officer Harmon were conferring, and rushed back to them, clutching her phone.

Officer Harmon cleared his throat when he saw her. "As you know, Mr. Alden gave us permission to search his entire house. He was completely cooperative. We questioned him again, extensively, and we're reasonably sure he had nothing to do with Luca's disappearance." The police officer folded his hands together in front of him.

"But all those dolls? What's he hiding down there? You didn't find anything of Luca's?" Hope asked, as her phone dinged. She glanced at it, noting Dan had left a voice mail before focusing back on the officer.

"No. And after questioning him again, we don't believe he knows anything in connection to Luca's disappearance," Officer Harmon said. "But we will keep an eye on him, in case we missed something."

"Then what did you find in his basement? Just dolls?" Hope rocked on her heels, clutching her cell tightly with her hands.

"Yes." The police officer nodded. "Apparently, Mr. Alden makes porcelain dolls as a hobby. Really realistic. We could see why you thought you saw children in his basement. They gave us quite a scare too. Some of them were life size—forty-eight inches tall. And the details on the face. Man—" He broke off and shook his head. "I'll tell you, I've never seen anything like it. So many dolls of all sizes, lined up on that platform and against the wall. I was convinced for a moment that he really did keep children down there."

"That's so . . ." Hope searched for the word. "Creepy." She shuddered, still wondering if she'd imagined seeing one of the dolls move.

Shaun spoke up. "Why does he keep life-size dolls down there?"

"He wants to tell you himself, so I was sent to see if you'd be willing to talk to him." The officer looked from one to the other.

Hope's phone dinged again, and she looked down to see Dan had sent her a text. Shaun said something to Officer Harmon, and Hope took that moment to read Dan's text.

I just left you a voice mail. Call anytime. Have my phone on me now. So sorry to hear about Cassidy.

Hope sucked in a breath. Had he not known that Cassidy had passed away? She had assumed he knew when she left him the message. That must have been a shock, if he'd found out from her jumbled voice mail.

"Hope?"

She looked up to see Shaun looking at her, a question on his face.

"Sorry." She shook her head slightly. "What did I miss?"

"You want to go hear what Mr. Alden has to say?" Shaun asked.

Hope turned to Officer Harmon. "You're positive he had nothing to do with Luca's disappearance?"

"No, not positive. But like I said, we're reasonably sure."

Hope blew out a breath. "Then I need to apologize. I said some pretty ugly things to him." As much as part of her was relieved that Mr. Alden hadn't turned out to be an evil man who kept children in his basement, she was crushed that they weren't any closer to finding Luca. If Mr. Alden hadn't taken him, then where was he?

They rose from the table and made their way back to the foyer. Shaun opened the front door, allowing Officer Harmon and Hope to pass through before closing it behind him. Silently, they cut across the lawn to Mr. Alden's property. The half dozen or so people gathered at the corner all turned to them the minute they walked outside. A few people shouted questions, but all three of them ignored them. Once at

Mr. Alden's front door, Officer Harmon opened it after giving a quick knock and gestured for Hope and Shaun to enter before him. Mr. Alden sat at the kitchen table with Officer Dillon. The police officer stood as soon as he saw Hope and Shaun, and gestured to the table. Hope sat, with Shaun standing behind her chair. She eyed their older neighbor.

"I'll let you all talk." Officer Harmon nodded at them before closing the front door behind him as he left. Officer Dillon stood against the wall, his radio crackling intermittently.

The room had felt small when Hope was here earlier, but now with the addition of Shaun and Officer Dillon, it felt even tinier. It was suffocating, and Hope struggled to take a breath. She knew she needed to apologize to her neighbor.

"I—" she started, just as Mr. Alden spoke too. She broke off and gestured for him to continue first.

He cleared his throat and looked from Hope to Shaun before speaking. "I want you to know, I would never hurt Luca, or any other children. I'm sorry if my dolls scared you."

Hope spoke up. "No, I'm the one who's sorry. I accused you of something horrible, and I admit I was convinced you were keeping children and that you had Luca." She paused, drawing in a breath. "I'm sorry, but I don't regret snooping. I needed to be sure."

"I know." Mr. Alden nodded. "Like I told the police, I haven't seen him in at least a day or so. I can't remember. But I definitely didn't see him yesterday." He clasped his hands together on the table. "I spend a lot of time down in my workshop, and the only windows there look out into my backyard or the shrubs on either side of the house. I can't see the street from down there."

Hope nodded, searching their neighbor's eyes. He looked so sincere, and she wanted to believe him. But what was with the creepy dolls?

As if reading her mind, Mr. Alden addressed the question. "You asked why I live alone. I was married, many years ago." He stopped to let it sink in, and Hope's eyebrows rose in surprise. "Mary and I had a beautiful little girl, an angel named Sadie." He stopped again and swallowed. "When Sadie was ten, Mary took her into New York City for a day of sightseeing and shopping. This was, oh, about thirty-eight years ago. In 1986."

Hope glanced at Shaun, and he widened his eyes at her. She knew Mr. Alden was about to tell them something bad. A pit formed in her stomach, and she braced herself for whatever tragedy Mr. Alden had endured. She could see the grief etched in his weathered face, even after all these years.

"Sadie was so happy that day. She was wearing her favorite yellow dress and carried a purse that my wife had made for her, as well as her doll, Samantha. My wife and I had saved and saved to buy Sadie this new doll that had just come out. It was expensive, especially back then, but the doll looked remarkably like Sadie and our daughter was entranced." Mr. Alden turned to Hope. "You know what I'm talking about? The company that's now American Girl."

Hope nodded, her heart in her throat.

"It was Sadie's tenth birthday and we surprised her." There was a faint smile on Mr. Alden's face, and he looked off into space, as if seeing his little girl again. "I worked for Bell Atlantic back then, and had to work that Saturday, so I couldn't go with them. But that was okay, since Mary wanted to make it a special girls' day just for them." Mr. Alden met Hope's eyes, and she noticed for the first time how cloudy they were. "Sadie was so excited, and when I hugged her goodbye, I remember thinking how her long dark hair was just like the doll's." Mr. Alden ran a hand over his thinning gray hair. "She got my hair—I used to have a lot of dark-brown hair too. Mary was a redhead."

He paused, lost in memories of his family, until Hope finally spoke. "What happened to them?"

He gave her a quick glance before looking down at the table. "They were crossing the street, and a truck making a left at the intersection didn't see them. He plowed right into them." Mr. Alden stopped again when Hope gasped. She felt Shaun pull slightly away from her chair behind her. "Witnesses said that they were in the crosswalk. It was a sunny day, and as the driver made the turn, the sun blinded him for a few seconds. That was all it took." He pursed his lips for a moment and then released them. "Sadie died at the scene of the accident, still clutching her Samantha doll. Mary lived another three days before she slipped away. And just like that, my family was gone."

Hope stared in dismay at their neighbor, and shame at having hurled those insults at him earlier curled her stomach. "I'm so sorry for your loss. And I'm even more sorry for what I yelled at you." She brought a hand up to her mouth.

"It's all right, dear. You didn't know. I don't talk about my family. Some of the old-timers here remember Mary and Sadie, but they respect my privacy. My life ended that day. I was alone and have lived here alone since. I continued to work for Bell Atlantic, and later Verizon, until retirement age, and they gave me a very nice package at the end. I never wanted to lose another person I loved again, so it's just been me all these years." He sat back in his chair, leaning against the seat back as he looked from Hope to Shaun. "I started making porcelain dolls years ago because I was afraid that I was going to forget what Sadie looked like. And she loved dolls. I decided to make one that looked like her so that I could always look at it and remember my Sadie."

"How did you know how to make them?" Shaun asked.

"Initially I got books out of the library, and then eventually, I found more info online." Mr. Alden stopped and laughed. "I made a lot of mistakes, but I realized that working on the dolls and trying to perfect them was the only time I could breathe easily after losing my family.

And over time, I got better and better, until I finally made one who looked just like my Sadie."

"You weren't, I don't know . . ." Hope fumbled for words, not wanting to insult Mr. Alden. "Wasn't it kind of freaky to see her as a doll?"

"No, dear. I kept the dolls downstairs, and it was like having company as I worked on the next one. And if I suddenly couldn't remember what Sadie looked like, I'd look up and there she was." He chuckled at the looks on their faces. "I know that may seem strange to you, but they brought me comfort. Do you want to see my Sadie?"

Hope's eyebrows rose as she looked at Shaun. He cocked his head to the side, and she knew he was letting her make the decision.

"Yes," Hope said, after taking a deep breath.

Mr. Alden stood, and they followed him to the basement door, Officer Dillon trailing behind them. He hadn't said anything as Mr. Alden had told them the story, and Hope wondered now if he had known Mary and Sadie.

They trooped down the narrow staircase and found themselves in a finished basement. It was spotless, with whitewashed walls, and much neater than the kitchen upstairs. There was the large worktable Hope had seen through the window. And there, along one wall, was the platform that contained all the dolls Mr. Alden had made over the years. Hope gasped, unable to stop the sound—there had to be close to a hundred dolls. As Officer Harmon had said, dolls of all sizes, the biggest ones the size of a seven-year-old. They were so realistic that Hope had to blink a few times to understand that they weren't moving.

Mr. Alden walked to a cabinet and opened it, taking out a doll about thirty-six inches tall. He placed it on the worktable and then turned to Hope. "This is Sadie."

"She was beautiful," Hope whispered. With lustrous long brown hair, a delicate chin and nose and heart-shaped lips, Mr. Alden's daughter's likeness was forever etched onto this doll.

"I know some people find my hobby strange—that's why I don't tell anyone about it. But it gives me comfort. A few years after I finally got good at getting the likeness of someone onto a doll, one of our neighbors' son died of leukemia." Mr. Alden walked back to his collection of dolls and, after searching for a moment, pulled out a male doll. "The parents were besides themselves with grief. I made them a doll that looked like their son. But when I tried to give it to them, they freaked out. It upset the mother so much that her husband yelled at me, told me to get that thing out of their house." Mr. Alden held the doll out to Hope. "I realized then that not everyone wants to remember their lost ones the way I do. I started keeping to myself more and more after that. If I heard on the news that a child was lost, I'd make a doll that looked like them to remember them. But I never tried to give one away again. I'd learned my lesson."

He stopped talking and looked down. Hope and Shaun shared another glance. Yes, she found it creepy, but it seemed to bring solace to Mr. Alden, who found comfort in creating and remembering the lost children in this way. No wonder he kept to himself, and didn't want anyone to know about the dolls he made. But it was sad that he hadn't wanted another family after his had passed away. That he didn't want to be hurt again, and chose to lead this solitary life, secretly making dolls in his basement.

"I'm sorry again about your family, Mr. Alden." Hope took a step toward him so that he could hear her. "And I'm sorry I was snooping and suspected you had something to do with Luca."

He held up a hand. "Don't apologize. I know what it's like to lose a child. If I were in your shoes, I'd be doing everything I could to find him too."

Hope walked to Mr. Alden, her hand trembling slightly. She was sorry for suspecting Mr. Alden, after hearing his story. But she still needed to be sure that he'd had nothing to do with Luca's disappearance.

"Mr. Alden," she said, once she was within good hearing distance of him. "I'm so sorry for what you've been through, and for what happened today. But I need to ask you, for my own peace of mind." She stopped, drawing in a deep breath.

"You can ask me anything." Mr. Alden stared back at her without breaking eye contact.

"Did you take Luca? Or do you know anything about where he went?" She focused on her neighbor's face, looking for any changes in his expression that could give him away.

But his gaze remained true, and he shook his head. "I swear on the grave of Mary and Sadie that I have no idea where Luca is."

They locked gazes for a moment, and then Hope looked away.

She believed him.

15

Hope couldn't eat. Shaun had picked up pizza and salad for them from Sal's two minutes from their house, but Hope had no appetite. She stabbed her fork through the salad and took a few bites of pizza before putting it back down. Luca was still gone. Her strongest lead, Mr. Alden, had turned out to be so wrong. What if every lead they gave to the police turned out not to lead anywhere? What if Luca really had just disappeared into thin air?

She'd also yet to get hold of Dan Stern. She'd called him back as soon as they'd returned to their house after talking to Mr. Alden, but it had gone straight to voice mail. Frustrated, she'd been tempted to throw her phone against the wall but stopped herself at the last minute. She needed the phone. She'd instead thrown it onto the couch, where it'd landed with a soft plop, which wasn't nearly as satisfying.

"You want me to get you hot and sour soup instead?" Shaun looked at her plate from across the table. "I can go back out." He knew that was always her go-to comfort food.

Hope sighed, playing with her slice of pizza. "No, it's okay."

"You need to eat something."

"I know. But my stomach is in knots." She stared at her phone, now safe on the table next to her, willing it to ring. *Ring, stupid phone. Ring.* "Dan said he was keeping his phone with him. Why didn't he answer?"

"I'm sure he'll call you back—" He broke off when Hope's cell sprang to life.

She lunged for the phone and fumbled it, almost dropping it in her haste to answer. "Dan?"

"Yes. Hope. Sorry, I went for a walk. Didn't realize I hit a patch with no reception."

Hope breathed out a sigh. "It's okay."

"It's been a while," Dan said, his familiar voice sending an ache of longing through Hope. It'd been more than ten years since she'd spoken to Dan, but his voice made memories of Cassidy come flooding back.

"It has. I'm sorry you didn't know about Cassidy."

"Yeah, that was a shock. I know we haven't been in touch in years, but I always hoped . . ." He broke off and there was a moment of silence. "You said Cassy has a son?" Dan's voice was defeated. "I didn't know." He sighed. "She was my best friend, and I didn't know she'd had a baby or that she'd passed away."

"What happened to you two?" Hope jumped right to her questions. "Why did you and Cassy stop being friends?"

"I . . ." He sighed. "It was mostly my fault. I knew she wanted to travel around the US, that she wanted to see everything, experience everything. You know she couldn't wait to get away from your parents' house. She always felt like she didn't belong there. That your parents hadn't wanted her." Hope winced at Dan's words.

"That's . . ." She was about to protest, but it died on her lips. Her mother had all but confirmed this yesterday.

"Cassy couldn't wait to get away." There was a grim note in Dan's voice. "But I thought we would do it together. I didn't want to live at home either. We were going to travel, maybe go to Colorado, and I could be a ski instructor and save up some money. But she took off without me as soon as she graduated from high school."

"You were still in touch after that, right?" Hope remembered Cassidy talking about seeing Dan.

"Yes. She'd come visit, and once I met her down in Texas for spring break." He paused and took a breath. "The year she turned twenty, she . . . I . . ."

"What?" Hope asked gently when he didn't continue. "Did you have feelings for Cassidy? Besides friendship?" She'd always suspected that Dan had a crush on her sister, but Cassidy had always brushed it off whenever Hope had brought it up.

"Maybe." He huffed out a breath. "Yeah. But she made it clear I was only her best friend, that she didn't see me that way. She always went for those bad boys. Guys she knew wouldn't last more than a one-night stand or a few weeks of fun. I thought I had a chance once . . ." He broke off and stayed silent for so long that Hope thought he'd hung up.

"I'm sorry," Hope said, for lack of anything better.

"But then she disappeared. One day, she just suddenly stopped answering my calls and texts. I have no idea what happened. What I did . . ." He paused again. "Well, maybe I have a slight idea. But I never heard from her or saw her again."

"Why do you think she cut you off like that?" Hope was having a hard time understanding her sister's actions. Dan had been a true friend to her, which was rare in Cassidy's life.

"Maybe because I told her I wanted more than friendship?" Dan's voice was low. "She didn't. It hurt. I can admit that now, though I didn't back then. I was angry. So I left. I moved to Colorado and became a ski instructor, just like we had planned. Except I was alone, no Cassidy. I didn't answer her texts for a while. And when I finally relented and called her back, she was stilted. It wasn't the same. And then she stopped answering, and that was it. The end of our friendship."

"I'm sorry." Hope shook her head, perplexed. "I don't know why Cassidy would do that."

Dan made a noncommittal sound. Then his voice softened. "So, Luca. What's he like?"

Hope told him about her nephew, and a bit about Cassidy and Luca's life. "He just disappeared from our driveway. No one saw anything. But I've been digging into their background, and I think whatever it was that drove Cassidy away when he was born is tied to Luca disappearing now. I was hoping you'd have more info about why they left."

"I have no idea." The regret was obvious in Dan's voice. "She cut me off before they left, from what you're saying."

Hope blew out a breath of disappointment. She'd been hoping, clinging to the thought that maybe Dan knew something. And now that had led to a dead end too. The despair washed over her, rendering her speechless for a moment. She was about to ask Dan to keep her posted if he remembered anything, no matter how small, when Dan spoke up.

"I'm actually coming back to New York in September for a friend's wedding. Andrea Fratelli. Do you remember her?"

"Yes." Hope had a vague recollection of a skinny dark-haired girl who had always followed Dan around, hoping Cassidy and Dan would let her play with them. Cassidy hadn't cared for Andrea, saying that she was in love with Dan and hated Cassidy for taking all his attention.

"I'd love to meet Luca, if it's okay?" Dan's voice sounded hopeful.

"Sure. I'm sure Luca would like that." And then she stopped. "If we find him, that is." She clamped her lips together, not wanting to even think about never finding Luca. He had to come home soon. He couldn't be lost.

"I'm sorry." Dan's voice was soft. "That was insensitive of me."

"It's okay. I forgot too." She heaved out a sigh. "He misses Cassidy so much."

"I miss her too." Dan's voice was tinged with regret. "I wish I'd made more of an effort to reach out, to repair things between us."

They were silent for a moment, both thinking about Cassidy.

"Anyways, I'll let you know my plans when we get closer," Dan finally said.

"Okay. And again, anything you remember . . ."

"Definitely."

After hanging up with Dan, Hope couldn't stay still. Shaun was sitting on the back deck with Toby in his lap, a bottle of beer in hand. She joined them and updated him on her conversation with Dan.

"Another dead end," Shaun said, looking as defeated as she felt. "I've been over every single person who Luca has come in contact with." He ran a hand through his hair, frustration tingeing his voice.

Hope bounced on her heels, feeling the need to do something. She couldn't just stay here and wait for word. She had to get out of the house. "I'm going for a walk."

"Make sure you have your phone on you," Shaun said.

She waved it at him and then went out the gate that enclosed their deck, walking down the stone path on the side of their house to the front. She winced when she saw that the media were still out there, crowded at the corner. She ducked her head and veered in the opposite direction so that she wouldn't have to speak to anyone. As she passed in front of Mr. Alden's house, a movement across the street caught her eye. Turning her head to the right quickly, she saw a boy on a bike shutting their mailbox.

"Hey," she said. "What are you doing?"

The boy, somewhere around Luca's age, turned, his eyes wide with fright. He looked like a deer caught in headlights, and she was across the street and in front of him before he could move.

She reached out and opened her mailbox and saw that there were two envelopes in there. She blocked the boy's path so that he couldn't pedal away.

"Did you put these in here?" She kept her voice low, not wanting to attract anyone's attention.

"Um . . . no," the boy managed to stammer out.

"I saw you." She took out the envelopes, sucking in a breath when she saw they were addressed to her in Cassidy's handwriting. "Where did you get these?"

"I . . ." The boy had turned bright red, his blond hair falling into his eyes. He looked vaguely familiar; she supposed she'd seen him around the neighborhood but didn't know his name.

"Please don't lie. My nephew is still missing, and this might help us figure out what happened to him." She clutched the envelopes in her hand tightly.

The boy's eyes darted from side to side, and then he said, "This woman. She approached me yesterday. Asked if I wanted to make some money. It sounded simple enough." He looked down and kicked a rock at his feet. "She said if I'd put these in your mailbox, two at a time every day, she'd pay me fifty dollars now and fifty after the last ones were delivered."

"Who was she?" Hope's voice was sharp, her heart suddenly hammering in her chest.

He shrugged. "Dunno. Never seen her before."

"What did she look like?"

He shrugged again. "Um, maybe a bit taller than you, dark hair like you but longer."

Hope's breath caught. Cassidy was slightly taller than her, and she'd always kept her hair longer than Hope's. "Was she Asian?"

He shook his head. "I don't think so." Then he stopped and his mouth twisted. "But maybe? I don't know. She had sunglasses on and a hat, so I couldn't really tell."

"Why didn't you tell anyone when Luca disappeared?" Was Cassidy the woman who had spoken to this boy? Was she still alive, as improbable as that was?

He kicked the ground again. "I didn't know what to do. She made it sound really important, and that I wasn't supposed to tell anyone. I didn't know it had anything to do with Luca."

Hope thought for a moment, then questioned him again. "But I only got one this morning. You said she told you to put in two a day. With these two"—she held up the ones in her hand—"that makes three today."

His shoulder jerked. "There were too many people around last night. And this morning, I barely put the one in before a police car drove by. I figured I'd put more in tonight to make up for it."

"Where are the others?" Hope had a thought and started scrolling through her phone.

"At home."

She found a picture of Cassidy and held it out to the boy. "Did the woman look like this?"

He studied the picture, his brows drawn together. "Maybe? It could be her." He shrugged once more. "I'm not sure."

Hope took the phone back and found another photo of Cassidy. Granted, they were more than a decade old, but Cassidy hadn't looked that much older when Hope had identified her body. And then she wondered why she thought Cassidy was still alive. She'd ID'd her sister with her own eyes.

She thrust the phone out at the boy again, and he squinted at it. "I really can't tell. It kind of looks like her, but I can't be sure."

Hope huffed out a breath. "Can you get the rest of the letters for me? What's your name? Where do you live?"

"I'm Steven." The boy pointed up the hill. "Just a block up on Lily Drive. I can be back in a few minutes." He seemed eager to get away from her interrogation.

"I'm coming with you." Hope gestured to his bike. "You can walk the bike back." She didn't trust him to come back.

"Oh, and the woman gave me a cell phone too, that I was supposed to put in the mailbox with the last of the letters." Steven looked at her as he wheeled his bike at his side.

"What?" Hope's thoughts spun. "What kind of phone?"

"An old iPhone. It's not charged, and I don't have the old charger anymore." Steven ducked his head. "I wanted to see what was on it."

Hope didn't say anything, and they walked for a bit in silence. Could it be Cassidy's iPhone? Luca had told them he couldn't find his mom's phone when he'd found her nonresponsive in her car. What was going on? Was there a chance Cassidy was alive and reaching out to Hope? Had she taken Luca and now she was trying to let Hope know? The letters in Hope's hands seemed to burn with an energy, as if urging her to read them. But she couldn't let Steven out of her sight. She needed the rest of the letters and the cell. She needed to figure out what was going on.

Within minutes, they stopped in front of a yellow one-story cottage, typical of the neighborhood. Hope started up the walkway but stopped when Steven ran in front of her.

"Am I in trouble? Are you going to tell my parents?" He was shifting from one foot to the other.

"No. But you should tell them yourself. I'm sure the police are going to have questions for you." Her tone softened at his frightened stare. "You can help the police, Steven. Help bring Luca home."

He nodded. "I'll get the letters and then I'll tell my mom."

"Okay." Hope gave him a small smile. "I'll wait for you here."

He ran off without another word and was back in minutes. "Here. That's all of them. And the phone."

"Thank you." She took them from him, guessing at first glance that there were about seven or eight letters. The phone was an older model, its screen cracked.

"Do you think these letters have something to do with Luca disappearing?" Steven's face was screwed up with worry.

"I don't know." Hope sighed. "But I need to show them to the police. They're probably going to want to talk to you."

"I'm sorry." He looked away, not able to meet her eyes.

"Do you know Luca?" Hope asked.

"No." He shook his head. "We're not in the same class. I've seen him around but never talked to him."

Hope let out a disappointed sigh. She'd hoped for a moment that Luca had known Steven and maybe said something to him that would give them a clue. Jalissa had questioned her boys, and they'd all said Luca never said a word about wanting to leave. In fact, he'd told them that if he couldn't live with his mom, he was glad to be with Hope and Shaun.

"How was the woman supposed to pay you again?" she asked.

"She said she'd leave an envelope in our mailbox once I'd delivered all the letters."

"Hm." Hope thought for a moment and then counted the envelopes in her hand. Including the two Steven had put in the mailbox and the one she'd gotten that morning, there were ten letters total. So, at two a day, he would have been done with his mission in five days. Maybe the police could put surveillance on Steven's mailbox, see if they could catch the woman who was paying him. Even though she knew in her heart that Cassidy was dead, she couldn't help but hope that maybe there was a small chance her sister was still alive and trying to reach out to Hope.

Just then, a woman with the same blonde hair as Steven stuck her head out of the front door. "Steven, what're you doing?"

"Um . . ." Steven shifted his feet on the ground and averted his eyes from his mom.

Hope waved. "I'm Hope Chen, Luca's aunt."

"Oh." The woman's face melted in sympathy. "I'm so sorry. Any word?"

Hope shook her head and was about to tell her about the letters when Steven spoke up.

"I'll tell my mom now," he said.

Hope nodded. "I'll call the police. They'll probably be over soon." She waved to Steven's mother. "Steven will tell you what's going on."

"I hope they find him," Steven said, and then ran to his mother.

As she headed home, Hope pulled out her phone and called the police. After she told them about the letters, they promised to send someone to question Steven right away, maybe have a sketch artist get a drawing of the woman.

Hanging up, Hope picked up her pace. She clutched the old iPhone in her hand, praying they still had an old charger that would work. Whatever was going on, Hope couldn't quite quell the fantasy that her sister was still alive. If this phone held any answers, Hope would find them.

As soon as she got home, she dropped the letters on the bench and picked up the top one. Toby jumped around her legs, but Hope's entire attention was on the letter. Tearing into it, she pulled out the same cream stationery as before, covered in Cassidy's flowery script.

Dear Hope,

It's been two weeks since I left and I miss you already. I know I always act like I don't need you, but I do. Now more than ever. And I can't tell you. They'll hurt Luca they said. I don't know where we're going. I'm scared, Hope. I wish you were here to help us.

Hope sucked in a breath and looked up. Who had threatened Cassidy and Luca? What had happened, and who had given these letters to Steven? She closed her eyes briefly, sending out a prayer before opening them again.

"Shaun," she called. "There's more letters." She couldn't make heads or tails of what was going on, and the letdown of not finding Luca in Mr. Alden's basement was still a fresh wound. But these letters from Cassidy were spooking her, as if her sister were reaching out to her from the grave.

16

Ten minutes later, Shaun gave a shout of triumph. "I found one!"

Hope whooped in response. She took the old charger from him and plugged it into the outlet at the breakfast bar. Putting the other end into the old iPhone, she set it down, knowing it would take a few minutes to power up. She prayed again that the phone really was Cassidy's and would provide some answers to all the questions the letters were bringing up.

"Do you really think Cassidy is alive?" Shaun asked. He'd read the first letter that Hope had, before they went in search of a charger.

Hope's shoulders lifted and then fell. She'd told Shaun about Steven and the woman who'd paid him to deliver the letter.

"How can she be?" Hope shook her head. "And if she is, then whose body did I ID?"

"Are you sure it was Cassidy?" In the next breath, Shaun made a face. "But it had to be. Luca was with her. He saw his mother OD."

"What if he knew that wasn't his mother?" Hope's forehead furrowed, as she tried to think outside the box. "What if whoever it was had taken Luca, and now the real Cassidy has come back to get her son?"

They stared at each other for a moment. "That sounds a bit far-fetched," Shaun finally said. "Are you saying Cassidy had a long-lost twin or something?"

Hope blew out a breath of disappointment. "I guess not. But then what the hell is going on?"

Shaun handed her another letter. "We keep reading. Maybe these letters will tell us."

Hope looked down at the one in her hand. It was dated about a year after Cassidy and Luca had disappeared.

Dear Hope,

I dreamed about calling you, of showing up again like I used to do and surprising you. You're our only real family. I know our parents hadn't wanted me. You were the one who made me feel like I mattered in our family. I was like a ghost. When you left for college, I was so mad that you left me alone with them. That's why I drank and did drugs. Because then, it didn't matter that I was all alone in the world.

When you told me you would help me raise Luca, I really thought this was it. I would finally get clean, go to rehab, and kick this habit once and for all. But life laughed in my face. I found a note stuck under my windshield wiper. It said, "Leave and never come back, or we hurt Luca." I wanted to think it was just kids playing a prank, but how did they know Luca's name? I didn't want to leave. Isn't that just like me—always wanting whatever I couldn't have?

A few days later, I was driving to Target and a car was tailgating me. I deliberately sped up, and the car stayed right with me. I slowed a bit, and that's when he hit me from behind. Not hard, but enough to make the car swerve. And then it was to my left, gaining speed, and I realized it was trying to run me off the road. I had a split second to decide if I was going to drive off the highway onto the grass, or call his bluff. Just as I cut the wheel hard, it veered away from me and roared off. I managed to pull over on the shoulder and then I sat there, shaking.

The baby was fine. He'd slept through it, but I wasn't. I barely managed to drive back to your place and the next morning, I found another note on my windshield. It said, "Yesterday was a warning. Next time, we'll kill you and Luca." I found another note in my tote bag. I have no idea when or how it got there, but it said if I didn't leave by the next day, they were taking Luca. It said if I left, money would be sent to me via MoneyGram every month for as long as I stayed away. And the scary part is, they knew my banking info. There was a picture of Luca sleeping in that car seat bassinette you bought for me on your back deck. And a small piece of cloth that I realized was cut from one of Luca's burp cloths you'd bought him with the little whales on them.

I had to go. I'm sorry, Hope.

Love,
Cassidy

Hope looked up, tears stinging in her eyes. She finally knew what had made Cassidy leave, and it wasn't her. She didn't know who it was, but at least she now knew the truth. Someone had been terrorizing her sister. Hope burned with anger and shame that she hadn't protected her little sister. Poor Cassidy. Hope wished Cassidy had told her what was happening back then. She would have done whatever she could to find out who was threatening her sister.

Hope handed the letter she'd just read to Shaun and picked up another one. She skimmed it, more sure than ever that these were from Cassidy. They referenced things that only Hope and Cassidy knew about. The small, dark apartment at basement level that they'd lived in, with windows so high up that they didn't bring in much light. The lumpy, scratchy sofa Hope had slept on even before Cassidy had been born, because there was only one bedroom. The bathroom was always either burning hot in the summer or freezing in the winter, and Cassidy made references to the way she'd danced and jumped, Hope scolding her to stay still as she'd tried to dry off a wriggling Cassidy.

Hope picked up another letter, her heart hurting for all that Cassidy had gone through in the years since Hope had last seen her. She told Hope in the letters that she thought there was something wrong with her. She wasn't like Hope. She wanted to stay clean for Luca, but she always fucked up. She mentioned Emmy a few times, and Hope wondered if Emmy's contact info would be in the phone.

And then a paragraph from the letter Hope was reading jumped out at her.

> I can't do this by myself. I need your help. I do the best for Luca and when I'm using again, I make sure someone, usually Emmy, is watching out for him. But it's not fair to Luca. I know you'd take care of him. He could stay with you while I go to rehab. But I can't do it. They told me if Luca is seen back in your neighborhood, they would take him and kill him. I wish I could call you, Hope. I need help.

"Shaun." Hope realized she finally had concrete evidence that whatever had made Cassidy run all those years ago, was responsible for Luca's disappearance.

Shaun looked up at the urgent tone in Hope's voice. "What's the matter?"

"Look. I think their disappearances are connected." With a trembling hand, she held out the letter to her husband.

While he read, Hope tried to calm her thoughts. Cassidy thought if Luca came back here, they would kill him. Was that what had happened? Was Luca dead? Hope wrapped her arms around herself, rubbing her arms. No, she refused to believe that. Luca couldn't be dead. *Then where is he?*

"We need to give these to the police," Shaun said.

Hope nodded. "Can you call them? I want to read this last one." She still held an unread letter in her hand.

Shaun stood, heading for his cell phone. But before he could pick it up off the counter, their doorbell rang. They turned and looked at each other for a moment, Hope's eyes widening. Shaun went to the door while Hope stood rooted to the spot, not daring to breathe. Was it Luca? She strained her ears, urging her feet to move and go to the front door. But they refused to cooperate. She recognized Detective Regel's voice, but couldn't make out any words. And then in the distance, she heard a scream, and the blood froze in her veins. It was a woman's voice and sounded like it was coming from the Caine house. Hope's legs finally started moving, and she rushed to the door, her heart pounding.

17

The first things Hope took in were the red and blue flashing lights of a police car lighting up their street from in front of the Caines' house. The Caines' front door was wide open. There was also an unmarked police vehicle in front of it, as well as one in Hope and Shaun's driveway. Hope's heart stopped.

"What happened? Have they found Luca?" Hope grabbed Shaun's arm, looking out into the dark night.

"No," Detective Regel said. "It's about Jack Caine."

Hope drew in a breath as the detective told them that Jack had been arrested for embezzling from his company. Hope's head jerked up when Jalissa came running out of her house, screaming for them not to take Jack away. The strobing lights hurt Hope's eyes, blinding her for a moment, even as she strained to take in every detail of the scene. Jack was being led toward the unmarked car with his hands handcuffed behind him. A detective had hold of his arm, and Jack was calling something back to his wife and children. When he turned around, his eyes seemed to meet Hope's, and for just a moment, Hope could have sworn she saw a spark of animosity before he turned away.

"How did you know?" Hope tore her eyes from the drama at the Caines' and focused back on Detective Regel.

"He was already under investigation by detectives in Manhattan. When Luca disappeared, we looked into the lives of all the neighbors you mentioned, including the Caines. When he refused to give us his front-door security footage, we dug deeper. He had a few visitors yesterday that he didn't want his wife to know about." Detective Regel continued, but Hope's thoughts had splintered.

She couldn't look away from Jalissa, who was now wailing on the lawn, her two youngest clutched in her arms as her older sons lingered in the doorway. Those poor boys, having to watch their father being taken away in handcuffs. Hope heard Detective Regel say it was NYPD detectives arresting Jack, but all Hope could think of was her friend and neighbor.

"I didn't mean for this to happen . . ." Hope trailed off.

"It's not on you." Detective Regel turned to her. "It was only a matter of time before they got him. The search for Luca just sped things up."

"Poor Jalissa." Hope looked across the street again. "I should go to her." But then she remembered the letters when Shaun spoke up.

"We were about to call you." Shaun told the detective what they'd discovered from Cassidy's letters. As he was finishing, Detective Hanson walked up to them.

"We'll need the originals." Detective Hanson was all business, the drama across the street background noise to their own turmoil.

"Can I make copies first?" Hope asked. She didn't want to let Cassidy's words go without something to hold on to.

The detective nodded, and Hope rushed back into the house, gathering the letters and heading for their printer in a corner of the living room. She could hear Shaun talking to the detectives, as well as the voices from the Caines' punctuating the night. Her nerves were shot, and she didn't know what to focus on: Luca, Cassidy, or what was happening across the street.

As she waited for each page to be copied, she took out the last letter that she hadn't read yet. Her eyes skimmed over it, and then with her heart pounding, she read it again.

Hope—

I love you. I'm sorry. Please take care of Luca. I came back but someone is following me. The payments stopped months ago. I thought it was safe to come back but I was wrong. If they get me, take care of Luca. Promise. They're watching me.

Hope flipped the paper over, looking for more, but there was nothing. Cassidy hadn't signed it like the other ones. She couldn't even be sure Cassidy had written this, since the handwriting looked nothing like her previous letters. Hope read the few sentences again and then looked up just as Shaun walked into the living room.

What had happened to Cassidy? And who had been watching her?

◆ ◆ ◆

An hour later, after the police had finally left and the neighborhood was quiet again, Hope threw herself onto the couch, lengthwise. Shaun sat next to her, putting her feet in his lap. They didn't speak for a few moments, both overwhelmed by everything that had happened that day. Hope couldn't believe it'd been only about twenty-eight hours since Luca had disappeared. She felt as if she'd aged ten years. And they were no closer to finding Luca.

"What's going on, Shaun?" Hope closed her eyes. "Luca disappearing is impacting so many people around here."

"Makes you realize that you never know what is happening behind closed doors." Shaun ran his fingers over Hope's calves, gently kneading to get the knots out. "Who knew our neighbors had so much to hide."

Hope's eyes opened. "I feel so bad about Jalissa. I wanted to go to her but . . ."

But they'd been busy with the detectives about Cassidy's letters. And the cell phone Steven had given her had finally powered up. Hope had skimmed it, and confirmed it was indeed Cassidy's phone. She'd gone through it, writing down names and phone numbers, including Emmy San Giacomo's, before giving the cell to the police. There hadn't been any text messages in the phone. Someone had wiped them clean, but the police would try to get whatever info they could from it.

The detectives had also updated them on what they'd learned from Steven. His family had just moved into the neighborhood a few months ago, so Steven couldn't tell them if the woman was a neighbor. They were going to send a sketch artist to Steven's house tomorrow to see if they could get a better idea of what the woman looked like.

Shaun continued to massage Hope's calf, making her sigh.

"I saw her sister pull up. She'll take care of Jalissa," Shaun said. "It's probably better that you're not there."

Hope knew what Shaun meant. Maybe Jalissa would blame them for shining the light on Jack's indiscretions. "Yeah, you're right." She turned to Shaun. "Why are Cassy's letters and cell phone suddenly turning up? What's going on?"

"I don't know." Shaun's fingers stilled on Hope's calf. "I have this feeling . . ." He trailed off and Hope pushed herself to sit up on the couch.

"About what?" She searched her husband's face.

"Cassidy was afraid of someone. It makes me wonder if she really just overdosed, or if someone killed her."

Hope gasped, staring at her husband, wondering if he was joking. But there was no hint of a smile on his face. He was dead serious. Her mind went back to that last letter she'd read. The handwriting had been all over the place, as if Cassidy had been drunk or high. That was what Hope had assumed. But what if Cassidy had just been scared?

"You think someone killed Cassidy, and now they're back to get Luca?" Hope's eyes widened in fear. "Maybe that's why we didn't get a ransom note. Because they don't want money. What if whoever had been paying Cassidy to stay away came back to finish off the job?"

A chill went down her spine. What had her sister gotten herself involved in?

18

Day three
7:00 a.m.

Luca had been missing for nearly thirty-eight hours now. There were no leads—no ransom notes, no phone calls, no sightings, no clues. The only things they had were the letters from Cassidy and her old cell phone. Shaun had convinced Hope to take a sleeping pill the night before because she couldn't shut off the questions running through her mind. She couldn't stop imagining what Luca was going through, if he was dead, if Cassidy really was alive, and what any of it meant.

Despite the sleeping pill, Hope woke up feeling as if she hadn't slept at all. The spot next to her in bed was empty. The smell of freshly brewed coffee told her that Shaun was up. She rubbed her temples, her head already throbbing as she thought about another interminable day of waiting for any word about Luca. With a sigh, she got out of bed and Toby followed her out of the bedroom.

Shaun was sitting at the dining table in one of the two seats that faced the TV in the living room. The news was on.

"Anything?" she asked, even though she knew the answer was no. If there were any news, her cell, which was practically glued to her hand at this point, would have alerted her.

Shaun shook his head, taking a sip of his coffee. "They ran a piece about Jack Caine."

Hope sank onto the chair across from him and put her head in her hands, her elbows propped on the table. All their leads had turned to nothing. All they'd managed to do was unearth their neighbors' secrets.

Where are you, Luca? Are you still alive?

She picked her head up. "I want to call the few people that are in Cassidy's contacts." She knew the detectives had called them all already, and no one knew where Luca was. Hope wanted to talk to them herself, especially Emmy San Giacomo.

Luca had told them that he usually stayed with Emmy when Cassidy "went on a bender." It had shocked Hope at first, how matter of fact Luca was about his mother's addiction, talking about it as if she'd caught a cold. But she guessed he was old enough to understand. And it was a reality of his life, something he'd lived with for as long as he was alive. Emmy had been kind to him, he'd said. They'd met her at a campground one of the times they hadn't had a place to stay. About the same age as Cassidy, she'd been camping with her sister, something they did every year. Luca had said that Cassidy and Emmy had hit it off right away and stayed in touch. They'd see her a few times a year, but often went months without speaking to her.

"Dan was in there, right?" Shaun asked.

Hope nodded. "I think he'd be happy to know that Cassidy had kept him in her contacts."

"Any other names jump out at you?" Shaun had been busy with the detectives and hadn't seen the phone himself.

"My parents are there." Hope had been surprised to see that. "I didn't recognize any of the other names, except Emmy's."

"She lives out West somewhere? It's too early to call her."

Hope picked up her cell. "But now that we know her last name, maybe I can find her on social media." She pulled up Instagram first and typed in Emmy's name. She found her profile right away.

Shaun came around to her side, and they studied the Instagram account. The profile picture was of a woman with brown hair caught in two braids. Her feed was mostly pictures of a goat and the brunette woman, along with some landscape photos of what looked like a farm.

"I remember Luca saying something about her goat." Hope chuckled. "Named Vincent van Goat."

"Vincent van Goat." Shaun laughed too. "That's pretty good."

"I'm going to DM her. That way, hopefully she'll call as soon as she sees it." The detectives had told them they'd spoken to Emmy last night, and Luca hadn't been in contact with her. She hadn't even known Cassidy had passed away. But she was the person Cassidy had been closest to in the last few years, and Hope desperately needed to know what her sister's life had been like.

Hope had just sent a DM to Emmy when her notifications showed she had a message.

"That was fast." Hope read the message and then looked up at Shaun. "She's up, even though it's just after four a.m. on the west coast. She said she can talk now."

Hope dialed Emmy's number.

"Hello? Hope?" Emmy's voice was younger than Hope had imagined.

"Yes. I'm sorry to bother you so early."

Emmy laughed. "I'm always up this early. That's what running a farm is like." She cleared her throat, and then her voice sobered. "I'm so sorry to hear about Cassidy. And that Luca is missing." Emmy's voice was heavy with regret. "I haven't heard from them in almost six months. It's not unusual for that to happen, so I didn't think anything of it."

"Were you close?"

Emmy sighed. "Yes. Cassidy felt like family. I knew I could trust her with my life and that, if I was in trouble, she would come help me, no questions asked. But at the same time, I didn't know very much about her. She never really opened up about her life."

"Has Cassidy ever said anything to you about why she left home?"

And me? Hope thought, but didn't say out loud.

"She said once that Luca's life was in danger. She'd been drinking . . . one of the times she fell off the wagon. She started talking about you. How she missed you, wished she could call you. And I was like, 'Why don't you then?'" Hope's heart leaped at Emmy's words. Cassidy had missed her.

"What did she say?" Hope held her breath, waiting for Emmy's answer.

"That she couldn't. Someone wanted her gone. That's all she would say." Emmy was silent for a beat. "I can't believe she's dead. That she's not just living her life somewhere, and then one day out of the blue, she'll call me up and say, 'Guess what—Luca and I are coming to visit tomorrow.'"

"Did she do that a lot?" Hope was so curious about her sister's life. "Just show up without any notice?"

"Yes." Emmy laughed. "That's why we got along so well. Neither of us are great about making plans. We just do things when we feel like it. I never leave the farm, except to go camping with my sister, and every few years, I'll treat myself to a real vacation."

"Do you live alone?" Hope was curious about this woman.

"Yes, just me and the animals."

She didn't elaborate, and Hope didn't ask, not wanting to pry. Instead, she got the conversation back on track. "Can you think of anyplace that Luca might have gone to if he had left by himself? Or anyone who might have taken him?"

Emmy was silent for a moment. "No," she finally said. "Like I said, I didn't know much about their lives when they weren't with me. I can't think of anyone that she talked about, except for you and some guy named Dan from her past."

Hope's heart sank again. Another dead end. She sighed. "Okay. Thank you."

"I'm sorry I wasn't more helpful," Emmy said. "For what it's worth, she missed you a lot."

They were quiet for a moment, and then Hope thanked her again, asking her to call if she thought of anything that might be helpful.

When she hung up, she stared at Shaun, who'd heard the whole conversation on speakerphone. He held out a hand and she walked to him, settling on his lap as he wrapped an arm around her waist.

"Cassy loved you." He kissed her softly on the lips. "Your sister missed and loved you." He knew how often Hope had blamed herself for Cassidy leaving, thinking her sister hated her and wanted to get as far away from her as possible.

"Yeah." The word came out on a sigh. It lightened her heart to know her sister had thought of her all these years. But they still had no clue about what had happened to Luca.

19

Hope was scrubbing the tiles in the shower of the guest bathroom. She needed something to do and was taking her worry and anxiety out on the grout, rubbing the dirt away with vigorous strokes. Shaun had looked in for a moment and shaken his head before leaving her in peace to her attack of mildew and soap scum. Most of the tiles were already done, gleaming in fact, and she had only a small patch left when her cell suddenly rang next to her. She jumped, then blew out a breath.

She reached for the hand towel that she'd left next to her for just this reason, quickly dried her hands, and picked up her phone. She looked at the caller ID and called out to Shaun, who was putting together sandwiches in the kitchen for lunch.

"It's Tessa." She hurried out of the bathroom and down the hall to the kitchen. Shaun paused with the knife in the air over the sandwich and focused on her.

"Hi, Tessa. Any news?" Hope said as soon as she picked up the call.

There was a pause, and then she heard, "Ayi?"

One hand flew to her mouth, and her eyes widened, not daring to hope. "Luca? Is that you?"

At the sound of the name, Shaun put the knife down and sprinted to her side. He gestured for her to put the call on speakerphone, which she finally did once she could move.

"When can we come home?" Luca's voice was faint, as if it were coming from far away.

"Luca! Oh, thank goodness. Where are you? What happened?" Hope asked, frantic.

Shaun spoke too. "Are you okay? Are you hurt?"

"I'm fine. So's Mochi." Luca's voice was so low that they both had to bend forward to catch his words.

Tears sprang to Hope's eyes and then she was crying, so thankful that Luca was alive. "Oh, Luca . . . I'm . . . I'm . . ." She couldn't speak, and choked out a sob instead.

"What's the matter?" Luca's voice rose in panic. "Why are you crying?"

Hope still had no words, so Shaun answered. "We've just been so worried about you. What happened? Where'd you go?"

"I'm with Shadow. You know that."

"What?" Hope and Shaun stared at each other, and suddenly, it dawned on Hope that Luca had called from Tessa's number. "You're with Tessa and Robert?" They shared another confused look.

"Well, yeah . . ." Luca trailed off, and they could hear muffled sounds coming through the phone. Suddenly he whispered, "I have to go."

"No, wait!" Hope shouted. "Where are you?"

"I don't know. We're in the RV." Luca was still whispering.

"Don't hang up. I . . ." Hope looked at Shaun helplessly, not sure what to say.

Shaun stepped in. "Have you been in the RV this whole time? Did they hurt you?"

"Yes. I mean no . . . I have to go." And he hung up.

"No, Luca!" Hope's voice rose and fell with those two words. And then she turned to Shaun. "We have to find him."

Shaun was already pulling out his phone. "I'm calling the police. They can probably trace her phone. Find out where she is." He looked at Hope as he waited for someone to pick up. "Why would they take him?"

She shook her head helplessly, her thoughts moving in too many directions to make sense. All she could think was that Luca was alive. He sounded fine, although she wasn't sure if Tessa and Robert had harmed him from his last answer. But he was alive. She sank back against her chair, holding on to that one fact. He was alive.

PART 2

Tessa

20

Six weeks earlier

I fell in love with Shadow the minute I laid eyes on him. I knew we needed to adopt him when I saw his pictures in her social media posts. Not only for me, but also for Robert. To fix the strain that had sprung up between us, a distance I didn't want to admit to but couldn't ignore.

"I think it's time we got a dog." I showed Shadow's picture to Robert and then I waited, my breath held.

He knew how much I'd always wanted one, but we were both so busy with work, and it wasn't fair to leave the poor thing at home by itself all day. And then Robert had gotten sick and all my energy went into taking care of him. I'd quit my job as sales manager of a large corporation when Robert's cancer came back. I hadn't returned to work, wanting to spend every moment with him.

When Robert didn't say anything, I spoke again, hating the pleading tone in my voice. "He's perfect for us. He's black, just like I've always wanted." I'd told Robert years ago that I always felt bad for the black dogs. They were usually the last to be adopted.

He nodded, his face softening, and my breath hitched with hope. But Robert's next words immediately plunged me back in despair.

"You'll need the company when I'm gone." His jaw clenched, and his face became like stone.

My arms dropped to my sides, and I pressed my lips together so hard I lost feeling. "Robert, you're not going anywhere. I won't let you." I really believed I could make him stay here on Earth just by the sheer force of my will.

His tone was impatient. "You need to face—"

I cut him off. "I'm filling out an application." I didn't look at him, but I could feel him staring after me. I would do anything to dissipate the tension that had been between us since his cancer came back. If I was being honest, that tension had started even before he got sick again. Getting a dog would heal us. I was going to make everything okay between us again.

And now here we were, in the Chens' driveway, about to meet our dog. I grabbed Robert's hand and squeezed, ignoring the fact that he pulled it away. Shadow's foster family waited in their fenced-in backyard. There were three dogs running around, and my mood lightened when I caught sight of the boy. Robert had no idea the surprise that waited for him.

The Asian woman opened the gate and greeted us. "Hi, I'm Hope. You must be Robert and Tessa. This is my husband, Shaun." She gestured to the lean man with long limbs and a narrow frame who stood next to her.

We shook hands and they stepped aside so that we could come into the yard, while the excited dogs barked and surrounded us. Shadow gave us a sniff and then ran back to the boy, who was crouched in the grass.

Hope closed the gate firmly behind us. She was about five four, a few inches shorter than me, with high cheekbones and black hair cut just to her chin so that it swung forward in a glossy sheet when she moved her head. She was so pretty in a cool way, as if nothing ever ruffled her feathers.

Shaun gestured to the boy. "Luca, come meet the Conrads," he called.

The boy reluctantly let go of Shadow and stood, coming toward us slowly, his hair in front covering one eye. Shadow stayed by his side, and my heart melted at the dog's loyalty.

"This is our nephew, Luca Wen," Hope said.

A sudden gasp made me turn to Robert. His face was as white as a sheet, and he had one hand clutched to his chest.

"Luca Wen?" he asked in a low voice. Wen wasn't a common last name around here. But the name Luca would be what tipped him off.

The boy stared at him, curiosity shining in his eyes. Robert swallowed so hard that I could see his Adam's apple bobbing. He looked like he was going to pass out. His mouth opened, but no words came out.

"Robert?" I laid a hand on his cheek. "What's the matter?" I asked, even though I knew. I'd wanted it to be a good surprise. He needed something to lift his spirits, to help beat this cancer. I hadn't meant to send him into literal heart failure.

"I . . . This is . . ." He shook his head, unable to continue. His voice was weak. The cancer was taking my Robert away from me, one cell at a time.

I focused on my husband but could see the concern on Hope's and Shaun's faces from the corner of my eye. "It's okay, Robert. Things happen for a reason." He was still staring at the boy, but then he finally met my eyes. I smiled and gave him an encouraging nod.

He swallowed again, his eyes searching mine, but I gave nothing away. My eyes only shone with love for him, telling him without words that I would always be here for him. He didn't speak, but slowly, my love enfolded him until the color returned to his cheeks and a tentative smile curved his lips.

"Thank you, Tess."

"Say it," I encouraged.

"You're my lifeline."

And he was mine. But I wished he'd stop calling me Tess. It was his special name for me, and I'd never had the heart to tell him I hated it, that it made me think of the woman in *Tess of the d'Urbervilles*, who stabbed her husband to death. I shuddered. All that blood. I could never do that.

I was aware of Hope and Shaun watching us, and once I was sure Robert wasn't going to keel over, I turned my attention back to the dog.

"Hi, Shadow." I dropped to the grass in front of him. The dog looked at me, and then his tongue lolled as he panted. I reached out a hand for him to sniff and he gave it a lick. I laughed.

"He likes you," Robert said, finally tearing his eyes away from the boy and focusing on the dog. My husband vibrated with nervous energy even as he held a hand out to Shadow.

The dog sniffed both of us and allowed me to put my arms around him. His short black fur was so silky.

"He's perfect," I breathed, as I looked up at Shadow's foster family. Hope and Shaun were smiling, but the boy was biting his lip and looking away.

I was about to say something, but then the larger of the two white dogs ran up to him, and the boy fell to the ground. He wrapped his arms around the dog, burying his face in her back. Hope put a hand on his shoulder.

"I'm sorry," she said to us. "Luca is a little sad that Shadow is leaving." She shot us a look full of concern.

"Oh no." I placed a hand on my heart. I didn't want to make a little boy miserable. But we needed Shadow.

The boy sniffed, and then his shoulders were shaking. He turned away, as if he didn't want us to see him crying. I looked at Robert, whose eyes were wide in alarm. He took a step toward the boy.

Shaun pulled his nephew to him, and the boy swiped a hand over his eyes. "Shadow is going to a great home," Shaun said. "Don't be sad."

Robert reached out as if he wanted to touch the boy, but then he dropped his hand to his side. There was a helpless look on his face.

"I'm sorry," Hope said again, sending us another apologetic look. "This is his first experience with having a foster dog leave. Luca only came to live with us about two weeks ago."

"Oh." I made a sympathetic face, even though I'd already known this.

"I'm sorry, Luca," Robert said softly.

We all watched as the boy turned to Robert, tears shining in his eyes. For a moment, no one moved. Robert and the boy locked eyes, and I held my breath.

"It's okay," the boy finally said. "I know he's found a good home. But please take care of him. He likes to go out after he eats. He doesn't always go right away, so you have to stay with him, but you need to take him out, okay?"

Robert nodded, then blinked. "Tessa and I will take good care of him."

The boy reached up to brush the tears out of his eyes, and Shaun tightened his grip on his shoulder.

I felt so bad for him that I almost offered to let him keep Shadow. But then I looked at the black dog and knew he belonged with us. To distract the boy, I said, "We have an RV and like to take trips around the country. I think Shadow is going to love going camping with us."

The boy turned to me for the first time. "You have an RV?" I had to admit, he was a very good-looking boy, with a shock of brown hair that fell into his eyes and large dark-brown eyes.

I saw the interest on his face and warmed to the subject. "Yes. We love our RV. Have you ever been in one?"

He shook his head. "Mom and I would see them when we camped out. I always wished we had one."

At the mention of his mother, my lips curled, but before I could say anything, Robert jumped in.

"It's like a small apartment on wheels. We have everything we need inside." He smiled, and the boy swung his curious gaze toward my husband.

"There's a bathroom and everything?" the boy asked.

"Yes. And we have a kitchen too." Robert turned to me. "Tessa thought of everything when we furnished it."

"Maybe you can come visit us sometime to see Shadow and we can show you the RV?" I offered. I realized this was a brilliant idea. The perfect way to connect with him.

His eyes lit up, and he glanced at Shaun and Hope, his tears forgotten. "Can I?"

Hope laughed. "If Tessa and Robert don't mind."

"We're only a ten-minute walk from here." Robert pointed to the other side of the lake.

The boy leaned down and gave Shadow a hug. "I'm going to miss you so much," he said. "But I think you're going to have so much fun in the RV. I'll come visit you, okay?"

Shadow gave the boy a lick on the face, making him laugh. He looked up at us. "Are you going to keep his name? He knows it and comes when I call him."

I nodded. "I think it fits him perfectly."

The boy finally smiled at me. "I'm glad. I got him a special toy that he loves to sleep with. Can I give it to you so he doesn't miss me too much?"

I nodded again, and he got up to run inside. I looked after him and noticed that Robert was doing the same thing. I slipped my hand into Robert's, and he looked down at me distractedly. His attention was focused on only the boy.

Shaun handed us a large bag with things for Shadow while Hope went over feedings and things we needed to know about our new dog. The boy came back with a large green stuffed alligator and handed it to Shadow.

We all laughed when Shadow picked up the alligator and trotted around the yard with it. The smaller white dog ran after Shadow, while the bigger one stayed by the boy's side.

"You're really good with the foster dogs," Robert said.

The boy nodded. "Aunt Hope and Uncle Shaun said I've been really helpful." He reached down to stroke the white dog's head. "They're like me. No place to go."

Robert turned and caught my eyes, and I could see by the way his chin wobbled that he was emotional. His thoughts must have been spinning, and I knew he was trying to contain his shock. Hope and Shaun probably had no idea the inner turmoil Robert was going through, but I knew him. And right now, he was freaking out. I had done the right thing in bringing him here.

Giving myself a virtual pat on the back for a job well done, I accepted the leash that Hope handed me. Robert and I posed with Shadow as Hope snapped pictures to send to the rescue. And then it was time to go.

The Chens and the boy walked us out the gate and to our car in their driveway. The boy was fighting tears again, and Robert stopped next to him.

"Thank you for taking such great care of Shadow, Luca." Robert reached out and, after hesitating a moment, laid a hand on the boy's upper arm briefly before letting go.

"You're welcome." The boy bit his lip and looked away.

I walked to them with Shadow, and the boy got down to give Shadow one last hug. I smiled at him and then opened the back door so Shadow could get into the car. After securing the seat belt we'd bought for him, I closed the door and faced the boy again.

He was openly crying now, and Robert and I moved at the same time toward him. With a questioning look at Hope, who nodded, Robert and I enveloped him in a three-way hug. For a moment, I closed my eyes and let myself imagine what would have happened if Robert hadn't said no all those years ago. This could have been our family. But then my eyes opened and I knew there was no point in looking back. I could only look forward and work with what I had.

We let go of the boy and got into our car. As I was closing my door, I heard Hope say, "What a nice couple." I smiled to myself, happy that this was how others saw us. We really *were* the nicest couple.

I pulled away and looked back to see the boy waving madly. I turned to Robert. Without saying anything, I knew what he was thinking. He put a hand on my thigh and squeezed, sending tingles through my body.

"I think we should order a box of stuffed toys and send them to him, so he can give them to the next foster dogs." I put a hand over Robert's, which was still on my leg. Robert couldn't drive anymore. "What do you think? It might cheer him up."

Robert glanced at me, a smile lighting his thin face. "That's a great idea." He searched my face, and I wondered what he was thinking. He'd been distant with me for months now, and I couldn't bear it. But it looked like my plan was working. He was already more affectionate with me than he had been for months.

I sighed and looked back at Shadow. "Our dog is going home with us."

"He is." Robert didn't look at me. He stared straight ahead. "You finally got what you always wanted."

I disagreed, but I kept my mouth shut. Soon, we would both get what we'd always wanted.

21

Two weeks earlier

The screen on the back door banged behind me as I jumped out of its way, mindful of my heels. That stupid screen had cut me so many times. I had a scar thick as a rope from the worst of them, when the door sliced my heel open, making me fall on the floor in pain and shock. I hated the sight of blood.

Shadow pulled on his leash to get outside, and I almost tipped over.

"Hold on, Shadow!" He halted at my shout but looked back at me with an impatient shake of his head.

I laughed at his eager expression. He loved going on walks. Whenever he heard the clink of his harness, he would give a few happy woofs and jump on me, tail wagging frantically. He'd been with us for a month, and we took a lot of long walks together, just Shadow and me. Robert was in bed most of the time now, and the only way I could stave off my worry was to get out of the house when he was resting. I'd installed a camera so that I could keep an eye on him while Shadow and I went on our walks. They calmed me, forced me to take in deep breaths of fresh air as we roamed the neighborhood.

I didn't want to admit it, even to myself, but I could see Robert was fading away. I was losing him. Despite trying everything—making sure he ate and stayed hydrated, talking to him softly, reading his favorite books to him, playing his favorite music at a comfortable level, keeping his lips from drying out—despite getting Shadow, despite getting the boy into our lives, I had failed to do the one thing I'd vowed to do, and that was not let the cancer win the fight for Robert. We now had someone coming to the house daily to help. Just the other day, the doctor had mentioned hospice. I clamped my mouth together hard to drive that thought away.

I refused to let him give up. I couldn't. What was I going to do without him? Even now, just thinking about it, the panic caught in my chest and clawed at me until I wanted to curl up in a ball and hide. I couldn't live without Robert. We were everything to each other. It was us against the world, and we were each other's number-one priority in life.

I took a deep breath and held it for a few seconds before blowing it out through my mouth, just like our yoga teachers had taught us. Shadow started walking down the front path and I followed, willing my negative thoughts to float away with each exhale. I invited in only positivity, only healing thoughts for Robert. He looked good today. He even had enough energy to sit up in bed and talk on the phone with his sister, who lived in Connecticut. I was thankful for Janie, who called Robert often and tried to visit every week or so, bringing us Robert's favorite foods to tempt his appetite, or a new book she thought he'd like. I could go on my walks with Shadow, knowing that for a little while, someone else would watch over Robert.

The summer air steadied me. We lived at the very top of the hill that surrounded the lake, which was man-made and only about a mile around. On three sides, the neighborhood went uphill with the lake in the middle down at the bottom. Sometimes in the winter, I could get a glimpse of the lake from here, about six streets up, but now, with the trees in full bloom, I couldn't see it. The boy lived on the other side, only one street up from the lake. I shaded a hand over my eyes, looking in his direction. Maybe I could get him to visit Robert today after school.

My eyes took in the pretty houses and lawns, and the wooded areas that were rampant in this community. The sun was warm on my neck as birds chirped and butterflies and bees flitted in flower gardens. The neighborhood was peaceful, the quintessential lake town on the verge of summer, with colorful flowers in bloom and geese and ducks floating down on the lake. I often spotted deer and fox at dawn and dusk. With all this natural beauty around me, all this *life*, it was so unfair that Robert was wasting away in our home, his body ravaged by a silent killer that was now in his brain.

Shadow pulled again and the plastic poop bag carrier attached to the loop of his leash swung out. The roll was empty.

"Shoot." Shadow looked over his shoulder at me. "I need to get a new roll of bags." I turned to go inside, but Shadow refused to budge. I tugged on the leash. "Come on, Shadow." He took a couple of steps but stopped again. I managed to move him a few more steps to the edge of the short flight of stairs leading to our front porch before I gave up. "Fine, you can stay out here and wait for me."

I looped his leash around a post of the handrail and Shadow plopped his butt on the ground. Giving a shake of my head, I went in through the front door, since it was closer than going around back. The front door closed quietly behind me, unlike our back door.

I could hear Robert's low voice and was glad that he was occupied. I headed for the kitchen at the back of the house and went to the drawer where we kept things for Shadow. As I grabbed a new roll of poop bags, my gaze fell on the bag of liver treats that the boy had brought over for Shadow the last time he came to visit.

My plan had worked perfectly. We'd kept in touch with Hope and Shaun and the boy, sending them pictures and videos of Shadow. Robert and I had ordered a huge box of stuffed dog toys and had it shipped to Master Luca Wen (Robert's idea—he thought it would make the boy feel more grown-up, to be addressed as master of the foster dogs). The boy had sent us a nice handwritten thank-you note, along with a drawing of Shadow and Mochi that was actually quite good. I'd hung it on our fridge. And we'd invited him to come over to see the RV. Shaun had brought him and Mochi over three weeks ago, so that the dogs could play in the yard and Robert could show off our RV.

I was right. The boy was good for Robert. Even though Robert's energy and appetite were failing fast, even though he was shrinking by the day, he had perked up the first time the boy came to visit. I'd gotten a glimpse of the old Robert. And he'd been like that every time the boy had come to visit after that, walking around the lake with Mochi by himself. I suspected his aunt didn't know he did that, but I wasn't about to stop him.

I closed the drawer, letting the sound of Robert's voice soothe me. I closed my eyes, trying to absorb it into my being. I drew strength from the sound. He was still here, alive, in our bedroom. I crept quietly toward the living room, taking comfort in his low rumbling voice and trying to drink in the moment, to hold on to the sound forever.

It took a minute before the meaning of his words sank into my consciousness.

". . . was going to do it before I got sick again."

My ears perked up. Do what? Maybe something special for me? I took a few steps closer, making sure I was behind the wall that separated the kitchen from the living room, which led right into our bedroom. I could hear Janie, since I'd set the phone on speakerphone before I left.

". . . tell Tessa?"

Tell me what? Janie said more, but her words were an unintelligible jumble. I steadied myself by pressing one hand flat on the wall and inched forward. I was a master at eavesdropping, having practiced all my life. First with my parents, and then later with Robert. I held my breath, straining to hear their words. Robert's voice was weak, and he stopped often to catch his breath. It was hard to understand him, especially from another room. But when the words finally penetrated my brain, my entire body seized and a rush of heat engulfed me, as if I were standing in the middle of a bonfire.

No, no, no. A voice screamed the word over and over in my head. I felt like I was going to explode. Literally combust, pieces of Tessa everywhere.

I let go of the wall and grabbed my head as my eyes prickled and warm tears pooled. I squeezed them shut, the tears leaking out, faster and faster, running into my mouth, the salty tang choking me. The grief overtook my body, and it felt like someone had taken a knife to my heart. Twisted it in my chest, hacking off pieces of the organ, until all that was left was a bloody pulp.

A howling sound filled my ears, as if I were caught in the vortex of a tornado. As I gulped for breath, my heart raced out of control, and I was convinced I wouldn't survive this. Images filled my mind and suddenly I was back there that night, the night Robert had saved me. My head was bleeding, from where the lamp had crashed into my skull, and I was crawling on the floor, my left hand a mangled mess. There was a trail of bloody handprints behind me, blood streaming down my face, my mouth swollen, my lips split. Blood, so much blood that night. On me, on him, on her. That night was the reason I couldn't stand the sight of blood. Or the metallic smell of hot blood gushing out of a human body.

I grabbed my head, gave it a shake, determined to drive that nightmare out. Robert had saved me, and he'd promised to be with me forever. He couldn't be leaving me so soon, not yet, when we still had so many years together. It couldn't be true. We were a unit. We were supposed to be together forever.

I sank to the floor and curled up in a ball, hiding my face in my arms. Heaving out a breath, I fought for control, to stop the swirling of memories in my head, hurt and anger expanding in my chest like a living creature. I had to fix this. I couldn't let it happen. I forced myself to take slow breaths, and my heart finally beat at a normal pace again and the tears stopped. I picked my head up, surprised Robert hadn't heard the sound of my heart breaking. Of my entire being shattering, right here on our kitchen floor. But he and Janie were still talking, although now their voices were lower and I couldn't understand a word.

Slowly, I stood, pushing against the wall since my legs were so wobbly. By the time I was completely upright, I knew what I had to do. With my mouth pressed together hard, I gave a grim nod, resolved. I couldn't let this happen. I would fix this and make things right for us again. Robert, my love. I knew what I had to do, and I would do it after my walk with Shadow. For us. I was doing it for us.

22

Five days earlier

The day was sunny, bringing cheer into our little home, filling it with light. I'd opened the windows that morning and a breeze blew through the house, the scents of freshly mowed grass and summer air drifting in. All was right in the world again. A miracle had happened and Robert was improving. As much as it had broken my heart, I knew I'd done the right thing. Because Robert had suddenly started to gain strength and energy in the last week. I was right and the doctors were wrong. My Robert was stronger than the cancer, and he was beating it. He'd even gotten out of bed today.

"Robert," I called from the foyer. I'd gone out to pick up his favorite pasta fagioli soup from the Italian deli in town. His appetite had returned, and I was so grateful, I would have walked to Italy to get the real thing if that was what he wanted. All my efforts to keep him alive were finally working. The fear that had gripped my insides for months was slowly melting away.

"In here, darling." His voice came from the living room.

I walked to the back of the house and set the bag on the counter. Our kitchen opened into the living room, and Robert sat on the couch with Shadow beside him, watching TV.

He smiled when he saw me. "There you are. I wondered where you'd gone." Shadow wagged his tail and jumped off the couch to come to my side.

My heart leaped to see Robert up and about, when only a week earlier, he'd been bedridden, needing help to get to the bathroom. "I got your favorite soup." I pointed to the paper bag. "Want it now?"

"Thanks, darling. But I'm not hungry. I'll have it later."

He reached out an arm, and I walked over and slid into his side. He dropped a kiss on the top of my head, and I closed my eyes to savor the moment. I wanted to remember the warmth of his lips and the smell of his aftershave forever.

"You take such good care of me, Tess." His voice no longer had that trembly tone it'd taken on in the last few weeks.

I opened my eyes and looked into his, still so bright and blue. "Of course. You're my family." He knew I would do anything for him.

My parents had kicked me out of the house as soon as I turned eighteen, a few days after graduating from high school. They said I was an adult and could take care of myself. I had, finding waitressing jobs and living with friends, but I'd longed to belong to someone. I was so lonely until I met Robert a few years later. From the moment our eyes met across the room at the sports bar where I worked, he had become my family. Only a couple of weeks after meeting, he'd saved me from that horrible . . .

I stopped myself before my mind could take me back to a time that I tried to put behind me. A tremor went through my body, and I hugged my arms around myself. Robert had saved me, and when I recovered, I knew we were meant to be together. That was more than twenty years ago, and he was still everything to me. We didn't have any children because Robert never wanted them and I'd agreed. But we had each other, and that was all that mattered.

This was why I couldn't lose him. He was the only family I had in the world, the only person who truly loved me. My parents hadn't loved me. My mother might have once, long ago, before my father's influence flattened her, turned her into someone for him to control and use. I'd craved her love all my life, but after I found Robert, it hadn't mattered anymore. I didn't need to worry about my parents. They were both dead, gone. Out of my life because they hadn't taken care of what was theirs.

Robert yawned and I laid a hand on his chest, wanting to memorize his form with my fingertips, marveling at how solid he felt, even with all the weight he'd lost. "Still tired?"

Robert nodded and rubbed the side of his head. "A bit. And I have a headache."

Alarm shot through me, and I studied his face. "Do you feel sick? Anything hurt?" I ran my hands down his body as if that would help me figure out what was wrong.

"I'm fine." He took one of my hands in his and squeezed. "Just tired."

"You still up for the RV trip?" I looked at him anxiously. We'd talked about taking a trip soon, if his strength continued to improve. Shadow stuck his nose into my hand, demanding a pet, and I complied, but my focus was on Robert.

We'd bought an RV the year Robert was diagnosed with prostate cancer. He'd always wanted to take trips in one around the country, and we decided to go for it because, you know, life is short. We'd taken many trips in the RV since then, even doing one cross-country. He was semiretired now because the cancer treatments had really kicked his ass this time around. He could work from anywhere, even though he'd kept only some longtime clients.

"I'll be fine. I feel better every day." He rubbed the back of my hand absently with his thumb, sending warm waves up my arm. I'd missed these little signs of affection. It only reinforced that I'd done the right thing the day I'd overheard Robert and Janie talking.

"Okay." I didn't say more; he hated it when I worried, so I tried to keep it to myself.

I thought of taking a yoga class, to calm my nerves and stretch the kinks out of my body. I'd signed us up for private yoga sessions soon after his first diagnosis because I knew yoga calmed the mind and kept the body supple, wringing out toxins. I wanted to rid Robert of as many toxins as I could, both physically and mentally. But lately I had been too worried about him and had slacked off in my practice.

"We should take a gentle yoga class tomorrow," Robert said, as if reading my mind.

My heart glowed that we were still so in tune with each other. "That would be nice." I gave him a smile. "Remember when I first told you I got you private yoga sessions and you said it wasn't for you?"

He chuckled and I felt it rumble through my body. "Who knew I'd get hooked, right? Anna did wonders for us." Anna had been our first teacher, the one who had taught Robert to do a mean chaturanga. Well, he used to, before this last round of treatments. Over the years, we'd taken several yoga classes a week together, until a few months ago. Now he could handle only gentle stretches. But I knew he was going to slowly get his strength back and it wouldn't be long before we were taking a vinyasa flow class together again.

He suddenly coughed, his body jerking forward and his arm sliding away from me. I put a hand on his back, worry thrumming through my veins as he hacked for what felt like an eternity. I jumped off the couch to get him a glass of water, but he waved it away and it sat untouched on the coffee table.

When he'd finally quieted down, I said, "Maybe you should go back to bed. Get some rest." I touched his cheek. It was pale.

He stood and gave me a weak smile. "Good idea. I'm tired. Don't worry so much, Tess. I just need some rest."

I nodded, biting my lips. It was a miracle, but I had to remember he was still recovering. I stood and gave him a kiss, my eyes roaming over the face I loved so dearly. He was still handsome at fifty-two, even with all the weight loss and skin hanging from his bones. I loved the silver at his temples, mixing with his sandy hair. Even though it hadn't quite grown in all the way from this last round of chemo, he was beautiful to me, with or without hair.

He kissed me back, running his hand through my thick dark-brown hair, which I kept long because I knew he loved to play with it. I gave him one last kiss and then watched as he walked into our bedroom and got in bed. I stayed where I was for a moment, thinking about what I could do to make sure he stayed with me for a long, long time.

I had tried a couple of months ago to get Robert the one thing I knew would make him the happiest man in the world, but . . . that hadn't ended well. Not at all. I hadn't expected the cops to come so quickly. I'd panicked and run because I hadn't had a backup plan. But I was starting to fix the mess I'd made. I'd kept my eyes on them, not only through the community gossip channels but also through her social media. I'd made contact with the boy. And now my plan to bring Robert back to me was working. I had to take it slowly, weighing each step, waiting for the right opportunity so that I didn't make another mistake like last time. I had to succeed, and I wouldn't rush it. Because Robert's happiness was the only thing I cared about in the world.

23

I peered out the window of the living room, looking for Robert. Where was he? He had grown stronger and stronger every day, and I couldn't believe how much better he looked. Almost back to his old self, his body filling out again with all the good food I gave him. His energy had returned, and we'd been able to do a yoga video together in our living room yesterday. But still I worried, especially coming home from the grocery store to find him gone. Was he taking a walk? But then why hadn't he taken Shadow?

Shadow barked as if I'd spoken his name out loud. I reached a hand down to rub his head, my thoughts still on Robert. Where was he? Shadow followed at my side as I paced the room, walking from one end to the other, growing more agitated with each step. I knew I hovered over my husband sometimes, but I couldn't help it. The need to make sure he was okay, that he was happy, was stronger than even my own comfort and happiness. If I could, I would have taken his place and been the sick one. Since I couldn't, it had been up to me to make sure we did everything we could to kick that damn cancer. I hadn't accepted it when the doctors had told us he didn't have much time left. I had known they were wrong. *I mean, look at Robert now.*

Needing something to do, I decided to heat up the clam chowder I'd bought earlier. Soups were easy for him to eat, and clam chowder was his second favorite. I walked to the fridge and took out the container, dumping the whole thing in a saucepan. I set the flame to low, since I didn't know when he would be back. I could have called his cell, but I didn't want him to feel like I was checking up on his every move (even though I was). And besides, I'd found his phone in the bedroom. He hadn't taken it with him.

I'd give him twenty more minutes before I gave in to a full-blown panic. I stirred the soup, letting it heat slowly, and took a calming breath. The minutes crawled by, punctuated by the wall clock above the sink. Tick, tick, tick. I closed my eyes, willing my breath to slow. Tick, tick, tick. Exhale, out through the mouth. Tick, tick, tick. My eyes flew open in annoyance, and just as I was about to yank the clock off the wall and hurl it across the kitchen, the back door opened. I blew out a breath of relief.

"Robert! Where'd you . . ." I bit off the rest of the sentence.

"I felt so good I went for a walk." He grinned at me as he came to my side. "Wasn't sure if I could control Shadow so had to leave him behind." He reached down to stroke Shadow's head. "Sorry, buddy."

Shadow snuffled and pushed his snout into the side of my leg as my entire body relaxed. Robert was dressed in bright-blue trousers with a colorful polka-dot, button-down, short-sleeve shirt, and fluorescent orange sneakers on his feet. He loved vibrant colors, and my heart lifted to see him up and dressed, and not stuck in bed in his pj's all day.

"You look so dapper." I threw a coy look in his direction.

He smirked back at me. "Didn't think you'd see me dressed like this again, did you?"

I laughed and threw my arms around his neck. "I did. I believe in you." Gone were all the tension and stress of the last few months. I had my Robert back again. I squeezed him hard and then looked up at him. "You doing good?"

"Very good. I almost feel back to my normal self."

"The doctors were wrong." I hugged him close again before pulling back to stare into his eyes. I'd thought I'd never feel his warm body against mine again. I'd thought I was losing him. But here he was, solid and real, still with me.

"It's all because of you, Tess." He kissed my forehead. "You take such good care of me." He had color in his cheeks, and the sparkle was back in his eyes. "You are seriously the best wife ever." Robert's arms tightened around me, as if he never wanted to let go. Just like in the early years, before he'd made that mistake. "Don't ever leave me. Please." His lips curved up in a gentle smile.

My heart tugged, but I matched his smile with one of my own. "Never. You're stuck with me, old man." He was only nine years older than me, but when we'd met over twenty years ago when I was twenty-three and he was thirty-two, he had seemed so much older and wiser.

When Robert leaned down and kissed me, relief coursed through my veins because his lips on mine felt so warm and alive and his hand stroking my back was so real. I had thought I'd never feel him kissing me again. I had thought I'd never hold him again. But we were still together. I'd been given a second chance and I wasn't going to waste it.

Robert pulled away and looked around. "What's burning?"

"Oh shoot." I'd forgotten about the soup. I rushed to the stove and turned it off, taking the smoking pot and throwing it into the sink. It sizzled when I ran it under water, and I stared at the steaming, burned mess.

"What was that, clam chowder?" He looked at the empty container still on the counter.

"It was. I'm sorry I ruined it." I gave him a helpless shrug.

"It's fine. I'm not hungry." A slow smile spread across his face. "I just had a great idea. Why don't we take a quick trip? Leave now, for a few days?"

"Now?" My eyebrows raised in surprise.

Robert threw his head back and laughed. I wanted, no, *needed*, to absorb that sound into me forever. He sounded so joyful and carefree, just like when we first met.

"Yes, now," he said.

He was spontaneous, while I plotted and planned. He always got me out of my comfort zone, to try new things. And leaving now on a trip sounded amazing. But I was supposed to help set up for an end-of-school party at the clubhouse tomorrow. Even though we didn't have kids, I always volunteered for stuff like that so the parents could focus on their children and make sure they had fun.

"Are you sure you're up to it?" Just a few days ago, he couldn't get out of bed. And now he wanted to go on a trip? But even I had to admit he looked great. Not 100 percent back, but better than he had in a long time.

"Just a short trip. We won't go far. But it'll be like old times. You and me and the open road. Except now we have Shadow." His eyes twinkled again, and I knew he was remembering when we used to take off on a whim in his old red Ford Mustang, and just drive to wherever the road took us.

I laughed at his enthusiasm. "Okay, let's do it. I'll have to call Nancy Meza and make sure they have enough people to set up for the party tomorrow, though."

"Perfect. It should be fine. They always have plenty of volunteers." He beamed at me, then added, "Oh, and we should bring our yoga mats."

I nodded, blinking fast to keep the tears away. My Robert really was back. There was nothing he liked better than practicing yoga outside in nature, the two of us breathing in unison, as we emptied our minds and invited in only positivity and strength.

"Let's load her up then." I walked to the kitchen door that led out to the garage and opened it.

Shadow followed me into the garage, where we kept an extra freezer stocked with food we could take on the road. I rubbed him on the head as I filled a cooler with what we'd need and then hit the button to open the garage. It would be easier to load up the RV parked in our driveway.

"Come, Shadow. Help me pack up your things." He followed me back into the kitchen as I filled a bag with food for him, along with treats, poop bags, and his toys. "Oh, I forgot to call Nancy."

I put the bag down in the kitchen and walked into the living room to get my cell. Nancy, the association president, picked up on the first ring, and I sighed in relief when she reassured me that they were okay for tomorrow. I hated to leave anyone hanging, and I was glad there were enough volunteers to make the party a success for the kids.

I went into the bedroom to finish packing. We kept almost everything we needed while on the road in the RV, so I only had to worry about clothing. I grabbed Robert's bag on my way out because he'd gotten a phone call. I gestured to him that I would load it into the RV. Once the bags were stowed, I went through the garage and back into the kitchen.

"Come on, Shadow," I called. "You're going on your first trip."

We hadn't taken an RV trip since we got him because Robert had been so sick. But now Shadow was finally going to get to travel with us. I made a note to let the boy know. Maybe he could come with us next time.

I looked around when I didn't hear an answering woof. *Where'd that dog go?*

"Robert, is Shadow with you?" I yelled toward the direction of our bedroom.

"No," he shouted back.

My eyes went to the open door that led to the garage, and then my heart sank as I tried to remember if I had closed it when I came in from loading up the cooler.

"Shadow?" I ran through our house quickly, looking for him.

No dog.

I ran out the kitchen door and through the garage, hoping Shadow was standing in our driveway. But he wasn't there. I ran to the end of the driveway, looked both ways, and just caught a glimpse of him way down the road before he disappeared around the corner.

Shit, shit, shit.

I ran back inside and grabbed my car keys. "Shadow got out. I'm going after him."

I didn't wait for an answer. My heart pounded with fear, hoping Shadow wouldn't get run over before I could get to him.

Jumping into the car, I started it and practically peeled out of the driveway, heading around the lake after Shadow.

24

I drove all the way to the other side of the lake. I'd caught a glimpse of Shadow way ahead of me, but then he'd disappeared around a curve. Pulling into the beach and clubhouse parking lot, I cursed myself for being so careless, for leaving the kitchen door open. If something happened to him, I'd never forgive myself.

Heart pounding, I got out of the car, searching for Shadow. The road that the beach was on was long and straight, and when I'd turned onto it, I'd seen Shadow somewhere around here. But he wasn't here anymore.

"Shadow, where are you?" I called.

Sweat beaded my forehead as I scanned the surrounding area, looking for any motion, listening for any sound. I ran down the road, looking in the front yard of the house next to the clubhouse, and screamed in surprise when a dog darted out of nowhere behind the fence and barked at me ferociously.

No one was about, except for the big boxer baring his teeth at me for trespassing on his property. I ran to the edge of the woods directly across the clubhouse, remembering there was a path. Maybe Shadow had gone in there. The boy lived on the next street up. I prayed that Shadow had gone back to him and Mochi.

I heard a faint shout coming from the woods, and my head jerked up. I plunged into the trees, my breath catching when I saw the boy sprawled on the ground, halfway up the hill, Mochi at his side. And then I heard a whimper and my heart stopped. Shadow was tangled in a bush.

"Shadow," I cried out, as I hurried up the path toward them.

"Tessa." The boy sat up, cringing when he saw the long gash on the underside of his left forearm. "Shadow came to my house. And then he ran in here and Mochi and I followed him."

The sight of blood trickling down the boy's arm made me sway with dizziness. I looked away, taking a deep breath. Shadow whimpered again, and I swallowed my nausea, stooping down by his side. He was tangled in a thorny bush.

"Oh, Shadow." I reached out to pet him on the head. Mochi stood right at his side, as if guarding him. "Hold still, we'll get you out." I blanched when I saw the open wound on Shadow's front paw, where it looked like the skin was stripped away, oozing blood. My breath came in short gasps.

The boy came to my side. "Are you okay, Tessa?"

I turned to him, and blanched again when I saw the boy had another cut on his leg, blood seeping down to his ankle. I closed my eyes briefly as a shudder went through me. I had to get hold of myself. I had to help Shadow.

"I'm fine." I swallowed, keeping my eyes away from the wounds. "I just don't like blood." I took in a breath to steady myself. "Can you help me get Shadow out?"

He nodded and crouched down at my side. He held back branches, careful to avoid the thorns, and I was able to ease Shadow out. The dog struggled to his feet, shaking himself as soon as he was free. His front right paw was lifted up, and then he started making this horrendous noise, something between a snort and a gasp. But on repeat. I stared at him in horror. Mochi stuck to his side, nudging him with her nose.

"Shadow, are you okay?" I dropped down next to him, hands fluttering, not sure what was wrong or how to help him.

"I know what to do," the boy said, hurrying to Shadow's side.

I watched as he closed Shadow's mouth with one hand and then plugged one of Shadow's nostrils with a finger. Within seconds, Shadow had quieted down and was breathing normally again.

"He's okay now," the boy said to me. "He always does that when he's scared."

"Oh, thank god." I heaved out a sigh of relief that the boy had been here. "I need to get him home. Clean up that cut." My whole body convulsed when I caught sight of the gash again. I closed my eyes, trying to think happy thoughts so that I didn't pass out.

The boy said something, but I didn't hear him over the roaring in my ears. But when he said, "I'll help you get him into your car," my eyes popped open.

Yes. This was brilliant. My spine tingled as it occurred to me how I could make things up to Robert for what I'd done to him. I'd been waiting for the right moment, and fate had dropped this opportunity in my lap. I wasn't going to waste it.

"Yes, please." I kept my face averted, my voice trembly. "That would be so helpful."

I could see the way the boy's chest puffed up in pride. He grabbed hold of Shadow's collar. "I'll try to support him so he doesn't have to put much weight on that paw." He called to Mochi, and slowly, the three of them followed me down the path and to the road.

"Wait here," I said. "I'll bring the car around." I ran to the parking lot and, within seconds, had pulled the car up next to where the trio awaited me at the entrance to the woods.

I got out of the car and, with the boy's help, lifted Shadow into the back seat. Once Shadow was settled, Mochi jumped up next to him.

"Mochi!" The boy looked at his dog, shaking his head. "You're not going with them. We should get home."

The white dog sat at Shadow's side and cocked her head at the boy. He called to her again, but Mochi refused to move. The boy leaned into the car, trying to pull Mochi out, but she'd become as stiff as a board, gluing her body to Shadow's. I almost kissed Mochi right then and there. She was helping me get the boy to Robert.

"I don't think she wants to leave him," I said. "Maybe you can come back with me and help me clean the cut? We need to bandage you up too." I gave a shudder. "I hate the sight of blood."

"I don't mind it," the boy said, backing out of the car to look at me. "I can help."

"Okay, let me text your aunt." I pulled out my phone and typed into it with my thumbs. I looked up. "She said it's fine." I smiled at the boy. "Thank you for helping."

He nodded. "I'm glad I caught Shadow. I didn't want him to get run over." He crawled into the back seat, next to the dogs. As he was buckling his seat belt, he asked, "What happened? Why was Shadow out without a leash?"

I got in the driver's seat, looking around to make sure no one had seen Luca getting into my car. "The garage door was open. Shadow must have wanted to see Mochi."

The boy nodded.

There was no one about. That didn't mean someone in their house wasn't looking out. But in my gut, I knew no one had seen us. The situation was just too perfect, the setup better than I could have planned. I took the main road home instead of backtracking through the neighborhood the way I'd come. So many cars passed on the main road, and it was less likely anyone would notice mine. I knew some of our neighbors had front-door cameras, and I didn't want to chance anyone seeing Luca in my car as we drove by.

When we got back to the house, the boy helped me get Shadow into the house to the kitchen, where I wet a washcloth to clean his wound. But I had to look away and the boy giggled, seeming to find it funny that I didn't like the sight of blood.

"I'll clean his paw," he offered.

"We should get you cleaned up," I said, glad to let him take over, handing him the cloth.

"I'll take care of Shadow first."

As he sat on the floor tending to Shadow's paw, I called out, "Robert, I found him."

"Oh, good," came the answering shout. "I'm in the bathroom. Be right out."

"Hi, Robert," the boy called, still focused on Shadow's paw. Without waiting for an answer, he started talking to the dog, telling him he was going to be okay.

I took out my cell and said, "Oh, it's your aunt calling." I put the phone to my ear and spoke into it, as if I were telling Hope what had happened. My eyes narrowed as I observed the boy, noting how absorbed he was in cleaning Shadow's cut, talking to the dog as if he could understand.

I took a chance. "Do you want to talk to your aunt?" I held the phone out, my breath held.

And released it when the boy said, "Not now, I need to get this clean."

"Okay." I turned back to the phone and spoke into it. "What? Is everything okay?" My voice rose in alarm. "What can I do?" I nodded and looked at the boy, but he was still talking to Shadow and not paying attention to me. "Your parents . . . I can get him right back." I stopped, as if a thought had just come to me. "Wait. What if we took Luca on an RV trip?"

At that, the boy looked at me, as I'd known he would. When Shaun had brought him over a few weeks ago with Mochi to visit Shadow,

Robert had given them a tour of our Allegro Open Road, and the boy had been entranced with it. Robert and I had gone all out and bought what he called the "mack daddy" of all RVs, a class A motor home, which meant it was one of the largest vehicles on the road, built with the same framing and construction as commercial trucks and buses. It was spacious and comfortable. I'd made fun of Robert for using that term, and when I'd told the boy that day, he'd giggled, even though I was pretty sure he didn't know what it meant.

"An RV trip?" Luca asked. I saw the way his eyes lit up, the way his hands stilled on Shadow as he focused on me.

I help up a finger as I listened into my cell. "Okay, let me ask him." I held the cell away from my ear. "Your aunt has a family emergency. Her mom. They have to leave now. I can either get you home so you can go with them, or how would you like to take a trip in the RV with me and Robert?" I gestured to the dogs. "And Shadow and Mochi, of course."

"What?" The boy's eyes widened, and he dropped Shadow's paw.

"It's up to you." I was counting on the fact that he'd told us he'd always wished his mother had an RV when they traveled to sway him into coming with us.

"Really?" He looked from me to Shadow, then to Mochi sitting on the mat next to him. "We can all go? For how long?"

I shrugged. "Until your aunt and uncle come back. What do you say? Robert and I were going to leave soon."

"Yes!" His eyes lit up, and he leaned down to hug Mochi. "It's okay with Aunt Hope?"

"She says it's up to you." I smiled at him and then put the phone back to my ear. "Luca wants to come with us." I listened for a bit, aware of the boy's eyes on me. "Okay, I'll let you go. Don't worry, we'll get him everything he needs. It'll be fun for Robert and me too. Okay, bye."

I hung up the call and smiled at Luca. "Looks like we're going on a trip."

"Yay!" He cheered and then turned to finish cleaning Shadow up.

"We're all loaded and ready to go. Let's get your cuts cleaned up and then we're off." I couldn't wait. Robert was going to be so surprised.

"I can wash off my own cuts." He jumped up and went to the kitchen sink.

"Okay. But quickly. We need to push off."

While he washed his wounds, I wrapped a bandage around Shadow's paw, glad to see it was no longer bleeding. I then put Band-Aids on the worst of the boy's cuts. My movements were rushed because I knew we needed to get out of here.

"Okay. Let me get Robert." I stood. "Can you put the dogs' harnesses on? There's an extra one that you can use for Mochi." I gestured to where we hung the leashes and, without waiting for an answer, headed for the bedroom to tell Robert the good news.

I knew he was going to forgive me now.

25

"Should I get the dogs?" The boy gestured out of the RV to the garage.

I'd kept the dogs in the kitchen while we finished loading the food because I didn't want them to get out again.

"Yes." I looked around the RV. Robert was setting the locking mechanisms on the refrigerator doors so that they wouldn't fly open in case of sudden stops. "We're ready to go."

The boy gave a whoop and ran down the side steps and into the garage. A pain suddenly shot through my head, and I squeezed my eyes shut. I fought against the hammering in my skull, which felt like an electric shot jolting my brain as images of Robert sick and failing flitted across my mind. He was fine now. I took a few deep breaths. I could do this. I was fine. Shadow was fine, and now, by a stroke of luck, the boy and Mochi were going on our trip with us. It was more than I could have hoped for.

When I opened my eyes, Robert was standing in front of me. No longer gray and pallid, no longer bedridden. My breath hitched and my body quivered, trying to remind myself that he was fine. He grinned at me and wiggled his eyebrows, and just like that, my chest loosened from the vise that had gripped it the last couple of weeks. Weeks filled with tension, worry, and sleepless nights.

"This is going to be so fun." Robert's voice was so sure that I wanted to cry in relief. But then the smile fell off his face and he winced, as if in pain.

My heart skipped a beat. Did he have a headache like me? Maybe this wasn't a good idea. What if he had a relapse? What if he suddenly lost his energy? But then I stopped second-guessing myself. This trip was meant to be.

I studied him, trying to gauge his pain level. "Why don't you relax in the recliner in the bedroom?" I'd gotten one for him so he could rest comfortably but still be strapped in. "I'll drive first."

"That's a good idea." Robert nodded at me.

My eyes followed him as he walked into the bedroom, and then the dogs came thundering up the stairs. The boy followed close behind. I hit the button to close the garage door.

"Where's Robert?" The boy asked.

"He's resting in the bedroom." I nodded to the back of the RV.

"Oh." The boy's eyes drifted to the bedroom door and then back to me. "Is he okay?" His forehead was furrowed in concern.

I nodded. "I think he's just tired. He needs to rest."

The boy considered that for a moment and then turned in a circle, taking in the RV. "It'll be just like being in a moving house."

A movement outside caught my attention. I suddenly had an idea how I could pay her back for taking the boy. It was only fair.

"Why don't you and the dogs get settled. I'm just going to do one last check, and then we're off to our first destination." I set my cell in the car phone holder and slipped my sunglasses on, pulling the hat on my head lower. I picked up my tote bag. "Stay in here, okay?" I threw over my shoulder.

The boy nodded and I slipped out of the RV, making sure he was occupied with the dogs.

Less than two minutes later, I was back in the RV, mission accomplished.

I settled myself in the driver's seat and started the engine. I backed out of the driveway and drove down the hill, toward the lake. As the lake came into view, I heard the sound of police sirens in the distance, drawing closer. They were coming from across the lake. Oh no, the Chens must have discovered that Luca was gone already. I was getting out just in time. I turned right onto Lake Circle, then made another right onto the main road that led out of the lake community. The boy was chattering behind me, giving the dogs a running commentary on all the RV's amenities, and I smiled despite my nervousness about the police.

"You like the RV, huh?" I asked, catching his eyes in the rearview mirror.

"Yes. Mochi and Shadow love it too." He ran a hand over the couch he was sitting on.

We'd had the interior luxuriously designed in Ultraleather furniture in the color "cocoon" with features of soft tan and cream earth tones and a light-blue and tan clear glass backsplash in the kitchen. The light-brown wooden cabinetry was all handcrafted, and we had a full state-of-the-art sound system and flat-panel TVs with soundbars. It was our luxury home away from home.

There was a dinette where we ate behind where Luca currently sat, with booth seating in Ultraleather on each side. The full kitchen was across from the dinette. The bathroom, complete with a shower and a washer and dryer, was across from the bunk bed nook. And at the very back was our bedroom. The vehicle was spacious, and because of the panoramic galley kitchen window, it was also bright and inviting. There was plenty of room for the boy.

"What kind of emergency did you say Aunt Hope had?" The boy chewed on his bottom lip.

Oh no. I didn't want him to start questioning me already. "I think it was one of her parents." I made my voice soft, so that he would trust me. I meant him no harm. I couldn't remember which parent I had said was sick.

"They're flying to California?"

"Is that where her parents are?"

He nodded. "That's where my grandparents live. But I've never met them. I don't think they like me or my mom much." He shot me a grin. "I'd rather go on an RV trip with you guys."

I grinned back. "We're glad you're here too."

He smiled at me, and I was struck by how sensitive and serious he looked in that moment, as if he were a lot older than nine. He had an old soul, and I could tell those young eyes had seen much more than he should have at that age. And even though I didn't really feel one way or another about the boy except as a means to an end, I was suddenly sorry for my part in putting that pain and burden in his eyes. I vowed then to make this the best trip of his life, not only for Robert's sake but also for the boy's.

He sat back on the sofa, bouncing a bit as if to test the cushions, which I knew were very comfortable. The excited light was back in his eyes again. He was going on a dream trip with the two dogs. What more could he ask for?

"This is so, so cool. One time, when me and my mom stayed in a campground, this really nice older couple let me look in theirs. But it was so much smaller than this one."

He rambled on, and I drove as fast as I could without going too much over the speed limit. The last thing I needed was to be pulled over. Once we got on the highway about fifteen minutes away from our community, I relaxed my grip on the steering wheel. No one had seen the boy with me. No one was chasing us, sirens blasting. We'd gotten out just in time.

As I drove, I thought about the RV park we were headed to. I'd decided on a campground in Pennsylvania for the night, about four hours away—far away enough to get us out of this area. There was plenty of space to explore and things to find in the park's woods to keep the boy and the dogs busy. The RV site was spacious, and I'd find a spot away from others. I would make sure no one saw him so we wouldn't get questions as to why he was with us.

"Did you and your mom go camping a lot?" I was curious about this boy for so many reasons and brought the conversation back to what he'd mentioned earlier about his mother.

"Some. When we had to sleep in our car, I always wished we had an RV. Then we could go wherever we wanted, and not worry about finding a place to sleep. It'd be a home. Our home." I couldn't mistake the wistful tone in his voice.

"Well." I spread my arms around, encompassing the RV. "You can pretend this is your home for the next few days until your aunt and uncle get home."

"But I don't have anything with me. Not even extra clothes." The boy worried his lip with his upper teeth again, reality intruding on his excitement.

"Don't worry, I can stop at a store and get stuff for you." I needed to put him at ease. "Thank you for your help earlier."

"I'm glad I could help. And I'm glad Mochi can come too."

I looked in the rearview mirror and saw him petting both dogs. "Me too. Shadow is so calm with Mochi." It was really heartwarming the way the two dogs interacted. It made me feel bad for separating them. Anyone could see they were a bonded pair. But maybe this was the chance for them to be together again?

The boy echoed my thoughts. "I'm glad they're together again."

"Me too." I turned quickly and shot him a smile, which he returned.

My heart was light. But just then, my cell rang and I saw it was Hope. Shit. Did I answer? Did I not? I debated too long and it went to voice mail. But then I realized it would throw too much suspicion on us if I didn't answer. I called her right back, holding the phone to my ear so that Luca couldn't hear. I had to stay one step ahead of them.

26

Day two
11:00 a.m.

The next morning, I drank my steaming cup of coffee as I watched the boy running through the woods next to where we'd set up the RV. I'd found a secluded RV hookup at the edge of the park, and there wasn't anyone close to us. It was perfect. Robert could enjoy his time with the boy. I'd stopped at a Target last night, and told the boy to stay in the RV with Robert and the dogs. He was more than happy to be in charge, proud that I'd trusted him with it.

I'd picked out clothes and underwear for him, as well as a toothbrush, some books because we knew he loved to read, squeaky toys for the dogs, and stuff I thought the boy would enjoy, including water guns. And I was right. Robert and the boy were currently having a water gun fight, running and ducking behind trees, aiming at each other. I studied Robert, at the energy just bursting out of him, and knew he'd defied his diagnosis. He *was* getting better. We'd be together for many more years, growing old together like we planned. The two dogs barked at my side, and my heart swelled with lightness.

The boy came into view, aiming his water gun at Robert. My heart gave a wistful thump as I watched them. They were so alike, even in the way they ran. This was how it should have been. How I'd always imagined our life would be, from the first day I met Robert. My eyes darkened as I thought back to what could have been. The boy should have been my child.

The thought threatened to take over my mood like a thundercloud about to let loose on unsuspecting picnickers. But I pushed it away, refusing to allow it space in my head and heart. I refused to give in to the sadness. I squeezed my eyes shut, the image of the boy and Robert seared into my retinas. They were here with me, and that was the most important thing in the world. Everything would be okay. Everything was going to be fine.

"You can't get me!" The boy's shout brought me back and I shook my head, clearing it of the despondent thoughts. I refused to give them any room to grow.

"Yes, I can," I shouted back, as Robert came up to me, his face lit up by his grin. I would focus on that. Hold on to the joy on his face, the way it crinkled his eyes. I needed to remember every detail of him.

I put my coffee mug aside and grabbed the water gun from Robert. I aimed it at the boy, right as he popped into view. With a shriek, he held his hands over his face as I drenched him from head to toe. Then he recovered and aimed his own water gun at me, and I ducked behind Robert.

"Hey," Robert said as I cowered behind him while shooting my gun without being able to see where the boy was. "No fair using me as a shield."

I paused for a moment, joy filling my heart to hear how light his voice was. Gone were the pain and weakness from the last month. Gone were the trembling voice and wavering body. This was my Robert, whole and healthy again.

I gave the water gun back to Robert, and he charged the boy. I sat down on the steps of the RV, the two dogs at my feet, and watched them. I wanted to hold on to this moment, when all was right in the world. The boy was where he belonged. I pushed all thoughts of Hope and Shaun out of my mind. They would be fine. It wasn't as if the boy were their child.

Reaching for my phone, I checked the time. I wanted to be on the road before lunch, and there was still plenty of time. I didn't want to interrupt their fun, to be the one to spoil the mood. I left them to it, and stepped back inside the RV. I needed to figure out where we would go next. I had to keep us safe, away from prying eyes. I had to find locations that were out of the way. Places where few people went. And I needed to find out the latest in the search for the boy. When I'd called Hope back yesterday, soon after we drove off, I was pretty sure I'd convinced her that we didn't know where Luca was.

An hour later, I walked back outside, noting that the boy was sprawled in the grass, both dogs with him. I was so glad he had them. Surely he felt safe with Shadow and Mochi. I knew he probably wouldn't have gone with us so easily if he hadn't had Mochi with him.

I felt, rather than saw, Robert behind me. He put his arms around me and I leaned back, content to let him absorb my weight, feeling the warmth radiating off him, reassuring me.

"We should get on the road soon," I said.

"In a bit." His voice was a whisper in my ear, the feel of his lips against the side of my face sending shivers down my spine. My Robert. My love. "There's no rush. We don't have to be anywhere."

He was right. There was no hurry. I'd disabled the TVs in our RV and played music from Spotify on my phone. The boy didn't have a phone or iPad, so he couldn't check the outside world. And I'd told Robert that we were unplugging on this trip, so all his devices were packed away in a bag. I only had my phone out for navigation.

I knew the boy's face would be plastered everywhere, that every news station would be leading with his disappearance, and I didn't want Robert or the boy to know he was a missing child. When I'd last checked the news on my phone in the bathroom, it had seemed the police were still trying to piece together what had happened. No one suspected that I'd taken him. Not even Robert. He'd believed me when I told him Hope and Shaun had a family emergency and needed to fly to California. I could tell he was happy Hope had trusted us with the boy, and grateful for this opportunity to get to know the boy better.

I felt his chest against my back and shivered, so happy that we were connected again. I closed my eyes, my back warm from Robert, my skin tingling from the sunrays that beamed down on us. I wanted to hold on to this perfect moment for as long as possible. To remember always how it felt to have him close to me, the heat of our bodies mingling and drawing us together. I wanted this moment to last forever. When I opened my eyes, I saw the boy coming toward us, the two dogs at his side. Shadow barked and limped his way toward me, and I knew I'd done the right thing.

27

The miles passed and I was blissfully content. Robert was relaxed, the boy was happy, and Shadow's wound had been cleaned again this morning and he was starting to put weight on the leg. Mochi was never far from Shadow's side, unless he was with the boy. We'd made a pact, Robert and I, not to talk about what would happen after this trip. For now, we were together, whole and happy, and that was enough.

Robert hummed a song, and I had to strain to catch what it was. A small smile played on my lips when I recognized a butchered rendition of our favorite song, "Every Breath You Take" by the Police. It was the first song we ever danced to, in the middle of the bar where I'd worked. It was a few months after that terrible night when Robert had saved me. Robert, who'd been waiting to drive me home, had grabbed my hand and pulled me to him. And there, in the middle of the yeasty, musty bar, on a floor sticky with spilled beer, he'd held me close and we'd swayed to the music as he whispered the lyrics in my ear. That was the moment I knew we would be together forever.

"Happy?" Robert's voice broke through my thoughts. He'd stopped humming and was focused on me.

I nodded, smiling at him. But then I glanced away again—sometimes seeing how tenderly he looked at me gave me an uncomfortable twinge about what I'd done two weeks earlier. I didn't regret it; it had been necessary to bring us to this moment. I didn't like to be reminded of it and strove to put it out of my mind. But when Robert looked at me like that, I couldn't meet his eyes. I knew he understood, though. There'd been understanding in his eyes that day too.

We were going west toward Pittsburgh, heading for an RV park in Ohio for the night. It was in the middle of nowhere, surrounded by a river and woods. The open road was in front of us, and Robert was strapped into the passenger seat, dozing on and off. I glanced at the gas gauge and realized that we'd have to get gas soon. We could stop at the next rest area to fuel up and then be on our way.

"Has Aunt Hope called?"

The boy's voice right behind me made me jump. My hands jerked on the wheel, but I quickly got it under control again. I took a breath before I spoke.

"She texted me this morning. They're fine, but her mom is in the hospital and there's no cell service. She said she would call as soon as she can." I kept my voice pleasant, but inside I winced. Would he buy my lame excuse? How was I going to keep him from suspecting anything? So far, the novelty of traveling in the RV was keeping him distracted. But I knew it was only a matter of time before he started to ask questions that I didn't have the answer to. Already, he'd asked why he couldn't watch his favorite shows on our flat-screen TV. I'd had to make some quick excuse about how the satellite was down. The last thing I wanted was for him to see his own face on TV.

"Do they miss me?" He held on to the back of my seat and shifted from foot to foot.

"I'm sure they do. You shouldn't be standing while the RV is moving." I shot him a quick look and saw how dejected he looked. I softened my tone. "They're fine, okay? I promise." That was a promise I could keep. They *were* fine, at least physically. "Let's let them deal with the emergency without having to worry about you too."

He didn't say anything, but he didn't move from where he stood behind me. I wondered if he was going to defy me and stay standing. Finally, I heard him shuffling away. Looking in the rearview mirror, I saw him sinking onto the sofa with Shadow and Mochi. He picked up one of the books I'd bought for him and stared at it.

There was a rest area coming up ahead. Signaling to pull into the right lane, I turned to check the lane behind me and saw that Robert had fallen asleep. Good. He needed his rest. Hopefully this meant that he'd have more energy once we got to the RV park later. I needed to talk to him about something important. Something I needed to get off my chest.

When I had maneuvered the RV up to a gas pump—I'd gotten really good at this; it was almost like a dance, positioning the RV just right so that I could exit easily—I turned to the boy. "Stay inside, out of sight of the windows, okay?"

His forehead scrunched up. "Why?"

I realized my mistake at the same time that he spoke. I tried to backpedal. "I need you to keep an eye on Robert, make sure he's okay." I gestured to where Robert dozed with his mouth open in the recliner.

"But he's not—"

I cut him off. "He needs you, okay? Please? Help me out?"

The boy looked back and forth from Robert to me a few times and then nodded.

I got out and, after putting in my credit card, stuck the nozzle into the fuel tank. Then I waited, since it took so long to fill up the RV. I listened to the news that they were blasting at each bay, noting that the man talking about the forecast for tonight had a nice voice. That was probably why he was on the radio. He'd probably been told all his life that he had the perfect radio voice. I smiled to myself as he said that tonight called for warm, clear skies. Hopefully, that would be the same in Ohio. It was fine if it rained since we'd be nice and dry in the RV, but it would be more fun for the boy and dogs if they could run in the woods and explore along the river.

I was looking into the big panoramic window of our RV, noting that the boy was moving around inside, when I suddenly heard the radio man say something about a missing boy. I stilled, and focused on his words.

"Nine-year-old Luca Wen is still missing from his aunt and uncle's home in Upper Westchester County in New York. A recent development just came in. There was an altercation with a neighbor, and the police are now investigating to see if the neighbor is responsible for the boy's disappearance. We'll update you as we get information. In other news . . ."

I tuned out when the perfect radio voice started talking about the Senate moving forward to fund something. My eyes darted around to see if anyone was watching us. Even though it was radio and a picture of the boy hadn't been flashed on a screen, I was suddenly wary of anyone paying too much attention to us. The man in front of me was scrolling through his phone as he waited for his gas tank to fill; a woman on the other side of the island was looking around but not in our direction; and a few people walked by, some with dogs on the grass, while others headed toward the store to get food or use the restrooms. No one was watching us. But my senses were on alert, and I tapped my foot impatiently, praying the gas pump would hurry up. Looking at the RV, I was thankful the boy was no longer visible in the window. We needed to be careful. I'd bought him a baseball cap, and I was going to have him pull it low over his eyes anytime we were around people.

The gas tank was finally full, and I put the nozzle back into the pump. I closed the gas tank and hurried to the driver's door, slipping into the seat and closing the door with a bang. Turning around, I studied the boy, who was back on the sofa with Shadow.

"Is everything okay?" he asked.

"Yes." I gave a little shake of my head. "Why wouldn't it be?"

"You look like you saw a ghost." The boy widened his eyes at me.

"No, I'm fine." I strapped myself in and jumped when the boy suddenly appeared at my elbow. He really needed to stop scaring me like this.

He leaned down to whisper in my ears. "What's up with Robert?"

"Why are you whispering?" I pulled back slightly to stare at him.

He shrugged, looking around. I glanced over at Robert, who was still asleep with his mouth open in the passenger seat.

"He's doing better, but I still worry about him," I said.

I'd told the boy a little bit about Robert's illness right after we'd caught Shadow, when we were driving back to our house. How the doctors thought he didn't have much time left and I was hopeful this trip would be good for him, revive him. The boy had nodded. He'd bonded with Robert the few times he'd visited us, talking about basketball and dogs. Robert had also shown him every feature of the RV. It had given me peace of mind to watch them together, knowing Robert had another reason to hang on, to keep living.

"But why is he . . ."

Just then, loud honking drew our attention out the window. There was a traffic jam just past the gas station, as an SUV blocked both right lanes trying to get into the left. I started the engine. We needed to get out of here before anyone saw us.

"Buckle up," I said to the boy.

He retreated and sat down, picking up his book after he fastened his seat belt. My shoulders loosened as I maneuvered back onto the highway, just as Robert woke up next to me. I smiled at him, glad that he looked rested. I thought about what I planned to say to him when we stopped for the night. I'd been keeping this secret for so long, and it was finally time to tell him the truth.

I knew he was going to be so shocked. Because he didn't know I knew his deepest, darkest secret.

28

We pulled into the RV park in Ohio, and I registered us before getting back in the RV. Following the directions on the map I was given, I drove to our site, as far away from the office as possible, with no one else in the adjacent lots. I'd asked for one away from others, and was glad the RV park was just as deserted as the last time Robert and I had stopped here.

Robert wanted to help hook up the RV, but one look at him told me he should rest.

"I'll do it," I said. "Give you more time with the boy."

I knew it was the right thing to say when Robert perked up, looking over at the child.

"Can you watch the dogs for us?" I asked the boy. "You can all come out once I get everything hooked up."

He nodded and I walked down the steps.

I took care of hooking the RV up to the power and water sources. Our Class A motor home used a 50 amp hookup, and I'd remembered this one in Ohio where I knew I could get a reservation, unlike the more popular sites that you needed to reserve months, sometimes years, in advance. Robert and I had stopped here before, when we did our cross-country trip, and I had enjoyed a week away from people and real life.

I turned off the circuit breaker and then used a surge protector before plugging into the pedestal for our site. Then while the boy watched me with curiosity from the RV's open door, I hooked up the white fresh water hose after disinfecting the water faucet. (I was always careful to clean it first—who knew what the previous camper had done with it?) And lastly, I hooked up the black sewer hose. Robert had always taken care of this, but now he didn't have enough strength to do it, so it was up to me.

When I was all done, I called to Robert and the boy, and they came outside with the dogs. I put out the camping chairs and then set about making a fire while Robert rested. The boy helped me by gathering sticks, and Shadow settled down near me, while Mochi stayed by the boy's side, sniffing and scratching at the ground. Once I had a fire going, I finally sank into my own chair and Robert and I sat there, watching as the boy and Mochi explored the banks of the river. I leaned down to check the wound on Shadow's leg. There was no blood on the new bandage I'd wrapped around his leg with the boy's help that morning.

I turned to see Robert watching the boy, and my heart ached. Everything I did, I did for my husband. Yet he hadn't always thought of only me. I opened my mouth, about to tell him that I knew, but then the boy came running up, Mochi at his side.

"I'm starving. Can we cook the hot dogs now?"

"Hungry boy, huh?" Robert said, grinning.

"I love hot dogs. Mom said they aren't nutritious, so she only let me eat them once in a while. But I can eat like ten of them." The boy sank onto the chair that I'd set out for him and beamed at me. "Can we roast them over the fire on a stick?"

I nodded, buoyed by his enthusiasm for something as simple as hot dogs. "Can you go get the hot dogs and the stew out of the fridge?"

He popped up out of the chair and ran for the RV before I could even finish my sentence. Robert and I shared a laugh, and then we watched him juggling the bag of hot dogs and the container with the stew in it.

"How about you find us some long sticks so that we can roast the hot dogs over the fire?" I asked him.

"Just two sticks, right?" he answered.

"Um . . ." I looked at Robert.

"Two is fine." He nodded at the boy. As strong as Robert appeared, the fact that he'd slept most of the day told me he wasn't feeling well.

"Yes, two," I said to the boy. "I can roast Robert's for him."

The boy turned and ran to the edge of the woods. By the time he came back with two long sticks, I had the materials laid out for our meal. I showed the boy how best to spear the hot dogs, and then we pulled our chairs up close to the fire and settled into the act of roasting hot dogs over an open flame.

Robert watched us, a smile on his lips, especially when the boy's hot dog burst into flames on one side and the boy gave a whoop. He blew on it, laughing when it went out and revealed a charred end. He stuck it into the fire again and, after a few moments, declared it perfectly crispy. I handed him the bag of buns and watched as he took one out and stuck his hot dog in it. He squirted ketchup on it and then sat back in his chair, taking a big bite.

"This is so good," he said around the hot dog.

I smiled, put a hot dog in a bun, and held it out to Robert.

"I'm not hungry yet," he said.

I stared at the hot dog in my hand, then glanced back at him. He needed to eat. If he didn't, he would get weaker.

I gave him a nod and doctored up the hot dog before taking a bite. The boy was right. There was nothing like a hot dog freshly roasted over a campfire, the juices flowing out in a delicious squish as you bit into it.

The boy devoured two more hot dogs before the stew was ready. He had two healthy servings, but I noticed Robert barely touched his. What could I tempt him with? His appetite had been so good the last week that its loss now had me concerned. And then I knew what would make him eat.

"Who wants s'mores?" I asked, holding up a bag of marshmallows.

"Me!" The boy waved a hand in the air with enthusiasm. He seemed to have forgotten all about his worry over his aunt and uncle. I was glad. Maybe I could hold off his questions for a bit longer while I came up with a plan.

"Me too," Robert said, chuckling at the boy's enthusiasm.

For the next few moments, the boy and I had Robert laughing as we roasted the marshmallows. When the one at the end of the boy's stick fell into the fire, Robert burst into a laugh so healthy and deep that my heart leaped in hope like the flames dancing in front of us.

"Oh man!" The boy pouted, but I could tell he wasn't really put out. He was having fun, and I was so glad. "Now I have to start over."

Just then, my marshmallow caught on fire, causing the boy to whoop. I quickly took it out and blew on it until the flames were extinguished. I was left with a charred mess, Robert's favorite. I squished it onto a piece of chocolate I'd laid over a graham cracker and then smashed the other graham cracker over it.

"You made that perfectly," Robert said. I turned, seeing the love shining in his eyes, and my lips quirked up, even as my insides went gooey like the marshmallow. "You know me so well."

"I do." We shared a quiet look.

"Look at the one I made!" The boy's shout had us turning back to him. He'd stacked another marshmallow on top of the s'more he'd already made, then laid a second piece of chocolate over that, before slapping a third piece of graham cracker over it. "A double-decker s'more!"

I laughed. "How are you going to get your mouth around that?"

He grinned at us and I couldn't help but grin back. "Watch me." And he smashed it as much as he could, before opening his mouth and stuffing it in. He looked at us triumphantly, his face plastered with chocolate and marshmallows. He was a mess. But he devoured that s'more with gusto, before going to the hose and washing the stickiness off his hands and face.

"Can Mochi and I go explore before it gets too dark?" His eyes gleamed in the firelight, and I couldn't believe how much energy he had.

"Yes, but don't go too far. Stay within sight of the RV, okay?"

He nodded and ran off, Mochi at his side.

"He's a good boy."

Robert's voice brought me back to the fire, and I smiled at him. "He is." I studied him, noting the way the flames threw shadows across his face, even though it was still light out. It made the hollows in his cheeks that much deeper and the dark circles under his eyes more pronounced, and suddenly, I could see what his skull looked like, as if the skin had all melted away. It scared me, and I screwed my eyes shut so hard that I saw stars. When I opened them, Robert's kind face stared back at me. The skeleton was gone.

I breathed a sigh of relief and finished the s'more in my hand. I sat back and stared into the flame, knowing it was time to tell Robert I knew his secret.

"Robert." I said his name quietly, not looking at him.

"Yes, Tess." His tone was teasing, but the nickname I hated had me grinding my teeth.

I forced myself to release the tension in my jaw before I answered. "I know what you did."

"What did I do?" His tone was still teasing. He had no idea I was about to drop a bomb on him.

I turned so that I could see his face. He knew the boy was his son, but he had no idea *I* knew. "That boy is your son."

29

I watched the emotions play across his face. First, blank, as he took in my words. Then the slight widening of his eyes when my words sank in. And then he couldn't hide the horror that flashed across his face when he realized I knew.

"Tess . . . I . . ." That was all he could get out.

"I saw you with her." I paused to let that sink in. "I saw what you did."

The air seemed to drain out of Robert, and his whole body deflated. "Oh, Tessa . . . I'm . . . oh god." He reached out a hand but stopped before he touched me. "I'm so, so sorry. More than you'll ever know."

I kept my face passive, not wanting to give away what I was feeling. "I followed you that night, because I knew you were upset. I wanted to make sure you didn't do something stupid. When you went into that bar, I waited in my car, thinking you'd come out after a drink or two. I didn't want to hover." I turned to stare into the flames, watching the way they danced and swayed, so cheerful and bright, when my insides were so dark and vile.

"Oh, Tess . . ." I didn't have to turn to see the sorrow on his face.

I kept talking, not acknowledging him. "You didn't come out. An hour went by. I got out, went to the door, and peered in. And saw you at the bar. Sitting next to her. I didn't think anything of it. Just thought you were letting off steam with a friendly stranger, so I went back to wait in the car." The fire sparked and I watched the way the embers disappeared up into the air. "Another hour went by, and you finally came out. With her." Here, I turned and focused my gaze on him.

"Tessa, I'm so, so sorry. It . . . it didn't mean anything. I was upset . . ." The look on his face, so sorrowful and full of regret, made me glad. He was still my Robert, and I still loved him with all my heart, but he *should* feel bad for what he had done to me. To us.

"I knew you were upset. But why didn't you turn to *me*?" I stabbed a finger at my chest, hard. "Why did you turn to *her*?"

Robert scrubbed a hand over his face, took a deep breath, and then looked at me. "I didn't turn to her. I just needed some space after hearing about my cancer diagnosis from the doctor that day. We had just finished dinner, and I could feel the sympathy and concern just pouring out of you. And suddenly, I couldn't breathe. I needed to get out of the house. I felt as if I'd let you down. We'd promised to be with each other for a long, long time, and here my stupid body had gotten prostate cancer. I had to get out of the house."

I stayed quiet because I couldn't speak. He'd felt suffocated by me, by my love for him, my concern for him? So much so that he'd had to run out of the house and into her arms?

"I was just going to have one drink, to give myself time to calm down, to numb the pain. But she sat down next to me and we started talking. And she was so young, such a breath of fresh air, that I could breathe again."

I sucked in air when I heard that. I had known what he'd done, but hearing it from his mouth made it that much more real. Made the pain even sharper.

"And then we'd had four, five rounds and I knew I couldn't drive yet. So we talked some more, and then she said she had to go. I walked her to the car because she'd parked around back and it'd gotten so dark out. And then somehow, we ended up in the back seat . . ." He hung his head, unable to meet my eyes.

"I saw you, Robert. I waited and waited, not wanting to intrude on your time. I was going to drive you home if you were too drunk. But then you came out with her, and I saw you go around the side of the building. I got out of my car and followed you. You didn't even notice my car in the parking lot, you were so engrossed with her." My voice sounded disembodied, as if it came from somewhere above instead of from within me. "It was so dark back there, and I hid in between two cars near hers. I heard what you said."

"What I said?" His face was a mask of anguish.

"Yes, she was asking if you had kids, and you said no, even though you'd always wanted them." I turned to him, so he could see what his betrayal had done to me. "Why did you say that, Robert? You told me you didn't want children. I would have had them with you."

"Tessa, it's . . . You were so broken. From that night. I didn't think you wanted kids. Not after what happened to you." He reached out a hand, but I turned away.

"I was fine." I gave a nod, keeping my gaze on the fire. Dimly, I was aware of the boy and Mochi running in and out of the trees ahead of us. Shadow shifted next to me, and I reached down a hand to calm him. "And I saw what you did with her. Not just the sex, but the drugs. In a car, Robert? Really?"

"You've known all these years?" His voice was hoarse.

"Yes. I also knew it wasn't the only time."

We were quiet for a bit, the only sounds the crackling of the fire and the boy's voice as he talked to Mochi in the distance. It was still light out, sunlight peeking through the trees, but it felt like we were in a bubble of darkness. I'd finally told Robert I knew his secret.

"You have no idea how much I regret what I did." Robert finally spoke. "I wasn't thinking clearly. I needed to *feel* like I was still a man. I regretted it immediately. It's weighed on me all this time."

"Not so immediately—you saw her again. At least two more times."

"How did you know?" He stared at me.

I ignored his question. "I thought you loved me?" My voice was monotone, no inflections at all.

"I do love you. Tess . . ." Robert dropped his head, looking at the ground. "I . . . I have no excuses. She . . ."

"She was broken. Like me when you first met me."

He looked up at my words. "I . . . oh, Tessa."

"She was a lost soul with a traumatic childhood, like mine." I turned to him. "I followed her to the Chens' home that night, and then I asked around about her. Did you want to fix her like you did me?"

He finally turned to me. "I've tried to make it up to you every day since, to be the best husband I can. I'm so sorry for those few nights when I strayed. I have no excuse. I was lost, and I made a stupid, stupid mistake. I've never done it before, and never done it since. You are the love of my life, Tess."

I nodded. "I know." I should have just told him to stop calling me Tess, but now didn't seem to be the right time. "I would do anything for you, Robert. You know that. That's why I didn't say anything. And I could see how hard you were trying."

"How did you know Luca is my son?" he asked in a quiet voice.

"The Chens had recently moved into the neighborhood. I found out she was Hope's sister, who had a troubled past, hooked on drugs and alcohol. You know how gossip gets around in the community. I watched the house, but she wasn't there often."

"You followed her?" Robert's voice was incredulous.

"I needed to see who she was. Why you would betray our vows like that." I kept my voice even because I was no longer angry. I'd gotten over his betrayal years ago. "One day, I happened to drive by and saw her on the front porch with Hope. She was high—I could see it even from a distance." My parents were both addicted to drugs, and I learned to see the signs from an early age. I pushed thoughts of my parents aside. "A few months later, I saw her belly. At first, I didn't think anything of it."

"You were spying on them?"

I turned at the judgy note in his voice. "Hey, the bitch had slept with my husband. More than one time. I had a right to find out what she was up to."

That came out harsher than I intended, and Robert flinched. "How did you know?"

"Sorry." I softened my tone. "You didn't think I wasn't going to keep an eye out after that first time?" I shook my head at him. "You should know me better than that, Robert. I turned on 'Share Your Location' on your iPhone so I could track where you were. I knew you'd gone over to that place she was staying in at the time."

"But . . ."

I almost smiled at the bewildered look on his face. "But what?"

"How did you know he's my son?"

"I did the math and the timing was right. But I wasn't sure until later, after the baby was born and I found out that his name is Luca." I hadn't even had to spy on them to find this out. Gossip in our community spread faster than wildfire.

"Luca." Robert said the name softly.

I nodded. "Yes, Luca. That was the name you said you would name a son if you had one, wasn't it? You told me years ago." I stared him right in the eyes. "Did you tell her that too?" I asked, even though I knew the answer. "Is that why she named him Luca? Because she knew he was your child?"

I watched his face and saw him blanch. "You knew all this time," Robert said, his face breaking.

"Yes." I looked at him tenderly. "But I forgave you."

A headache was starting at my temples, my heartbeat throbbing there, as if a drum were playing inside my head. My thoughts swirled, until I was no longer sure if I was sitting at the campfire with Robert or if I'd gone back to that time when I found out about his betrayal. I'd waited and watched, tracked his every move, until I was sure she meant nothing to him. I was used to being unloved. I was used to people betraying my trust, leaving me. But I wasn't used to them coming back. No one had ever come back for me, until Robert. Just like he said, he was so sorry and spent the next few years showing me what I meant to him. That was why I'd never said anything. I knew then he truly loved me. If he hadn't, he would have left too.

A buzzing sounded in my ears, like an angry swarm of bees circling inside my head, until I slapped my hands to either side, pressing, trying to make it stop. A voice within the buzzing whispered, "He only came back because you made the problem go away."

I wouldn't acknowledge the voice. I wouldn't give it importance. I started to rock, to get the thought out of my head. Out of my mind. Out of my body. I choked on a sob, but clamped a hand over my mouth to stifle it. I wasn't going to cry. If the boy saw, he'd be scared. I blew out a shaky breath, looking for the boy. He was now sitting on a rock, picking at something at his feet, with Mochi hovering next to him. Shadow still sat silently by my side, his injured paw too raw for him to step over the rocks.

"Tessa." I heard Robert's voice as if from a million miles away.

I shook my head. I could clearly hear the boy talking to Mochi, even from a distance, so why was Robert's voice coming at me as if in a tunnel? A light flashed in front of my eyes and blinded me for a few moments.

"Tessa? Tess!" Robert's voice still sounded as if it were coming from underwater. I blinked, seeing nothing but swirling lights, and felt as if I were being rotated around and around, as if in a washing machine. Something twinged in my temple and I winced in pain, a hand flying up to the side of my head as I clamped my eyes shut. "Tessa?" I heard again from far away.

I couldn't move. I couldn't think. Thoughts danced in and out of my head. People flitted into my subconscious and then blew away. Harry, the drug dealer who Robert sometimes got painkillers from when he needed something stronger than what the doctors prescribed, something to make him forget how his body was betraying him. The boy and his mother appeared in my mind. They'd left, gone from this area, never supposed to come back. Robert, telling me to face reality, that he was dying, not going to get better.

Lights flashed again and the vise on my head clamped down until I gasped with the pain. Just as I thought I would burst into a thousand pieces, his voice brought me back.

"Tessa!" Louder now, more insistent. Right in my ear, hands holding my shoulder until I stopped spinning, until my head felt attached to my body again.

I stayed still until the world was no longer moving, and when I opened my eyes, I could suddenly see. And what I saw was my Robert staring at me with concern. My heart gave a grateful leap that he was here still. Everything would be fine. We'd vowed to be there for each other in sickness and in health, in good times and bad, and we had weathered the worst storm a couple could face. We were still here.

I looked him right in the eyes. "I'm sorry, Robert. I'm sorry for what I did to you."

"Oh, Tess." He laid a hand on my cheek, and his hand came away wet with my tears. "I understand. I forgive you."

The tears continued to fall down my cheeks. I was glad to hear him say that. Even though I'd seen the forgiveness in his eyes that day, hearing him say it released the knot in my chest. I had done what I had to, in order to protect our love and keep it pure.

30

The boy was asleep on the bottom bunk, with both dogs sleeping on the floor next to him. Moonlight shone through a window, bathing all three forms in a luminous glow. The boy had been tired from running around, and even from across the RV, I could see how his chest rose and fell under the thin sheet. Robert too was asleep in our bedroom, having retired soon after our talk. He was exhausted. So was I. Our talk had drained me, but now I was too wired to sleep.

I walked quietly to stand by the boy's side, observing how he was sprawled on the bed. He didn't stir, but Shadow and Mochi lifted their heads when they heard me approach. They were so in sync with each other. I made a shushing sound, and they put their heads back down, but their eyes remained open, trained on me. I looked at the sleeping boy, at the way the moon illuminated his face. He really was a handsome boy, but then again, he took after Robert, so that was to be expected. I wanted to feel something for him, some sense of belonging or certainty, but there was only a void. I felt nothing, no affection or hatred, just indifference. I'd needed him desperately, because I knew he was the only way to make it up to Robert. Maybe I would come to care for him, the way a mother does for her son. I would keep the boy forever if that meant I didn't have to lose Robert.

I had always imagined when I was a teenager living with my parents how I would treat my own children one day. If I had a girl, I would brush her hair, braiding it the way I'd always wished my mother had done for me. I'd bake cookies for my kids after school so they always came home to a house that smelled like a bakery and not a pub at two in the morning. I'd hold them tight and whisper *don't be scared* when they woke from a nightmare or *you got this* if they were about to do something scary. I'd drive them to and from school every day instead of leaving them to take the bus, where the mean kids would pick on them for their secondhand clothes and mismatched socks.

And now I'd lost my chance of ever having a child because Robert had lied to me, told me he didn't want any. When the truth was that he hadn't wanted any with *me*. He thought I was too broken, too beaten up to ever be a proper mother. Anger sizzled at the edge of my consciousness, and I had to force it away. Tamp it down. I had no right to be angry, not after what I had done. If Robert had wronged me, I had wronged him even more in turn. That was why I'd taken the boy. I *needed* him, even more than Robert did. With him here, what I'd done no longer mattered. I was once again Robert's adoring and adored wife, and he was once again my strong, loving husband.

With one last lingering glance at the boy's sleeping face, I walked to the front of the RV, to where we kept the security system. Turning on the camera for the inside so that I could keep an eye on everyone, I stood for a moment, looking around. Everything was in order. The TV was still unplugged, keeping the rest of the world away. Thank goodness the boy didn't seem to be a big TV watcher.

I checked the camera app on my phone to make sure it was working, then opened the side door. I could see Shadow's eyes gleaming at me. I would normally take him, but he was content with the boy and Mochi, and with his hurt paw, it was better if he stayed. And I needed time alone. To think and figure out what to do. I couldn't sleep, I couldn't sit still. I felt like I'd jump out of my skin any minute. I hadn't felt like this in so long. And the only way to fix that was to walk, be on the move. I went down the steps and closed the door quietly behind me.

I was going on my night walk. I'd started doing them when Robert's cancer came back. I couldn't show him how worried I was during the day, so I'd wait until he was asleep and then slip out of the house. I had cameras installed inside so that I could keep an eye on him in case he needed me, and then I'd walk in the dark through our neighborhood. Down the hill, then all the way over to the other side of the lake, past the Chens' house, up into the hills on that side, and then back down the hill. I walked in the night as if daring something bad to happen to me. I didn't take a flashlight, and only had my phone so that I could keep an eye on Robert.

The night walks soothed me. They allowed me to work out my fears, and my feet pounded on the ground as if I could shake out all the worries that filled me during the day. I walked until my legs were tired, my feet hurt, but my heart was calm, even if for only an hour.

I even did my night walks when we traveled in our RV. I knew it wasn't always safe, a new place I wasn't familiar with, a lone woman out at night by myself with only my phone flashlight to keep cars from running me over. But I dared the Universe to hurt me. I almost welcomed it. Maybe if something bad happened to me, Robert would be spared.

And tonight, I left the four of them in the RV and went out into the night. I needed to run away from my thoughts. I didn't want to think about the search for Luca or what I was going to do if we were caught. I wanted to believe we could keep going like this, traveling around the country in the RV, just the three of us with our two dogs. I didn't want to worry about keeping him out of sight, or what I would do if someone recognized him. I didn't want to worry about this itchy feeling I had, the urge to scratch at my skin, feeling as if it didn't fit my body. I remembered the last time I'd felt like this. I remembered how hazy my mind had been then, when I couldn't trust what was real and what was only in my head.

As my feet pounded the pavement and I picked up my pace, I realized I couldn't outwalk my thoughts. The night walk wasn't soothing me as they always had in the past. Instead, it stirred up memories that I'd buried deep, memories from that awful night, back when I was twenty-three. The night Robert had found me, my nose broken and my left hand mangled, limping badly from when my father had assaulted my mother and me. I picked up my pace, trying to outrun my father's fist, as it raised above me and plowed into my face. I ducked, my breath coming in gasps, as my mother's face loomed large in front of me. I had to watch again as she turned away, doing nothing to protect me, even though she was the one who had called me for help that night. They'd wanted me to leave as soon as I'd graduated from high school, yet when my mother called me, like the fool I was, I had gone back. It served me right, and I got only what I deserved. But I had finally had enough, that brutal night. I'd gone back the next week and taken care of them. I'd ended my father's reign of terror.

I willed myself to slow down, to set a pace that didn't have me gasping for breath. I concentrated on the sound my sneakers made as they slapped the pavement one after the other. Slap, slap. Slap, slap. There was no one about, just me and the big dark sky, and my pace finally slowed enough for me to catch my breath.

The week after my father assaulted me for the last time was a hazy blur. I never told Robert who had done that to me, and he'd never asked. Yet he'd known. He'd put it together and protected me, gotten me the help I'd needed. He'd gathered me in his arms and told me he would take care of me, make me whole again. He hadn't asked any questions. He believed in me. How could I not love him after that? How could I not give everything to him, knowing he understood and didn't judge me?

My camera app beeped, signaling movement within the RV. My pulse jumped until I saw it was only Shadow and Mochi pacing in the vehicle. The boy was still in bed, and our bedroom door was still shut. Everything was fine. It was just the dogs, restless, probably waiting for me. I blew out a breath and looked up. The stars were so bright tonight, twinkling and winking high above. I held still, staring at the brilliance, and was able to pick out some constellations. My mom had once taught them to me, many years ago, when I was a little girl. Before she'd chosen my father and drugs over me. Orion and his belt. The Big Dipper. Scorpius. Sirius, the Dog Star, and also the brightest star in the sky. That one made me think of Shadow and I smiled, spinning around slowly, my head still tilted up so that it was as if I were dancing with the stars. I wanted to believe the brilliant sky was a sign that I'd done the right thing.

I spun around some more, until everything was a blur. I finally stopped, and had to wait until my head settled. And I was able to finally think clearly. I had to find a way for us to disappear with the boy. How long would it take before someone saw us? How long before someone recognized the boy? How long would they search for him?

We could be on the road for years, never staying in one place long, keeping away from other people. I could go to the store and get supplies, since no one knew he was with us. But the boy was already starting to get restless, wanting to call his aunt. I knew I wouldn't be able to placate him for long. I'd need to come up with a plausible story by tomorrow. I needed the boy with us, needed to keep my family together. I'd do anything for Robert.

31

We were all up early the next morning and saw the sunrise. It was so peaceful, sitting in the middle of nowhere, warm mugs of coffee for me and Robert and hot chocolate for the boy. Shadow and Mochi gnawed at bones at our feet, and all was quiet. The sky was incredible, changing from pink to gold as the birds chirped and forest noises surrounded us.

Once the sun was fully up, I laid out our yoga mats in the grass, and Robert and I did a simple flow that Anna had taught us. The boy watched us with curiosity, even trying a downward-facing dog and a cobra, as I listened to Robert breathing next to me. *Inhale, reach up to the sky, exhale, dive over, inhale to a flat back, exhale, hands on the floor.* Robert's movements were choppy, not graceful, the way he'd started moving after years of weekly yoga practices. But he was flowing next to me, and I closed my eyes the next time I reached up to the sky, thankful he was at my side.

I made us a simple breakfast of scrambled eggs and bacon in the pan over the fire, and opened a bag of rolls so the boy could make himself a breakfast sandwich. I thought about staying for a few days, since we were already hooked up. But until I could come up with a plan, it was safer if we kept moving. I could feel the boy watching me all morning, even if he didn't say anything. I knew he was getting antsy.

We headed west again soon after breakfast, and Robert opted to sit in the back with the boy and Shadow. They were both silent, but I could feel the boy's eyes on me. Every time I glanced in the rearview mirror, he met my eyes. He'd positioned himself behind my seat, as if he were keeping an eye on me. His gaze made me uncomfortable, and I moved the mirror until I could no longer see him.

We'd been on the road for more than four hours when the boy suddenly said, "I need to pee."

Technically, he could go to the bathroom while the RV was moving, but Robert had always had a strict rule that we didn't use the facilities or walk around unless the RV was parked.

"I'll pull over at the next rest stop." I raised my voice so that the boy could hear me over the music I was playing from my phone. I had to use the bathroom too. And I needed to stretch my legs.

"The sign there said the next rest area is in five miles." The boy pointed back behind us.

I nodded to let him know I'd heard, and we drove on in silence until the turnoff for the rest area approached. I pulled over, and as soon as I had maneuvered the RV into a spot, he jumped up and ran for the bathroom, making Robert and me laugh.

I looked toward the service area, noting it was busy, lots of people on the road today. I had no idea what day it was. I'd lost all track of time.

"You need to go too?" I turned to Robert. When he nodded, I said, "You can go next."

"Thanks, Tess."

"I don't . . ." I opened my mouth to tell him to stop calling me Tess, but the boy came out right then.

"Can I go in and get a snack?" the boy asked, once Robert was in the bathroom.

"We have snacks." I pointed to the kitchen, which I'd stocked with everything I thought a boy would love: potato chips, Doritos, candy bars, popcorn, beef sticks, chocolate, and even fresh fruit.

"I want to look at the stores, get something fresh. Maybe a milkshake." A petulant look crossed his face, the first time I'd ever seen him in anything but a good mood.

"You can't go in . . ." I stopped because I realized how that sounded. Why couldn't he go?

"Why not?" He was digging in his heels, his brows furrowed as he squared off against me. "Where are we? When can I talk to Aunt Hope?"

"I'll go." I sighed and grabbed my purse, avoiding his question about his aunt. "I'll use the bathroom inside. What do you want?"

"Why can't I come with you? My mom always kept me with her whenever we traveled." He fixed his eyes on me.

I was searching for an answer when Mochi suddenly pounced on Shadow, and they started to tussle. Low growls emitted from Shadow as Mochi tried to put his whole head in her mouth. They batted at each other and rolled on the ground, their play sounding more ferocious than it really was.

"I need you to keep an eye on the dogs," I said. "Make sure they don't hurt each other. And Robert too."

"Robert doesn't need to be watched." The boy pointed to the dogs. "And they're fine. They're just playing."

"I know, but you never know. Please?" I looked at him imploringly. "Watch them for me?"

He looked like he was going to argue, but then he said, "Fine."

"Great." I fixed a bright smile on my face. "What do you want?"

"A vanilla milkshake. And chicken tenders with barbecue sauce."

"Okay. Tell Robert I'll be right back." I opened the door and then turned back. "Stay in the RV." I softened my voice so as not to raise any more suspicions. "I don't want you to get lost."

He looked at me, and even I knew that was lame. Because really, how could he miss this big-ass RV? But he didn't answer, so I left the motor home and headed to the rest area. I looked back but didn't see him in the windows and breathed a sigh of relief.

I used the bathroom quickly, then got in line to order the food. It took longer than I expected, and my foot jiggled, nervous energy shooting through my body. I didn't like to leave them alone for so long. Just as I was about to give up, the line moved fast, and I was finally able to order. I also got a chocolate milkshake for Robert—his favorite. I paid and then walked outside, heading quickly toward the RV. I was still in the car parking area when the boy suddenly appeared in front of me.

"Can I also get french fries? I'm starving." He panted slightly, as if he'd run all the way.

"What are you doing?" My heart leaped into my throat.

I looked around, checking out the scene. Was that man by the black truck staring at us? What about the group of women, all wearing bright-pink T-shirts and speaking over one another as they headed from their tour bus toward the rest area? Was one of them looking at the boy? I stepped in front of him, blocking their view before turning back to him. I couldn't grab his arm because my hands were full, but I stepped right up to him and spoke into his ear. "What're you doing? I told you to stay in the RV."

"But I wanted more food—" He broke off when I shoved the bag of food into his hands, along with his shake.

Someone jostled us from behind and I whirled around, expecting to find accusing eyes aimed at me. But it was only a teenage girl, arguing loudly with her mother and not watching where she was going.

I turned back to the boy. "You can't be out here." Out of the corner of my eyes, I saw a woman paying way too much attention to us. "Let's go."

With my hand free now that the boy was holding the bag, I grabbed his arm and practically dragged him along with me. I chanced a look behind and saw the woman pointing at us. My heart dropped. She had definitely noticed us.

". . . looks like the boy that's missing . . . you know . . . on the news," she was saying loudly to the portly man by her side.

Shit, shit, shit.

I leaned down and hissed in the boy's ear, "Get back in the RV and stay there. Don't come out again. Understand?"

He stared at me, his eyes wide, but he must have seen something in my gaze, because he simply nodded. I shoved Robert's shake into his hand.

"Take this back for Robert and eat your food. I'll be right back." I gave him a little shove, and to my relief, he ran toward the RV, disappearing around it to the door on the other side.

Blowing out a breath, I turned and saw that the woman who had been pointing to us was now pulling out her phone, walking quickly toward the rest area building. The man she was with was no longer in sight. I followed her as she veered off to the side of the building, where there were picnic tables. Most were occupied, and I saw her head for an empty table. I ran to catch up to her, my harsh breathing loud to my ears.

I heard her words just as she reached the table.

". . . think I saw the boy that's been missing. I saw his picture on the news and—"

I grabbed her elbow from behind and pulled her cell phone out of her hand, ending the call.

"Hey . . ." She whirled away from me, but I had a firm grip on her. Keeping her close to my side, I fast walked her away from the picnic tables and toward the back of the building. She tried to pull away from me, but I was stronger than she was. She had no choice but to walk along or risk being dragged. "Let go of me! What do you think you're doing?"

I ignored her but twisted the arm I had hold of hard, until she yelped in pain. By then, we had rounded the building, and I was glad to see it was deserted. No one around. I marched her to an area behind a row of bushes and finally stopped.

I held her slightly away from me and studied her without a word.

"What the fuck are you doing? Let go of my arm." She was red in the face, her tight, dark-brown curls springing from her head. She was around my age, midforties or so. But she was much shorter than me. She fought against my hold but couldn't break free.

"What were you doing?" I shot back at her. "Calling the police?"

"Yes, that boy. He looks like—" She yelped when I twisted her arm again.

I leaned down and spoke close to her ear. "You didn't see anything, okay?"

"What the—"

That was all she got out before I let her go and, with one swift punch, caught her on the chin, snapping her head back. She fell in slow motion to the ground as I stared down at her. I didn't have much time, and I had to make sure she didn't call the police again. I threw her cell phone against the wall and then stomped on it hard until the glass cracked. And then I looked around. My eyes landed on a large rock that would have to do. She was moaning, her arms thrown to the side. I picked up the rock, brought it over my head, and in one powerful motion, brought it down hard on her forehead. I couldn't chance having her get up anytime soon. I looked away as soon as the rock made contact with a sickening crunch. *Blood, ugh.* I shuddered, keeping my gaze averted. But this had been unavoidable. I'd had to silence the woman. I couldn't have her jeopardizing everything I'd done to get my family here.

"I'm sorry," I said to the inert figure. "You shouldn't have interfered."

I quickly left the scene, walking to the corner and back toward the RV. I wasn't worried about leaving my fingerprints because I'd never been arrested or printed for any reason. I headed straight for the RV when I didn't see the man who had been with the woman I'd just attacked. As I got closer, I could see the boy in the window, holding something up by his face. The moment he saw me approaching, he ducked out of sight.

I ran for the driver's door and yanked it open, hopping up into the seat and slamming the door shut. I looked down. Ugh. There was blood spattered on my pale-pink shirt. I reached behind me and grabbed my hoodie, sliding my arms in and zipping it up. I turned and found the boy sitting at the table dipping a chicken tender into the barbecue sauce. He gave me an innocent look, but I didn't have time to grill him. We needed to get out of here, fast.

"Is Robert in the bedroom?"

"No." The boy's voice bordered on hostile. He'd never spoken to me like that before.

I glanced back, noticing that the bedroom door was closed, and sighed. I needed to get the boy back on my side. I had to gain his trust again so that he wouldn't be so difficult.

"I'm sorry." I shot him a smile, but he turned away. I sighed again. "Buckle up, okay? I don't want you to be hurt." I started the engine and pulled away slowly, without waiting to hear the click of his seat belt.

I headed for the ramp that would take us back onto the highway, my attention focused on the heavy traffic. Once we were safely merged, I finally spoke up.

"What were you doing, right before I got back to the RV?"

Silence. Just when I thought he wasn't going to answer me, he said, "Nothing. What do you mean?"

"When I saw you in the window, standing up. What were you doing?" My eyes dropped to the cell phone holder, where I usually kept my phone, and my breath hitched when I saw it wasn't there. Had I put it in my purse before leaving the RV? One hand groped for my purse on the floor next to me.

"Just drinking my shake." He held it up so that I could see it in the rearview mirror. "Thanks for getting me the food."

My eyes darted to him in the mirror, and then I saw my cell on the dining table across from him. I must have put it there when the boy asked me about going out to get food. I looked quickly behind me and saw that the bedroom door was still closed. Robert's chocolate shake was in a cup holder next to the boy. I was concerned that Robert hadn't wanted it, but I was suddenly parched. If Robert didn't want it, I'd drink it.

"Can you hand me the shake?" I reached a hand behind me.

The boy silently put it in my hand, and I took a grateful sip. I knew we had to get away from the rest area as soon as possible, but the reason why was already slipping through my mind, like sand through a sieve. Adrenaline pumped in me, flushing my cheeks and making me feel as if I'd just run a marathon. I gulped at the shake, needing the cold sensation sliding down my throat to ground me. All I knew was I'd done what I needed to, in order to protect Robert. I wasn't sorry. With one final sip, I put the shake in the cup holder and focused on the road.

32

The boy wouldn't sit still. He was suddenly in the passenger seat, buckling himself into the seat.

"Here." He handed me my cell phone, and I took it from him with a quick thanks before snapping it back in its holder with one hand.

"Aren't you too young to be sitting up here?" I threw him a look before refocusing on the road.

He shrugged. "My mom used to let me sit up front with her sometimes, if we were just driving around our neighborhood and not on a highway."

"Oh." We were silent for a moment. "But we're on a highway." I peeked over at him, wondering what he was thinking. "You're making me nervous."

"Where are we going?" He was frowning so much that his forehead crinkled.

"Wherever the wind takes us," I said in a flip tone. This was the first time he'd asked since we started the trip. I'd told him when we left that we were headed west, and he hadn't asked for specifics. I wondered why he was asking now.

"What state are we in?" he persisted.

"I don't know. Ohio still? Or maybe Kentucky?" I hadn't been paying attention. I was just driving, heading west and slightly south. But I realized I needed to tell him something to make him stop asking questions. I needed him to start thinking of the RV as home, and me and Robert as his family.

"Listen—" I started, but he interrupted.

"When can I call Aunt Hope?" The sharp tone in his voice made me turn, and I caught a glimpse of despair on his face before focusing back on the highway.

"That's what I wanted to talk about. There's been . . ." I paused, softening my voice and relaxing my face so that I would be as convincing as possible.

"I need to speak to Aunt Hope." He turned so that the full gaze of his brown eyes was upon me. I didn't turn my head, but I could feel his stare penetrating into the side of my face. "I know something's wrong. I need to call them now."

"Luca." That was the first time I'd called him by name. "I'm sorry, but there *is* something wrong, and I didn't know how to tell you. There's been a . . . an accident." I took a shuddering breath, not meeting his eyes. "Your aunt and uncle didn't make it."

"What?" The word burst from his mouth.

I threw him a sympathetic look. He didn't say anything for several moments, and I figured he was processing what I'd just said. I had to make him stop asking to talk to his aunt. This was the best way to put an end to it.

"I'm sorry," I said after a while, when he still hadn't spoken.

He'd turned back to stare ahead, out the windshield at the road. If he started crying, I should pull over so I could comfort him.

I was just signaling to move into the right lane in case I had to stop when he sprang to life. He glared at me and shouted, "You're a liar. I just spoke to Aunt Hope. She's not dead."

"What?" I shook my head slightly. What did he mean? How could he have possibly spoken to his aunt?

"She's fine, and she didn't know you took me." His hands were balled into fists at his sides. "Why did you take me? Where are we going?"

"I . . . I don't know what you're talking about. Your aunt was the one who asked me to take you because they had an emergency . . ." My eyes fell on my phone. Suddenly, my entire body turned to ice. Had I taken the phone out of the holder and left it on the table before I went into the rest area? It was such an automatic habit, to swipe the phone from its place whenever I left the car. But now I couldn't remember doing it. I hadn't left the car directly. I'd been waiting with Robert for my turn at the bathroom. I'd been distracted, and I tried to remember if I'd left it on the table. With a sickening feeling, I knew I hadn't. I'd left it in the holder—whenever I took it out, I automatically slipped it into the front of my purse.

"You lied to me." Luca's voice had me turning to him. He swallowed and then said, "Aunt Hope was crying. She had no idea where I went. Why did you take me?"

"I don't understand . . ." My mind scrambled. Had he called his aunt? Or was he baiting me? My mind tried to come up with something to say, but I couldn't do that and concentrate on driving at the same time.

Before I could react, Luca had unbuckled his seat belt and was standing next to me. "Take me home now," he shouted.

I flinched at his tone but kept a steady grip on the steering wheel and looked straight ahead. "Calm down. I don't know what you think you know, but it's not what you think."

"I want to go home. Now," he said again.

When I ignored him, he suddenly reached out and grabbed the steering wheel, causing us to veer widely. My heart leaping into my throat, I let out a yelp and tried to straighten the motor home. But he wouldn't let go. I tried to push him out of the way, but he was surprisingly strong for a nine-year-old boy.

"Stop the RV!" He gripped the steering wheel hard and, with one fast yank, turned it toward him. I heard horns honking, and a car whizzed by us on the left.

I screamed as our vehicle careened across a lane into the slow lane, horns blaring and the squeal of brakes in our wake. I got control of the wheel and tried to correct our direction, pumping the brakes so that we wouldn't suddenly stop. But I must have overcorrected, because now the RV swerved in the opposite direction, heading for the guardrail in the center. The boy shouted and turned, calling to the dogs. I was too preoccupied struggling to keep the RV from hitting anything to see what he was doing. The RV scraped along the side of the guardrail, and the screeching sound of metal against metal made me want to hold my hands over my ears. But I had to get the RV under control. I swung the wheel the other way, praying there were no cars in the lane next to ours, and managed to correct the motor home so that we were back in a lane. I blew out a breath, my heart thundering in my ears. Thankfully, we hadn't hit anyone.

"Stop," Luca shouted, holding the dogs' leashes. "I'm getting out with the dogs." They were both barking frantically, and the boy lunged at the wheel again, just as I had it going straight. For a few seconds, we fought for control. Without warning, he let go as I was trying to turn the wheel my way, which made the RV swing wildly to the left. He screamed, diving behind me to the ground. I heard things flying out of cabinets, crashing to the floor. Shadow and Mochi barked as the boy yelled for them.

Another scream tore through the air, mine or his, I wasn't sure, as we hurtled across the left lane, narrowly missing a car that sped up out of the way. I stomped on the brake, trying to slow the inevitable crash, but we were already upon the guardrail again, this time head-on. I braced myself for impact, throwing my arms over my face as I remembered with dread that Class A motor homes like ours were not equipped with airbags. They were also made with cost savings for manufacturers in mind, meaning our RV was about to crumple like a sardine can. That was the last thing I remembered as the world around me shattered and the sickening crunch of steel on steel vibrated through my entire body.

PART 3

Hope and Tessa

33

H O P E

Day three
12:52 p.m.

"He's in Kentucky."

Hope's whole body sagged with relief on hearing Detective Hanson's words on speakerphone. Shaun reached out and grabbed her hand, holding tight. They'd called the police as soon as they figured out that Luca had called them from Tessa's cell, and they had been able to locate her position within minutes.

"Thank god. What happens now?" Hope asked when she could speak.

"We're contacting the local police. They're in northern Kentucky, over seven hundred and fifty miles away. As soon as they have him, we'll let you know." Detective Hanson's voice was calm, and Hope was grateful for it.

"Thank you," she whispered into the phone.

"We're sending someone to your house so we can keep you updated." The detective said a few more words, but Hope didn't hear them. Her head was literally spinning in relief, trying to wrap her mind around the fact that Luca was alive and well.

Shaun reached out and hung up the phone, then sank onto the chair next to Hope at the dining table.

"What if they can't find them? What if they get away?" Hope voiced her fears as soon as she could speak.

"The police will find them. Even if she turns off her phone, they know the general area where Luca called from. And in a big vehicle like that, they'll be easier to spot." The police knew they were looking for an RV, and even though they hadn't known what kind of motor home it was, Shaun had looked back through his texts with the Conrads. Now they knew to be on the lookout for a Tiffin Allegro Open Road. They even had the license plate number, thanks to a picture Shaun had taken of Luca in front of the RV.

"But why?" That question had been running through Hope's mind ever since Luca had told them he was with Tessa and Robert. "Why did they take him without telling us? What do they want with him?"

They'd racked their brains and looked back at all the texts and email chains with the Conrads, and nothing suspicious had come up. They were just a nice couple who'd adopted a dog Luca had taken care of, who'd invited him over to explore their RV. How had Luca ended up with them?

Shaun shook his head. "I don't know. I guess we'll get answers soon."

"Do you think they harmed him?"

"He said he was fine." Shaun met her eyes. "He didn't sound scared."

"They better not have hurt a hair on his head or I'm going to kill them." Hope clenched her teeth, her hands fisting in her lap. She'd tried calling Tessa back over and over after Luca hung up, but it had gone straight to voice mail. Someone had turned it off. Or something had happened.

A soft bark drew Hope's attention to Toby, sitting on the ground next to her chair. In one movement, Hope dropped to the floor and wrapped her arms around the little dog.

"They're going to find them. Everything's going to be fine." It had to be.

Toby leaned against her, panting softly in her ear, as if he understood. Hope hugged the dog to her and then looked up and met Shaun's eyes. In them, she saw the same helpless despair that must have been mirrored in her own as they waited for news about Luca. They had spoken to him. He was alive. It was hell not to be able to do anything except wait. Hope buried her face in Toby's back, praying with all her might that they found Luca soon.

34

Tessa

Day three
1:01 p.m.

There was an ominous silence before I opened my eyes. And then the sound of sirens in the distance, getting closer and closer. I blinked and tried to focus, to figure out where I was. And then in a rush, the crash came back to me. I was still in the driver's seat, strapped in by my seat belt, but the RV I knew was no longer.

It was too quiet inside the cab. Outside, I could hear the roar of traffic and a cacophony of voices raised in concern. Turning my head, I winced at the pain that shot through my brain. I brought a hand up to my face, and it came away with blood. I closed my eyes when the nausea hit me like a tidal wave. I did some deep yoga breaths until it receded. Tentatively, I opened my eyes again, purposely keeping my gaze away from my bloody hand. I looked behind me. The RV was a mess, broken glass everywhere, even though the windshield was still intact. Our stuff had flown out of cabinets, coins strewn about (where had they come from?), the refrigerator door open with food spilling out because I had forgotten to latch it.

As I gingerly tested my body, a movement behind me caught my attention. It was Luca, emerging from the wreckage. Objects fell away from him as he stood, and I saw Mochi struggling to her feet. Where was Shadow?

"Tessa, are you okay?" he asked, his voice loud in the silent RV.

He had a cut on his arm, a bump forming on his forehead, and a dazed expression on his face. I was surprised he wasn't hurt worse. He hadn't been wearing a seat belt like I had. Yet he was in better shape than I was. How was that possible? I felt as if I'd been pummeled by a giant mallet.

"Tessa?" he asked again, and I realized I hadn't answered him. "I'm sorry. I didn't mean for us to crash. I just needed you to stop." He sounded like he was on the verge of tears, and looking around, I saw how bad things were.

The sound of sirens growing ever closer jerked my attention away from him, and my heart hammered in panic. Were they coming because of the accident? Or had that stupid woman at the rest stop given them more info than I'd thought and they'd found us?

I struggled to undo the seat belt, which was digging into my chest and shoulder, but I couldn't. I ached all over. The sirens were right outside. My eyes darted in panic, even as I tried to take a breath to slow the way the world was spinning when I moved my head too fast. What was I going to do? I had to protect myself and . . .

My head whipped toward the back of the RV so suddenly that I saw stars. Oh god. Robert.

"Help is coming," Luca said. He took one of my hands and held it in his, forcing my attention back on him. "I'm sorry."

I heard a commotion outside, voices talking, radios going off, the sirens finally silent. And in that split second before someone started wrenching open the side door, as Luca held my hand so sweetly in his own, panic overtook my body. Was Robert okay? Had he buckled himself into the recliner? Or had he crawled into bed to rest? If he had,

I knew he would have been badly injured. Alarm coursed through me and I screamed his name, praying with all my might that he was fine.

As the side door of the RV was finally yanked open, my head lolled back and I tried to keep from blacking out. I squeezed my eyes shut so tight that lights danced in front of me. I was so dizzy. I felt Luca let go of my hand, and I moaned, the pain searing through me even as I fought to stay awake. I had to save Robert.

There were voices, Luca's saying he was fine and asking them to check out Shadow, who wasn't moving. Unfamiliar male voices answered him, although I couldn't understand what they were saying. A female voice too, who said into a crackling radio, "We got him."

More bursts from a radio and staticky replies before I heard someone approaching. I kept my eyes shut until a hand touched me lightly on the shoulder.

"Ma'am. Ma'am, are you okay?"

My eyes flew open, and I turned toward the voice. I blinked a few times, trying to bring the speaker into focus. A kind face peered at me, male and about my age. "My husband," I whispered. "He's in back, in the bedroom." My voice grew stronger. Panic took over, my breath coming in gasps. "Someone, help him. Robert? Robert! Help him!"

I started to thrash my arms and legs, trying to leave the driver's seat, but my body felt like lead. The man tried to calm me, speaking in a low, gentle voice, but the panic was clawing at me now and I couldn't be subdued.

"Please, ma'am, you need to calm down. What's your name? Focus, look at me." The man spoke louder this time, until I stopped and stared at him.

"Tessa," I whispered. "Tessa Conrad."

"Okay, Tessa. You're going to be fine." He examined me and then said, "We're sending someone back to get your husband. But let's get you out of the RV so the medics can examine you." He turned and called over his shoulder to someone.

Slowly, I nodded, and he reached to unbuckle my seat belt. He had a hard time because the driver's door had crushed in toward me. It finally unlatched and I tried to stand, but my legs weren't working. He caught me and supported most of my weight against him. The interior of the RV flashed by as he helped me out, and my heart ached at the debris that used to be our beautiful motor home.

I was placed on a stretcher once we were outside. Radios crackled, emergency lights still flashed even though the sirens were off, and I caught the boy's name, staticky through the radio. My head was spinning, seeing everything off-kilter, and I fought against the waves of dizziness that threatened to pull me under.

I tried to sit up on the stretcher, pointing frantically to the RV. "My husband. Please, help him." Tears flowed and I grabbed the medic who was trying to examine me.

He said something, but my attention was on the police officers gathered near the RV. I heard someone saying, "He's fine."

My heart gave a leap of hope. Were they talking about Robert? Or Luca? "Please," I pleaded again. "Robert is sick. He's dying, not thinking clearly. He didn't mean to . . ."

"What are you talking about, Tessa?" It was the man who had unbuckled me from my seat.

"The cancer, it went to his brain this time. He's not himself. He didn't mean to do it." Tears dripped out of my eyes, and I bent my head so that they fell into my lap. My dark hair hung on either side of my face like curtains.

"Do what? Are you talking about Luca?" I could feel the man's eyes fixed on me as he spoke. "You do know he's been reported missing, right? That there's an ongoing search for him?"

I nodded, just a slight motion, as if I were too tired to do more. "Robert didn't mean to. He's not thinking clearly. Don't judge him harshly. He only wanted to be with his son."

"His son?" I heard the note of surprise in the officer's voice.

"Yes." I nodded. "The boy is his son. Robert would never hurt him. He only wanted to spend time with him." I looked up suddenly, back at the RV. My breath was too loud, harsh and rasping, hurting my chest. "Is he okay? Is he hurt? What's going on?"

"They'll get him out. Please, lie back." The officer patted me on the shoulder as the EMT dabbed something on my forehead. I turned away when I saw the blood, taking in deep breaths until the nausea subsided.

"I'm sorry, I'm sorry." I could hear the hysteria rising in my voice, but I couldn't stop it.

"We'll get to the bottom of this." The man's radio crackled, and he turned away to speak into it. Someone responded, and my ears strained to hear what was going on, since the paramedics were hovering over me and I couldn't see anything.

Forgive me, Robert, I whispered in my head. "Robert, where are you?" I turned and grabbed the EMT trying to take my vitals. "Please, help him! He's hurt. If he weren't he'd have come out by now!"

I tried to jump up, to run back to the RV to save Robert, but the paramedic had a hold of me, and someone came rushing over to help him.

"Let me go," I shouted. "He needs me!"

A swarm of people surrounded me so that I could no longer see the RV. It was too much, all those forms hovering over me, and I threw my hands in front of my face. I prayed silently that Robert wasn't hurt, that the crash hadn't injured him. I couldn't lose him again. I couldn't. I wouldn't be able to bear it. I heard a commotion coming from inside the RV, and I shoved all the faces in my way aside to look.

"Robert!"

"Please, Tessa, you need to calm down." Someone tried to get me to focus, but my attention was on the RV as I waited for my husband to emerge.

"Lie back . . . stay calm . . . ," more voices said to me.

"No, I can't. You don't understand." I pushed against the hands holding me down.

"Tessa, stop."

"No!" I screamed. When they didn't let go, I screamed again. Out of the corner of my eye, I saw Luca watching me, his forehead puckered. I was struck by the concern on his face, the way he worried his bottom lip with his teeth. And in that moment, I knew I needed Luca. He'd made me see how life could be with a child. I realized I was no longer indifferent to him. I cared about him, and I'd be fine as long as I had Luca and Robert.

35

H O P E

"They got Luca."

At Officer Dillon's words, Hope sagged back against the couch in relief.

"Thank goodness. Oh my god." She clasped both hands to her chest, closing her eyes for a brief moment in thanks. "Is he okay? They didn't hurt him?"

"There was an accident. The RV hit the guardrail." Officer Dillon held up a hand when Hope gasped. "He's fine. A few bruises and cuts, but considering he wasn't wearing a seat belt at the time, he's remarkably unharmed."

"But the people who took him. Did they do anything to him?" Hope had to ask.

"From what they've been able to gather so far, they've treated him well. He thought they were taking him on a trip because you had a family emergency."

"Family emergency?" Shaun jumped in. "Where did he get that idea?"

"I don't know." The officer shook his head. "The scene is chaotic right now. They'll be in touch when they have more information."

"But what caused the accident? What happened?" Hope reached out to take Shaun's hand. Luca had just called them, not even an hour ago. Was the crash an accident? Or had something happened?

"I don't have any answers at this point." The officer looked apologetic. Hope swallowed a wave of frustration. She had to remind herself he was here, just like they were, and not in Kentucky, where the accident was. He was getting the information secondhand as things were happening.

"The dogs are fine too. The black one was injured, but nothing life threatening. The white one came out unscathed. Luca won't leave their side."

"Oh, thank god," Hope breathed out.

"They've got the woman, Tessa Conrad. Her husband might be seriously injured."

Hope and Shaun exchanged a look. Robert had seemed like a nice guy when they'd met, but knowing now that he and Tessa had taken Luca, Hope felt a spark of anger at the couple. Of course, she didn't want anyone to be hurt, but if they'd done something to Luca . . .

"Can we talk to Luca?" Shaun asked.

"They'll have him call as soon as the scene is stable."

The officer didn't say any more, but Hope could guess what he was thinking.

As soon as Luca was safely in police custody and away from the Conrads, then they could talk to him. There were still so many unanswered questions. What had caused the accident? Why had the Conrads taken Luca without their knowledge? Hope didn't know whether to be angry or relieved that Luca had been with them this whole time. But for the first time since realizing Luca wasn't in the driveway, she released a cleansing breath, her body finally unclenching from the tight coil it had become the minute she realized Luca was gone.

Shaun squeezed her hand and she squeezed back, holding on for dear life. They were finally optimistic that they would see Luca again.

36

TESSA

Day three
1:25 p.m.

Forcing myself to stay calm, I swatted at the people hovering over me until I could see the RV. My breath caught when a police officer came out the side door and walked down the ruined RV's two short steps. He turned to look back as a second officer emerged.

"Robert!" I called. "Where is he? Is he okay?" I tried to jump off the stretcher, but hands held me down. Whether to keep me away from the accident site or to keep me from hurting myself, I didn't know. All I knew was I needed to get to them.

One of the officers was shaking his head. Someone else walked over to them, and they had a hushed conversation. I was too far away to hear what they were saying, but the two officers kept glancing my way, gesturing at me. My heart seized and one hand flew to my mouth. Was Robert dead? Dread spread through my veins like poison. Were they trying to figure out how to tell me that Robert hadn't made it?

"What happened? Where's my husband?" I struggled against the arms holding me back until one of the officers walked toward me. I scanned his face, desperate to know how bad the news was. "Robert? Is he okay?" I tried to keep my voice from trembling, but I steeled myself for the worst. If they hadn't come out with him, that meant something bad had happened.

The officer stared at me for a moment. "Mrs. Conrad." He paused to study my face. "There's no one in there. You said your husband was in his recliner in the bedroom?"

"Yes." My voice rose in alarm. "What do you mean, there's no one in there? Did you check the floor? Maybe he fell under the bed." I grabbed his arm. "He's not well. He's sick. If he fell, he wouldn't be able to get up by himself."

Another man had walked over, and I saw the two of them exchanging a look before the first one turned back to me. "We searched the entire RV, even the bathroom. There's no one in there."

"What?" I let out a moan that turned into a sob. "What do you mean? He's in there. Robert! Where are you?" I struggled to get off the stretcher, but those hands immediately stopped me again.

"Tessa, please . . ."

"What's going on?" I shrieked. "My husband is hurt and you're telling me he isn't in there! Was he thrown out of the RV?" I turned my head frantically, searching the highway, which had been blocked off with emergency flares and vehicles. "You need to search the ground!"

One of the officers gestured to Luca, who was standing by a police car with an officer, Mochi at his side and Shadow in the back of the vehicle. When Luca reached my stretcher, the officer asked, "Luca. Have you seen Robert? Do you know where he went?"

Luca looked at me first, then turned toward the officer. "I don't know. It's just been me and Tessa. And Mochi and Shadow."

Silence followed his declaration, and I felt everyone's eyes swing to me. The one questioning Luca said, "Are you sure? Robert hasn't been traveling with you?"

The boy shook his head, sending me worried looks. "No. It's just been me and her. She kept talking to Robert, but he wasn't with us." I took in a shuddering breath. "Luca, what are you saying?" I swiped at the tears streaming down my cheeks. Someone pressed tissues into my hand, but I batted them away. "What have you done to Robert?" I screamed. "Where is he? Did you kill him? Is he hurt?"

With a flying leap, I jumped off the stretcher and ran toward the RV, but I stumbled over rocks and fell facedown on the pavement, skinning my knees and hands. Sobbing now, I struggled to stand, and felt hands reaching down to help me. But I didn't want their help. I fought them until they let go and I managed to stand on my own. I could hear shouts all around me, someone calling for the paramedics, and officers surrounding me. The woman whose voice I'd heard before was suddenly by my side, speaking to me in a soothing tone. I was beyond calming. I sobbed and shouted for Robert, clawing at anyone who came too close, yelling for them to let me see Robert, see for myself that he was okay.

"There's no one in there, Tessa. Your husband isn't in the RV." The woman continued to talk, but I ignored her. I thrashed, and my fist connected with her face. She yelped in pain, and her grip on me loosened. I was desperate to get to the RV, to help Robert, but now at least three or four people surrounded me. My arms swung out, and I kicked my legs, connecting with the shins of the EMT who'd been treating me. Arms restrained me and I wailed, hysteria bubbling up from inside me. I was dimly aware of Luca, so still and watching me, while someone made a call.

I cried out for Robert, even as hands steadied me, put me back on the stretcher, kept me in place. And then I felt a presence in front of me. I didn't look at the man or pay him any attention because my entire being was focused on the RV, willing Robert to get up, to walk out of the vehicle, and show them all he was fine. Just fine. But then words penetrated my brain. Words that hit me like a bullet from a gun.

"Ma'am, we made some calls. Your husband, Robert Conrad . . ." Here he hesitated, and I finally lifted my eyes to meet his, grief and frustration welling up inside me. "He died two weeks ago. At your home."

There was a sudden silence, made even more apparent because we were in the middle of a highway. I was dimly aware that we'd stopped traffic on this side, closing off the entire westbound lane. Vehicles in the eastbound side had been slowing as they drove by, rubbernecking to get a look at whatever accident was causing this backup. But for a few seconds, there was absolute silence, as if the entire world had stopped and was holding its breath.

And then I let out my breath and screamed as loudly as I could, holding my head between my hands, rocking forward and back, forward and back. Screaming, "No, no, no, no, no! Robert's not dead. He's fine. He's in the RV. He didn't die and leave me, he wouldn't do that." I turned to the boy, whose eyes were wide with terror. "Tell them, Luca. Robert has been with us these last few days. We're a family. You, me, Robert, and the dogs."

Luca shook his head slowly, pity replacing the terror in his eyes. "No, Tessa. I haven't seen Robert at all."

We stared at each other for a moment, and then I collapsed, screaming as if I'd never stop as people surrounded me and something pricked my skin, and then suddenly, there was nothing.

37

HOPE

Day three
3:05 p.m.

An hour and a half dragged by, as Hope and Shaun waited for word and to talk to Luca. Hope paced, and Shaun rolled out dough to make baos, fluffy pillows of white, soft buns filled with a vegetable mixture that he whipped up. He always cooked when he was stressed. Officer Dillon updated them as information came in. They knew now that only Tessa had been in the RV with Luca, that Robert had died two weeks ago of cancer. They had more questions than they had answers, since the police in Kentucky were still sorting through all the conflicting information. But they had taken Tessa into custody after they'd subdued her because she was inconsolable when they told her Robert was dead. They'd been afraid she was going to hurt herself.

Hope's cell dinged, and she looked down to see a text from Dan Stern.

Any word on Luca?

Hope typed fast. Yes! They found him. The police have the woman who took him. We're waiting to talk to him.

That's a relief! I feel as if I know him.

Hope sniffed, a small smile on her face. **I wish we'd both known him as he was growing up.**

The three dots danced, and Hope waited for Dan's reply.

Keep me posted. I can't wait to meet him.

Will do.

Hope's cell finally rang, and she picked it up right away.

"Luca?"

"Aunt Hope."

"Luca! I'm so, so glad you're okay." Hope took a breath to stave off a sob, not wanting to scare him. "Are you okay? Did she hurt you?"

"I'm fine. I didn't want to be in the RV anymore. At first, it was fun, an adventure. She told me you said I could either go on the RV trip with them or go to California with you. An emergency, she said." The words rushed out of Luca. "I'm sorry. I just wanted to go in the RV."

"Oh, Luca, it's okay. It's not your fault." She and Shaun exchanged a look. "We're just so glad you're fine. We had no idea what happened to you. Are you sure she didn't hurt you? Don't be afraid to tell us." Hope gentled her voice, not wanting to scare him, but at the same time, she needed to know that Tessa hadn't done anything to him.

"She didn't hurt me at all. I wanted to go and we had fun. She even played water guns with me. But she kept talking to herself, and acting as if Robert was with us." He paused, and Hope could hear him breathing on the phone. "I asked where Robert was, but she didn't always answer. He'd been so sick the last time I visited."

"How many times have you been to see them?" Shaun asked. They'd known of only the one time, when Shaun had driven Luca over with Mochi.

Luca paused again. "I'm sorry." His voice wasn't more than a whisper. "Mochi missed Shadow. I'd take Mochi for a walk, and sometimes, she just went all the way around the lake to the other side. And when we walked by their house, Shadow would be in their yard, and then they'd invite me in so Shadow could play with Mochi." He stopped, drawing in an audible breath. "Are you mad?"

"No." Hope rushed in to reassure him. "No, Luca. We're not mad. We're just so glad you're okay." So that was where he'd gone, the few times they hadn't known his whereabouts. There was so much she wanted to ask him. Things like, how Tessa had gotten him to leave without telling them or why she had taken him, what exactly she'd said to him. But now wasn't the time.

"Can I come home?" The hesitant note in his voice broke her heart, yet at the same time, her spirits leaped that he considered their house "home" now.

"Of course you can." Hope took Shaun's hand and squeezed. "We're going to take the first flight out to get you, okay? You're safe with the police until we get there."

"Okay." He breathed into the phone again. "What happened to Tessa?"

Hope looked over at the officer. He'd told her that Tessa was going to be charged with Luca's kidnapping. And possibly for another offense at a rest area. He hadn't gone into details, but they'd apparently caught her on camera committing another crime.

"Ayi?"

Hope started, realizing they hadn't answered Luca's question. "Don't worry about Tessa, okay? She won't hurt you."

"I'm not worried about her hurting me. I'm worried about her. She was really upset. Is she going to be okay?" The concern was clear in his voice.

"They'll take care of her, make sure she gets the help she needs." Hope had no idea what would become of Tessa, but Luca didn't need to worry about it.

"But what about Shadow? Can I bring him home?" His voice raised an octave, and Hope knew he was really concerned about the dog.

She and Shaun shared a look, and he nodded. "If they let us, we'll bring him home with us." They would rent a car and drive home, so that they didn't have to put Mochi and Shadow in the cargo hold of a plane.

Luca breathed out a sigh of relief. "I wouldn't let them take him away from me. He's here with me and Mochi."

"Okay, Luca. Sit tight. We're going to get there as fast as we can."

"Okay," he echoed.

They said goodbye and Hope hung up. Shaun was already looking for flights on his laptop, and she got off the couch, walking to the bedroom to pack. Toby followed her, and Hope shook her head at the thought of having three dogs. But the most important thing was that Luca was safe. Hope could finally breathe again.

38

H OPE

Day four
12:15 a.m.

Hope and Shaun silently followed the police officer who'd greeted them at the police station's front desk. They were headed down the hallway toward the room where Luca waited for them. Someone from Kentucky's child protective services had interviewed Luca extensively, establishing what had happened since Tessa had taken him and verifying again that he hadn't been physically harmed. They'd been told that Luca exhibited no signs of trauma.

Hope and Shaun had caught the first flight they could find from the airport in White Plains into Louisville. Mr. Alden had kindly agreed to look after Toby until they got home with Luca and the other two dogs. Hope had been antsy for the entire flight and the layover, when she'd paced the waiting area, too wound up to eat. They'd barely spoken, both lost in their own thoughts, but Shaun had taken her hand a few times, giving it a reassuring squeeze. Hope was grateful he was with her. She wouldn't be able to relax until they finally saw Luca again and could hold him in their arms.

The officer they were following opened a door, and the first thing Hope saw was Luca, sitting at a table, his back to her. The man across from him looked up, his eyebrows rising in question when he caught sight of them.

Hope rushed forward, then stopped. "Luca?"

Luca swung around, and then he was off the chair and across the room and in Hope's arms. "Ayi, you found me!"

She squeezed him tight, and then Shaun's arms were around both of them as Hope ran a hand over the back of Luca's head. Tears sprang to her eyes, so thankful that he was fine, alive in their arms. Shaun's arms tightened around them. Hope breathed out a sigh, so grateful they had him back.

"You have no idea how glad we are to see you," Hope finally said.

"You're not mad?" Luca asked, his voice muffled as he held them as tight as they were holding him.

"No." Shaun's voice was firm. "It's not your fault."

Luca gave them one last hug and then pulled away. It was then that Hope noticed the dogs, standing patiently at his side.

"Shadow and Mochi are glad you're here too," Luca said. Hope noted how the two dogs were practically glued to each other. "You said Shadow could come home with us, right?"

"Yes."

"They had a vet check Shadow. He got hurt in the accident." Hope saw that Shadow had a bandage on one of his front paws. "But they said he'll be fine. He just needs to rest."

"I'm glad." Hope reached over to pet both dogs and then caught the eyes of the detective who was in the room with Luca.

The man stood. "I'm Detective Brown. We've been keeping Luca comfortable and entertained." He smiled and extended a hand to Hope and then to Shaun. "We tried to get him to take a nap, but he didn't want to."

Luca scoffed, even as he stifled a yawn. "Naps are for babies."

Hope hid a smile. "Thanks for taking care of him."

"Can we go now?" Luca was anxious to leave, clipping leashes on Shadow and then Mochi.

"Let's get you out of here, shall we?" Detective Brown ruffled Luca's hair, and Luca shot him a quick smile before refocusing on Hope and Shaun.

Hope put her arm around Luca's shoulder while Shaun took the two leashes. She knew there was some paperwork needed before they could go to the hotel Shaun had reserved for them for the night, but for now, she was just so grateful that Luca was actually standing in front of them, unharmed.

The next morning, seated in a booth at a nearby diner, Hope couldn't take her eyes off her nephew. He sat with Shaun on one side with Hope across from them. Part of her still didn't fully believe that they'd found him. She knew the statistics, that if a missing child wasn't found within the first twenty-four hours, the chances of him being found alive started dropping. Luca had not only returned to them, but he was unharmed. He'd been asleep almost as soon as she'd pulled the sheets up over him last night, and then she and Shaun had fallen into the first real sleep they'd had since their nephew had gone missing.

"Can you tell us more how you ended up with Tessa?" she asked, as she watched Luca fork a bite of buttermilk pancakes, liberally doused with syrup and melted butter, into his mouth. They knew the gist of what had happened, but she wanted to hear from Luca how Tessa had gotten him into the RV.

He swallowed the bite before answering. "I was playing basketball outside."

Hope nodded. That heart-stopping moment when she'd realized he was no longer in the driveway would stay with her for a long time.

"All of a sudden, I looked up and Shadow was standing at the top of the driveway. When he saw me, he ran down to Mochi."

Luca's eyes were clouded as he looked from Hope to Shaun. "He wasn't on a leash and I didn't want him to get run over, so I opened the gate. I was going to put him in there with Mochi, but Mochi got out, and they were so happy to see each other. Then Shadow took off, up the driveway and toward the woods next to Mr. Alden's house. Mochi and I followed him."

He put down his fork, his face scrunched in worry. "We chased him all the way into the woods, and then Shadow somehow got tangled up in this thorny bush. I ran to help him, but I tripped and fell." Luca held up his arm to show them the long, healing scrape on the underside of his forearm. "I scratched up my leg too. It stung a lot. But Shadow was hurt. That was when Tessa appeared at the bottom of the hill."

Hope lifted an eyebrow and exchanged a look with Shaun. That must have been where they'd found Luca's key chain and blood.

"She was so relieved to see him. He'd gotten out of the house while they were loading the RV for a trip." Luca took a swallow of orange juice.

"Shadow escaped?" Hope asked.

Luca shrugged. "I guess? I was worried about him. He was bleeding and started doing that reverse sneezing thing he always does when he's scared." He put down his cup. "You taught me how to stop it, remember?"

Hope nodded. "You helped him?"

"Yes." Luca looked proud of himself. "I closed his mouth and plugged up one nostril just like you taught me, and he immediately calmed down. Tessa was so grateful. She kind of freaked out when she saw the blood. I don't think she likes blood much. I helped her get him into her car. I was going to come home after that, but then Mochi jumped in the car with Shadow and she wouldn't come out."

"I guess Mochi missed Shadow," Hope said.

Luca nodded. "Tessa asked me to help her get Shadow back to her house. I saw her text you, and she told me you said it was okay."

Hope shook her head. "She didn't. I had no idea where you went."

"I'm sorry." Luca met her gaze. "We were back at their house when she said you were calling and she picked it up. I saw her talking to you on the phone."

"She never called me. She must have been faking it." Hope couldn't believe Tessa had lied to Luca like that.

"How did you end up in the RV with her?" Shaun asked.

"I heard her say something about your parents and she looked worried. She said something about you and Uncle Shaun needing to fly to California. She asked if I'd rather go on an RV trip with them." His gaze didn't waver. "She told me it was up to me. That it was my choice." His bottom lip stuck out, and he looked on the verge of tears.

"Wow." Hope exchanged a look with Shaun. Tessa must have really played into Luca's love of the dogs and their RV.

"I wouldn't have gone, but Mochi wouldn't leave Shadow. Shadow was bleeding, and one of his paws was cut pretty bad. I helped Tessa clean him up." Luca looked away, unable to meet their eyes. "I really wanted to go in the RV." He picked up his fork and poked the half-eaten pancakes on his plate.

Shaun put his arm around Luca's shoulder. "It's not your fault. You knew her and trusted her. And you cared about Shadow."

"The RV was even cooler than I remembered." Luca was still talking to his pancakes. "Mom always told me never to go anywhere without telling her first, and I knew she would have been disappointed in me that I went with Tessa without speaking to you."

Hope reached out and touched Luca on the hand. "She manipulated you. I don't blame you for being excited at the prospect of going on a trip in the RV." He'd been so awed that time he'd first seen the Conrads' RV. Even Shaun had been impressed with their motor home, saying it was like a luxury apartment on wheels. "But from now on, please don't go off with anyone, even someone you know, without telling me or Shaun, okay?"

"Yes. I'm sorry." Luca's eyes brimmed with unshed tears. "I did keep asking her if I could call you, but she said you were busy and that you would call when you could. But you didn't."

"Because we didn't know she'd taken you." Hope knew that Luca had been told what happened, but she wanted him to hear it from her. "I would never just leave you without telling you myself. I'm sorry she lied to you."

"It was fun at first, and Mochi and Shadow were so happy to be together. But then I kept getting the feeling something was wrong. She said Robert was going with us, but he wasn't there. I asked her where he was, and she said he was in the bedroom. But he never came out." He took another bite, chewing and swallowing before he spoke again. "She told me the TV wasn't working. It was just the two of us and the dogs. It was really weird."

"We were so worried about you." Shaun squeezed Luca's shoulder.

Hope put her coffee cup down. "One minute you were in the driveway, and the next, you were gone. I was so scared."

"I'm sorry." He bit his bottom lip.

"Don't apologize again, okay, Luca? It wasn't your fault. It was Tessa's, for taking you without our permission." Shaun pulled Luca closer.

"Is she going to be okay? She wasn't the last time I saw her." Worry lines creased Luca's forehead.

"I don't know." Hope lifted one shoulder and then let it fall.

They finished the rest of their breakfast in silence, and Shaun paid the bill. Smiling over the table at Luca, Hope said, "Come on. Let's go back and get Mochi and Shadow and hit the road. I don't know about you, but I can't wait to get home."

Luca sprang out of the booth and stood next to Shaun, waiting for Hope to get out on her side. Then he wrapped his arms around her middle. "Thank you for coming to get me."

She squeezed him back. "Always, Luca. Always." She caught Shaun's eyes over Luca's head and could see by the way he exhaled that he was as glad as she was to get Luca back.

In her head, Hope whispered, *I've got him, Cassy. He's safe.*

39

H OPE

Day five
5:30 p.m.

Hope and Shaun got to know their nephew better on the road trip
back. He opened up to them, more than he ever had before. Maybe it
was the relief of going home, of knowing Shadow was with him and
Mochi. He told them about the places he and Cassidy had seen and
the people they'd met. He also told them about their favorite foods, his
eyes lighting up when he told them about the ikura fish eggs he and
Cassidy both loved.

"Mom gave them to me when I was really little. But I like to bite
the whole thing with the rice and seaweed together, so I'd get a whole
mouthful of them." He giggled, the sound soothing to Hope's heart.
"Mom couldn't believe it when I did that. She thinks they should be
eaten one at a time. But I like squishing them all in a mouthful."

"Do you know why she ate them one at a time?" Hope asked.

Luca shook his head.

"Because I used to feed them to her." Hope turned around to look
at Luca in the back seat. Shaun was driving. "When I was ten, our mom

had gotten a waitressing job in a Japanese restaurant. I'd meet her and Cassidy there after school. They let us sit at a back table, where I'd do my homework and look after your mom." She gave Luca a smile. "The sushi chef used to give me a little bowl of ikura because he knew how much I liked them."

"Me too!" Luca grinned at her. "I really love how they pop in your mouth."

"Yup." Hope nodded. "I used to eat them one by one with chopsticks, instead of as sushi with rice and seaweed. I fed them to your mom once, and she clapped her hands. She loved them so much." She laughed. "Maybe I shouldn't have been feeding raw fish eggs to a two-year-old, but it was one of the happiest memories I have of us."

"I have a lot of happy memories too." Luca's eyes gleamed. "She was a good mom." And then he sobered and grew quiet.

Hope turned around and saw him fighting tears. She reached a hand back, and Luca put one of his in hers.

"She couldn't stop doing the bad drugs," Luca said in a low voice. "She tried. But no matter what, she was always a good mom to me."

"I'm glad. I know she really wanted you when she found out she was pregnant." Hope twisted so she could see Luca's face.

"Really?" Luca's eyes were wide.

"Yes." Hope sighed. "I couldn't believe that my baby sister was going to have a baby. I wanted you both to stay with us so badly. She said she wanted to get sober and clean. For you."

"I miss her." Luca's voice was raspy.

"I know you do. I do too." Hope squeezed his hand. They fell silent, but their hands stayed interlaced until Hope got a cramp and had to take hers back.

They stopped at a hotel in Pennsylvania that night and then powered the rest of the way home the next day. Hope let Mochi and Shadow into the yard while Shaun went next door to get Toby. When he returned, the three dogs had a joyful reunion, with Luca in the midst of them. Luca squealed when Toby stuck his tongue in Luca's mouth, and then Mochi and Shadow jumped on him. He fell to the grass until all Hope could see was a wriggling mass of fur and little-boy limbs. Shaun put his arm around Hope, and she leaned into him, so grateful that Luca was back with them, safe and sound.

Shaun was busy in the kitchen, making *dan dan mien*, a spicy Sichuan noodle dish made of Chinese sesame paste, chili oil, ground Sichuan peppers, soy sauce, and more Asian spices served with a ground pork mixture and fresh Chinese greens. They'd discovered that Luca loved spicy foods—another thing he'd gotten from Cassidy, who had once, as a toddler, popped a whole chili pepper in her mouth and eaten it without blinking. Shaun had made the *dan dan mien* for Luca once and Luca had declared it a favorite. To go with the spicy noodles, Shaun was also making a clear soup with daikon and cilantro to tone down the heat.

While Shaun finished the meal, Hope sat in a chair on the deck watching Luca play with the three dogs in the yard. She wasn't letting him out of her sight, at least not for a while. It had been an exhausting and emotionally draining few days and she couldn't fully relax, even though Luca was right there in front of her.

"Here." She looked up to see Shaun walking out to the deck, holding two frozen drinks in his hands. "I made margaritas. Thought you could use it."

She took one from him and took a small sip. "Perfect on a hot July night." A gentle breeze blew her hair into her face.

"I don't think it would pair well with *dan dan mien*, so I thought we could enjoy them now, before dinner." He clinked his glass to hers. "You okay?"

Hope looked at him and nodded. They'd been told that Tessa had a breakdown and was being treated in a hospital. The detectives said that she'd had a psychotic episode when her husband died, and she'd convinced herself he was still alive and needed what Tessa believed was Robert's son. Hope and Shaun would be kept updated as information became available.

"I feel bad for Tessa." Hope clenched her jaw before taking another sip, trying to relax. "But what she did, taking Luca and Mochi like that . . ." She broke off with a shake of her head. "I don't care if she didn't realize what she was doing. It was wrong."

Shaun nodded. "I know. But I don't understand why she thought Robert was Luca's father."

"I guess we have to wait until they can get answers from Tessa." Hope shook her head again. "I don't want to think about Tessa right now. I just want to enjoy having Luca back."

Shaun raised his glass. "To Luca."

"To Luca," she echoed, and they turned when their nephew gave a shout as Mochi ran into his legs, causing him to fall down. Hope sighed, feeling the tequila sliding smoothly down her throat, warming her insides. The sound of Luca's laughter was a balm for her nerves. It was good to be home.

After the delicious meal, where Luca slurped up the noodles happily, asking for seconds and then thirds, the three of them had mint chocolate chip ice cream for dessert, another favorite of Luca's. The three dogs sat under the table, hoping for a drop of ice cream to hit the ground.

Hope's mind was on the letters from Cassidy. She needed to ask Luca questions about her sister. She wondered if she should wait, and worried her lip with her teeth as she studied her nephew.

As if he felt her watching him, Luca turned. "What's the matter?" he asked.

Hope gave him a quick smile. "Why do you think something's the matter?"

"You look . . . worried." His own forehead puckered.

"I'm just thinking about your mother." Hope and Shaun exchanged a look, and he gave her an encouraging nod. "I've been getting these . . . letters. They look like they're from her."

"What?" Luca sat up straight, turning completely around to face Hope. "She used to leave me little notes all the time. Did she leave some for you?"

"No." Hope thought of the notes she'd found in Luca's drawer. "I found the ones she left for you when I looked in your room trying to figure out where you went. I'm sorry for snooping."

"It's okay." He shrugged.

"But no, the letters I got from her were real letters, in envelopes. Someone was paying a neighbor to leave them in our mailbox. I just wondered where they came from." Hope lifted her hands in question.

"Can I see them?" Luca asked.

"Yes." Hope stood and walked into the house and down the hall to their bedroom, where she'd kept the photocopies of Cassidy's letters in the drawer of her night table. She brought them back outside. Luca came to her side and took them from her. He read the first letter quickly.

"These are from Mom. That's her handwriting." He traced a finger over the words before looking up at her. "I remember her writing to you. She never sent them, just kept them in her tote bag. I found a stack of them one time when I was looking for Chapstick and asked why she didn't mail them."

"She really wrote them?" Hope's breath caught.

Luca nodded.

Hope looked across the table at Shaun. "They really are from Cassy." As the words left her mouth, something in her stomach unclenched, knowing her sister had been thinking of her all these years, that she hadn't hated Hope so much that she hadn't wanted to be in touch. "What did she say when you asked her why she didn't mail them?"

"She said it would be too dangerous for me." Luca looked back and forth between them. "She wouldn't tell me why. She just said she couldn't stand to lose me and that's why she could never mail them. What was she talking about?"

Hope shook her head, unable to speak.

"We have no idea, Luca," Shaun finally said. "We've been trying to figure it out since we got the letters."

Luca asked Shaun something and they continued talking, but Hope had stopped listening. Instead, she was thinking about Cassidy. Her sister hadn't died hating Hope. She'd wanted to reach out, to come home, ask for help, but for some reason, she couldn't. Hope might never know who had threatened Cassidy and why, but for the first time since Cassidy disappeared, Hope was at peace regarding her sister.

Cassidy had loved her.

40

TESSA

A month and a half later

They drugged me, that day the RV crashed. The medicine had coursed through my veins, and I'd floated away to a place where everything was fine. All I remember was the bump and sway that I realized meant I was in a moving vehicle. But I didn't care where they were taking me. I'd drifted in and out, not sure what was real and what was in my mind.

Memories flashed before me, blinding me as if someone had shined a bright light in my eyes. Of my parents, stoned out of their minds, draped on the couch while I'd cried on the floor, hungry and dirty, only six years old. Of the day I graduated high school and my gift from them was an order to leave because they had done their duty. The times when I'd couch surfed, shuffled from friend to friend, sometimes with an unknown man because he'd taken pity on me in exchange for a few favors. The years when I took any job I could, saving up for my own place because I refused to be homeless, something I feared.

But most of all, I remembered the first time I met Robert and how our eyes connected from across the bar. I knew this was it. He was home. He was mine. Robert was the only thing that was clear to me during this time.

I slept, on and off, never fully aware of where I was or who was with me. If I stayed in this haze, Robert was there and my heart could rest. When the fuzziness lifted and my mind remembered, I'd scream and scream until people came running and my veins hummed and sang with whatever they injected into me. I knew I didn't want to remember, to remember what I had done, because to admit the truth would be like ripping the skin off my body piece by piece until there was nothing left to protect my core.

But sometimes, in that soothing place between oblivion and awareness, my mind would override the medication's effects. Then the one memory I'd tried to forget my entire life would pop into my subconscious, as clear and true as a movie on a big screen. It was the day when my mom had called me, a few years after they'd kicked me out. She could barely speak; he'd beaten her so bad. All I could make out was "Help me."

My heart had seized with fear, because I knew what he could do. He'd once thrown me down the stairs because I'd eaten the last frozen waffle. He'd terrorized me my whole childhood, and I'd been glad to escape when I was eighteen. I couldn't pack my bags fast enough, and my only regret was leaving my poor mother. I didn't want to leave her there, cowed by the man who claimed to love her, but who had instead made her an addict, dependent on him for drugs, for money, and for love. Or what she thought was love. But I knew, watching them from the time I could understand, that what they had wasn't love. I knew I didn't want to be like her. But that day when she'd called me, I could hear the desperation in her voice. She wanted me to save her.

I thought I could. Before my shift at the bar, I drove home for the first time in years. I confronted him, told him I was taking Mom and we were leaving for good. He didn't say anything, and I thought for just a moment that we could escape. Mom shot me a fearful look, but I put my arms around her, leading her out of the room to pack a bag.

I should have known he wouldn't let us go so easily. But I thought I was strong, having survived on my own these past years. I thought I could stand up to him, defy him, and get Mom out. He struck when I least expected it. I was taking Mom's clothes out of her closet, my back to him. He hit me with a lamp, and I crashed to the floor. Then he was pummeling my face with his fists, my nose breaking with a crack, the blood spurting out. I screamed, holding my hands to my face, pain exploding through me even as I almost fainted at the sight of my own blood. He stomped on me with his heavy boots, crushed my hand, and hit me again. I curled up into a ball, trying to protect myself from the brutal beast he'd become. I cried out, "Mommy, help me! Make him stop." But she did nothing.

When his brutal rage finally subsided, I saw my mom in his arms, her lips bleeding, her eyes swollen, but her body pressed against his. She wouldn't look at me, not even when I pleaded again, "Mommy, please help me."

She didn't. She chose him over me. They left me on the floor as they went into their bedroom, the door closing with a bang and noises I didn't want to hear leaking out. I managed to crawl outside and into my car. I was late for work. I couldn't lose my job. I needed it. I could barely see, but I drove to the bar and stumbled out of my car. The blood running into my eyes blinded me, and the throb of my poor broken nose mocked me.

And that's how Robert found me. Beaten and broken, leaning against my car because I was mustering up the strength to walk into work. He took me home and took care of me, and I cried against his chest after he cleaned me up. I didn't tell him that night what had happened. I didn't speak at all. But he put me to bed in his guest bedroom, and I slept without dreams for fifteen long hours.

I don't have clear memories of the days after that. Only a feeling, as if I were watching someone else's life from up above. I slept more than I was awake, and there was always that moment, right before waking, when memories would flit across my consciousness. The memory of wanting to end my father's cruelty. A feeling of pride because I knew how I could use their weakness against them. Had I really asked Robert if he knew someone who could get me what I needed? Had he stared deep into my eyes, then told me he did? Had he really gotten it for me, asked me what I was going to do?

Or was it all a dream, something I wished I had the spine to do, but would never go through with in the light of day? I'd never told Robert it was my father who had beaten me so badly. He didn't know about my childhood, and all I'd endured. But one morning, I woke to him shaking my shoulders.

"Tess, Tessa. Wake up." I opened my eyes to see him staring at me, his eyes wide with alarm. "The police just called your cell. They couldn't find you."

I sat up in bed, still woozy from sleep, all cozy in his bed. "Why did they call me?"

"They found your parents in their home last night. A neighbor noticed the front door was open." Robert stared intently into my eyes. "They think they overdosed."

I stared back at him. "Are they gone?" When he nodded, I fell back in the bed, my eyes closed. "Oh, thank god." It was finally over. They hadn't taken care of what was theirs, and now they were no longer my problem. Karma had finally come for them.

"Tessa? What did you do?"

I opened my eyes at the worry in his voice. "Nothing." I stared at him, my innocence holding my gaze steady. I hadn't done anything.

And now, stuck in the present without Robert, I didn't want to remember the past anymore. I fought it, the memories threatening to take over my mind, telling me that Robert was gone and it was my fault.

"Robert," I called, every time I broke out of the fog and swam my way to consciousness after the RV accident. "Robert, where are you?" I turned to whoever was tending to me and grabbed their arm, their sleeve, their shirt, whatever I could latch on to. "You have to find him. He's in the RV. He's hurt."

I thrashed and flailed, wanting to get out, get out of this bed and look for my husband. They didn't know where to look. They didn't know he was still in the RV, waiting for me. I had to get to him. I had to. I had to save him. It was all my fault. All my fault.

But my panic would bring people running into the room. People I didn't know, who'd inject something into my IV until my body relaxed and I was floating again. I can't say I hated the sensation. Because it was nice. It was good not to have to worry anymore. Not to worry about all the people who wouldn't leave me alone. They asked me questions, so many questions. Always with the questions.

Why did you take Luca?

Where were you going?

Did you plan this?

How well do you know Hope and Shaun Chen?

Why Luca?

Do you remember calling 911 the day you found Robert unresponsive?

Do you know your husband is dead?

At that last question, I clapped my hands over my ears and screamed at the top of my lungs. *No, no, no.* I wouldn't, couldn't allow anyone to say that out loud. Robert was fine. He wasn't dead. I didn't find him not breathing. He wasn't dead in our bed. *No.* They had no idea what they were talking about.

But then sometimes, late at night, when the effects of whatever they gave me wore off slightly, I'd suddenly be awake. Jolted out of a deep sleep where my thoughts wouldn't form coherent memories, I'd dimly be aware of making that 911 call, crying hysterically and saying over and over again that he wasn't breathing. *He wasn't breathing.* He'd stopped breathing, and I couldn't get him to wake up. My Robert. My poor, poor Robert.

And then I'd be gone again. I didn't want to think about a life without Robert. But then the police were back with their questions. Always the questions, going on and on until I thought I'd scream again and never stop. Asking me questions about someone named Marian Franks. I had never heard of her, and told them so. I didn't know who she was, and I didn't know why they were talking about her to me. She meant nothing to me. I tried shutting them out, refusing to listen, and when they wouldn't leave, I'd scream again, until I was hoarse and the nurses made them go. And then the IV with the medicine, until my lids drooped and I was pleasantly drowsy again, no longer caring about the stupid police officers.

Except the next time I opened my eyes, they were back.

Why did you assault Marian?

We have footage from a security camera behind the rest area.

We saw you drag Marian back there, punch her in the jaw.

We saw you hit her in the temple with a rock.

Did you overhear her calling 911?

She recognized Luca. She has two kids herself . . . She finally woke from her coma. But her brain is damaged.

You're lucky she woke up . . . charged with second-degree murder if she'd died . . .

I couldn't get them to shut up. I needed them gone, their voices, talking, always talking. I pounded my fists against the side of my head, wanting to get those voices out of my head. Someone restrained me and held my arms until I stopped. I kicked my legs, determined to get them out. Something was holding my legs down. I screamed and screamed, yelling for Robert, telling him I loved him, I'd do anything for him, I was sorry.

No, no, no.

I kept asking for Robert, over and over again like a broken robot. When they asked me about the boy, I answered, *Where's Robert?* When they asked me about Marian, I answered, *Find Robert!* When they asked about the accident in the RV, I answered, *Robert is in there! You have to find him!*

And in that pleasant haze caused by the medicine, I heard snippets of conversations, things I stored away because they didn't realize I was awake and heard what they said. I knew I was being moved. I knew I was going back to New York. Someone mentioned a forensic hospital. I knew I'd been arrested, on multiple counts. I knew I needed a lawyer. Because they didn't believe me.

I was kept medicated. I was moved, sometimes aware, sometimes not. More people came to see me, more questions, always the questions. Sometimes I answered them, and sometimes I chose not to. A woman I came to realize was my lawyer visited me often. She said Janie had hired her for me. It took me a moment to remember who Janie was. Robert's sister. Who'd been kind to me after Robert died, but I couldn't see her. She reminded me that Robert was no longer on Earth, when all I wanted to do was will him back to life again.

This lawyer asked me gently about Robert, about what happened after he died. I told her what she wanted to know. I knew she was on my side. She asked me if my grief over Robert's passing had made me do those things. Things like taking the boy.

Time passed. The lawyer came and went. She told me Hope wanted to see me. I shook my head. I couldn't remember my lawyer's name. More tests, more questions, more people. I did as I was told, I did as was expected. I played the part, and I took my medicine. No more need to be restrained. No more need for security outside my door. I was transferred to the forensic hospital.

I stared now out the window at the moon, which was half-full, shining brightly in the dark sky. I saw the stars, almost as bright as that night when I was content and did my night walk. I tried to find Orion, but my eyes wouldn't focus. I stared at the sky until the stars blurred and I felt at one with the night. It was so late, but in a place like this, night didn't necessarily mean quiet. The beep of machines, people rushing by, someone wailing off in the distance. The click of feet on the floor, the whoosh of a car outside. I was in a hospital, somewhere back in New York. I had to protect what was mine. *No one can blame me. I will survive this.* When I was strong again, Luca and I would be together. We would be a family, me and Robert's son.

41

Hope

Three months later

The months passed. Hope had called her parents the day after Luca came home, and Luca had suffered through a stilted conversation with them. When he hung up, he turned to Hope, his eyes full of confusion.

"Do they hate me?" He looked down, as if afraid to see the answer in her eyes.

"No, Luca." She took him by the shoulders and waited until he looked at her. "That's just the way they are. No one could hate you. You're safe now, with us. Okay?"

Luca nodded, but didn't say anything.

"Maybe next year, we'll take a trip out there and visit them." Hope searched Luca's face, trying to gauge his reaction.

He nodded. "Okay." And then they let the subject drop, because there was nothing else Hope could say about how detached her parents were.

Summer turned to fall, leaves falling all over their backyard. Luca had fun raking them up and then running through the piles with Mochi and Shadow following while Toby stood by and watched.

Hope couldn't get Tessa out of her head. She'd been arrested on multiple counts, including kidnapping, endangering the welfare of a minor, and assault. But she had a lawyer fighting for her, who believed that Tessa had suffered a psychotic break when Robert passed away. In her grief, Tessa had convinced herself that Robert was still alive. She'd told them that she'd taken Luca because she knew Luca was Robert's son. In her grieving mind, she thought having his son with him would cure Robert of his cancer and bring him back to life. Tessa's lawyer had convinced the trial court to order a psychological evaluation. Hope and Shaun had hired an attorney also, but until the evaluation was completed, there wasn't much they could do.

Hope had so many questions. If Tessa believed that Robert was Luca's father, it meant that Tessa thought Cassidy had slept with Robert at some point. Hope shuddered at that idea. Robert had been at least twenty years older than Cassidy. She couldn't imagine the frail older man who had come with Tessa to pick up Shadow sleeping with her vibrant, colorful sister. Although back then, he'd just been diagnosed, so he would have still been healthy and looked completely different.

Was it Tessa that Cassidy had been afraid of? Could Tessa have been the one to pay Steven to put Cassidy's letters in her mailbox? They did resemble each other, with similar face shapes and the same long dark hair. But if so, how had Tessa gotten Cassidy's letters to begin with? None of it made sense, and the only one who could clear it up was Tessa. Hope had their lawyer contact Tessa's to request a visit, but was told that the woman was being treated and not allowed visitors. And when Tessa was declared incompetent to stand trial, Hope *really* needed to talk to her. But once again, her request was denied. She was told that Tessa didn't want to see her.

At the end of September, Dan Stern flew to New York and came by to meet Luca.

"Wow." Dan's eyes widened in surprise. "You look so much like Cassidy." Hope stood behind Luca in the foyer, one hand on his shoulder.

Luca gave him a shy smile. "You were my mom's best friend. She told me about you."

One of Dan's shoulders lifted in a rueful shrug. "Yeah. I thought I was her best friend. But then she left and I never saw her again." He sighed and crossed his arms in front of his broad chest. He looked more like a California lifeguard than a ski instructor. "I wish I'd known you and watched you grow up. I would have helped Cassidy."

"She talked about you a lot. She told me about all the trouble she used to get you into." Luca's eyes sparkled when he said this, his lips twitching.

Dan threw his head back and laughed. "Yeah, she did. I always had to bail both of us out." But then he sobered. "We had a lot of good times. We talked about everything."

"Like what?" Luca cocked his head to the side, his gaze focused on Dan.

"Like what we wanted to do when we grew up." Dan's mouth quirked. "I wanted to get married. Have two kids, dogs, a house, all of it. Cassidy wanted none of that. She wanted to travel and see the country, be free. She wanted to go to Europe, Asia, Australia." Dan looked at Hope, and Hope remembered what he'd said about being in love with Cassidy and wanting to marry her if only she'd felt the same.

"She didn't get to go to those places. But she told me about them and showed me on a map." Luca's voice was quiet. "We did go all over the United States in our car, though. It was fun."

"I'm sure it was," Dan said, running a hand through his sandy hair.

They stood there for a moment, an awkward triangle, as Hope looked back and forth between Luca and Dan. Then she remembered her manners and invited Dan out to the back deck, where Shaun was prepping the grill. Dan had spent the rest of the day with them. It was a beautiful fall day, and Luca had come alive when he found out Dan loved basketball as much as he did. They played in the driveway while the three dogs romped in the yard, sometimes wandering over to the fence and barking at the players. Hope stood on the deck looking down at Luca, at his glowing face as he sank a basket, remembering the day he'd disappeared and feeling thankful that he was here where he belonged.

"I'm moving back to New York," Dan told them as they consumed the hot dogs, corn, and skirt steaks that Shaun had grilled for dinner, along with the salad Hope had made from their garden.

"Yay," Luca cheered, digging into his salad. He loved vegetables as much as he loved hot dogs. His cheeks were still flushed from playing basketball.

Hope smiled, surprised at how easily Luca had taken to Dan. "Where are you going to live?"

Dan shrugged. "I don't know yet, but I'm looking. I'm getting too old for the ski-bum life."

"Right, old man." Shaun shot him a disbelieving look. "What are you, thirty-two?"

"Yes. Same age as Cassidy."

Shaun snorted. "Wait until you're forty-two like me. Then tell me how old you feel."

Hope laughed. "What are you going to do here?"

Dan shrugged again. "I don't know. But I think it's time I settled down a bit. Get a real job, start saving money." He looked off into space. "Maybe meet someone, get married, have kids." He leaned over and tousled Luca's hair. "And get to hang with Cassidy's kid."

Luca swatted his hand away, but he laughed. "Mom would have liked that. That we'll get to hang out."

Dan sat back in his chair and looked at Luca for a moment without speaking. "Yeah. Cassy would have liked that," he finally said, his voice husky.

And Hope began to wonder if something had happened between Cassidy and Dan after all, and if Dan could possibly be Luca's father.

◆ ◆ ◆

Fall turned to winter with the first freeze, which killed all the vegetables in their garden, and Hope moved in the herbs so that they could use them during the cold months. A blanket of frost coated the lawn every morning, and they bought Luca a winter coat along with a hat, gloves, and a scarf because he didn't have any.

Hope's attorney tried to get her access to Tessa again, but Tessa's attorney, Samantha Rodriguez, said that Tessa still refused to see her. Frustrated, Hope paced the house. The detectives who had questioned Tessa hadn't gotten much out of her about her connection to Cassidy. Tessa had kept asking for Robert, sometimes aware he was gone, sometimes not. She refused to answer their questions. But Hope was sure the other woman held all the answers, and she resolved to keep trying. She would break down Tessa's walls eventually.

Dan found an apartment in a town ten minutes from theirs and often took Luca out on the weekends. Hope was glad to have someone else in Luca's life who had known his mother and could tell him more about Cassidy and what she'd been like. She'd tried to ask Dan if he and Cassidy had ever slept together, but Dan had turned away and not answered. She'd left it alone after that, even though she wondered.

The Caines' house had a **FOR SALE** sign in the front, which made Hope sad every time she drove or walked past it. Jalissa and the boys were still living there for the time being. Jack was incarcerated, awaiting trial. Hope tried to do what she could, inviting all the boys over for dinner, dropping off stews and breads or pots of soup every week. She knew Jalissa was too proud to ask for help, but neighborly gestures like these were appreciated.

She'd gone over soon after Luca was home—she had needed to apologize to Jalissa.

"I don't blame you. At all." Jalissa puckered her lips for a moment, as if she'd tasted something sour. "I'm just so damn mad at Jack. What was he thinking?" She turned to Hope, despair flooding her face. "We have four boys. How am I supposed to feed and clothe them? How will they ever hold their heads up, knowing their father is a criminal? A thief?"

Jalissa's Jamaican accent was heavy that night.

"I'm so sorry," Hope said again. "I blame myself. You've been such a good friend to me over the years, and I feel responsible for ruining your life." She bit her bottom lip hard enough to make her wince. "I just wanted the police to be thorough, to check out everyone that had contact with Luca. I didn't think . . ." She had no other words. How did she say to Jalissa that she'd not only suspected her husband of having something to do with Luca's disappearance but also that she hadn't thought about the consequences of the police's questions, much less cared?

"You were only making sure that all avenues where Luca was concerned were covered." Jalissa reached out and patted Hope on the hand. "I would have done the same if one of my boys disappeared." Her hand fisted and she slammed it into her other hand. "God, I could kill him . . ."

"Don't say that." Hope didn't want Jalissa to say something she'd regret later.

"I could." Jalissa shook her head. "I'm going to have to get a job again. I wanted to wait until Justin was older, but now . . ."

They had sat in silence after that, until Jalissa gave her a wry smile. "I'm glad Andrew has Luca as a friend. He's going to need him."

Hope nodded. "Definitely. The friendship is good for Luca too."

Hope had left soon after that, but not before enveloping Jalissa in a long hug. "You'll get through this," she whispered into her tight braids.

Just that morning, Jalissa had called to say they'd gotten an offer on the house. Hope stood on her front porch now, looking over at her neighbors' place. She could still hear the sirens and see the flashing lights from the night when Jack had been arrested. It was going to be a long time before she could look at the house and not feel a pang of regret for her part, no matter how small, in tearing apart her neighbor's life.

"Hope?"

The male voice to her left made Hope jump. Turning quickly, she saw it was Mr. Alden standing at the edge of their property line.

"Hi," Hope said, a hand over her heart.

Even all these months later, she was still jumpy, still expecting Cassidy to show up at her house one day. They'd never figured out where the letters had come from. The police had kept surveillance over Steven's family's mailbox, but no one had appeared to drop off payment. The photo that the sketch artist drew from Steven's descriptions had looked eerily like Cassidy, but because the woman had sunglasses on and a big hat, they couldn't be sure of the shape of her eyes or head. Even though Hope knew her sister was dead, a part of her still waited for Cassidy to ring her doorbell one day.

"How are you, dear?"

Hope flushed and looked away. She was still ashamed of the way she'd attacked Mr. Alden, the accusations she'd hurled at him. But he didn't seem to hold it against her. He had been so relieved when they brought Luca home. He'd invited Luca to come over to see his doll collection. When Hope had taken him over, Luca had been impressed and told Mr. Alden he should sell them online.

Mr. Alden had deflected, but eventually, with Luca's help, he'd figured out how to start an Etsy shop. And when the first doll had sold two weeks later, Luca had been ecstatic.

"I told you!" he crowed in triumph.

"Dear?" Mr. Alden's voice jolted Hope back to her front porch.

"Oh, I'm fine. Good." She smiled at him. "Very good."

"I'm glad." He smiled at her before turning away, making his way to the road. "Off on my walk." He stopped and faced her again. "Luca was the one who told me I needed fresh air, that I shouldn't spend all my time in a basement. He's right. These daily walks are good for me."

"Yes." She was happy for him. How lonely Mr. Alden must have been all these years, holed up in his basement on his own, with only his dolls for company.

"Luca is a special boy." And with one more wave, Mr. Alden took off down the street.

He was right. Luca was a special boy.

42

H O P E

Five-and-a-half months later

The call came just as Hope was expecting Luca home from school.

It was her lawyer. "She'll see you."

Hope blew out a breath. "Tessa?"

"Yes. Samantha Rodriguez just called us."

"What changed her mind?" Hope's heart gave a bump of anticipation.

"No clue." The lawyer's clipped voice came through the phone like little staccato pellets. "Maybe something in therapy. Maybe she needs closure. Whatever it is, she said she'll talk to you."

Hope was silent for a moment, as conflicting thoughts swirled through her.

What made Tessa change her mind?

Did she really have a psychotic break when Robert died, causing her to kidnap Luca and assault that woman?

Is she really so mentally unstable that a judge declared her unable to stand trial and she was transferred to a forensic hospital about an hour away?

"That's great. Did Samantha say anything else?" Hope was curious.

"No. Just that she'd help facilitate the meeting."

"Okay." Hope was somewhat resentful toward Samantha Rodriguez. She was the one who had ordered psychiatric evaluations for Tessa, claiming that her client had had a traumatic event following her husband's death and wasn't fully aware of her actions. Hope thought Tessa had gotten off too easy. She wasn't being held accountable for her actions. Even though Hope was sorry that Tessa had lost her husband, she couldn't forget the terror she'd felt when Luca had disappeared and the feeling that she was letting her sister down again.

But it didn't matter. Because Hope was finally going to get a chance to ask Tessa all the questions that had burned in her mind these past months. She would get her answers, no matter what.

◆ ◆ ◆

Six months later

Two days before Christmas, Hope found herself in a sterile room in the hospital, sitting across a plain wooden table from the woman who'd taken her nephew. Hope had been told Tessa was a model patient and had earned the privilege of a visit without supervision. But there were people out in the hallway, should they be needed.

They stared at each other, and then Hope cleared her throat. "Thanks for seeing me."

Tessa gave a nod, her eyes downcast. Hope studied her. This was not the Tessa she'd met the few times they'd had contact since Shadow's adoption. This woman was subdued, her formerly long dark hair now cut short to just above her shoulders. Gone were the waves and volume that Hope remembered; instead, her hair was straight and lifeless, hanging from her head as if it didn't quite belong. She was dressed in a loose pink sweatshirt that engulfed her slight frame, and Hope noticed she'd lost a lot of weight.

The silence hung heavily between them, and Hope wondered which one of them would break first. If she hadn't known what Tessa had done, she would have felt sorry for her. She looked forlorn, so folded in upon herself. Hope guessed that was what grief and having a psychotic episode did to a person.

"I have something to tell you," Hope finally said.

At the same time, Tessa said, "I'm sorry."

They both stopped, and then Hope made a gesture for Tessa to continue.

The other woman kept her eyes on the table. "Everything I did, I did for Robert. I thought I was saving him."

Tears sprang to her eyes, and even with her head down, Hope could see the way Tessa was blinking rapidly.

"I loved him so much," she whispered. "I tried everything, yet I couldn't do anything to stop him from dying. That day when I found him . . ." She took in a shuddering breath. "It was as if I'd died myself. I literally felt like my heart stopped too. It was unbearable. I held him for so long, not wanting to believe he was gone. I don't remember eventually calling 911, I don't remember them coming to take him away. I don't remember much after that day. Except what they've told me."

Hope's lips pressed together, feeling pity for Tessa. She would be devastated too if Shaun had passed away from a brutal illness. "I'm sorry for your loss," she said quietly.

Tessa looked up at that. "Thank you. They told me my mind had conjured Robert up. That I was so grief-stricken by his death that I willed him back to life." She blinked rapidly. "They said I convinced myself he had made a miraculous recovery. That I felt guilty over something, and that's why I needed to get Luca for him. To make it up to him, by giving him his son."

Hope held up a hand. "That's what I don't get. Why do you think Luca is his son? Can you really believe that my sister and your husband . . ."

"Yes," Tessa said. "I saw them together. It was the day he first got his cancer diagnosis. He was upset and left the house. I followed him to the bar in town to make sure he was okay and saw him with your sister. They . . ." She stopped and bit her lip hard. "I saw them come out of the bar together. They didn't see me hovering outside because it was dark. I heard your sister ask why he didn't have children. And he blamed me. He said if he ever had a child, he'd name him Luca. They had sex in her car at the back of the parking lot."

Hope winced. She knew Cassidy had slept around, but hearing Tessa describe the encounter sounded so tawdry. And now it made sense why Tessa had been convinced that Cassidy carried her husband's child.

Tessa looked at Hope, her forehead puckered. "*He* was the one who said he didn't want children. I knew she was your sister. I saw you with her one day. You were walking around the lake, and I saw the baby she was pushing in a stroller."

"But how did you know Cassidy named her baby Luca?"

Tessa gave her a disbelieving look. "You know the lake gossip. Even though we didn't know each other back then, people talk. I knew your sister had a baby named Luca. That was all it took."

They sat in silence for a while, as Hope absorbed this. Then she frowned. "I've been asking to see you for months now. Why wouldn't you see me?"

Tessa shrugged. "What was the point? Robert is gone, your sister is gone. There's nothing to say."

"So why now?" Hope couldn't help thinking she was missing something.

Tessa shrugged again. "I'm on medication that is helping me think clearer again. I'm working things out through therapy. They're helping me to see that I had a psychotic episode, that Robert did not in fact have a miraculous recovery and become my loving husband again." Tessa finally raised her head and met Hope's eyes.

Hope stayed silent, waiting for the other woman to continue.

Tessa took in a shuddering breath. "They talk about the support of my friends and family." Tears shone in her eyes. "Robert *was* my family, and now he's gone. His sister, Janie, has been helping me. She's the only family I have left. And Luca."

Hope's eyebrows rose. "Luca?"

"Yes. I'm his stepmother." Tessa pressed her lips together for a second. "I still get confused. Sometimes I don't know what's real and what's made up in my head. But I'm getting better, and the one thing that I know is that Luca is family."

Hope's forehead furrowed. It disturbed her, the way Tessa talked about Luca. She couldn't figure out what Tessa's motivation was.

"They made me talk about your sister in therapy." Tessa gazed off into the distance. "Why I thought Robert got together with her." Her brown eyes clouded. "Why do you think?"

Hope regarded Tessa. "You resemble Cassidy. Steven was the first to point this out. You have almost the same long dark hair, same shape face, similar builds."

"Steven?" Tessa tilted her head in question.

"The boy you paid to put Cassidy's letters and cell in my mailbox." Hope studied Tessa closely as she said this.

"Oh." Tessa looked startled for a moment, then dropped her eyes.

"It was you, right?" Hope wanted Tessa to confirm what she'd suspected. Tessa nodded.

"How?" Hope shook her head in confusion. Even though she'd suspected, it was still a shock to hear Tessa confirm this. "How did you get Cassidy's letters?"

Tessa held up a hand. "I'll tell you. But back to my question first. Why do you think Robert was attracted to Cassidy, besides her physical appearance?"

"I have no idea." Hope stared hard at Tessa. What was she getting at? "We were both poor lost souls, that's why." Tessa's voice was flat, without intonation. "We were broken, and he wanted to fix us."

"What?" Hope cocked her head to the side. "I don't understand."

"This wasn't the first time something like this happened to me. The first time was when I was twenty-three, right after I met Robert. When my parents died." Tessa's gaze was intense, burrowing into Hope. "Robert took care of me. Got me to doctors. I was broken. Thought I didn't deserve to live. But he loved me back to life, made me feel worthy again. He never blamed me for what I had done, or asked what happened to my parents."

"What happened to your parents?" Hope's mouth dropped open, and a tingling began at the back of her neck.

Tessa shook her head sorrowfully. "They overdosed. They were addicted like your sister was." She met Hope's eyes. "My father hit us. He beat me. He almost killed my mother that last time and me . . ." Her voice trailed off, and she cleared her throat before continuing. "I had to stop him."

"Tessa . . ." Hope was at a loss for words. She was almost afraid to think of what Tessa was trying to say. But Tessa didn't appear to have heard her. She was lost in her thoughts.

"Your sister was like me when he first met me. I don't do drugs, because of my parents. I was stronger than them. But just like me, your sister needed help. Robert always was a sucker for a damsel in distress. When I saw her with the baby, I knew I had to do something."

Silence hung as thick as fog in the room as the two women stared at each other. Hope knew without a doubt she was staring at the face of the person who had paid Cassidy to go away.

"You're the person Cassidy wrote about in her letters. She said someone paid her to go away and stay away. That if she or Luca came back to this area, they would harm Luca."

"Yes." Tessa dropped her gaze, staring at her clasped hands on the table. "And everything would have been fine if only she had stayed away like she was supposed to."

A tear slipped out of one of Tessa's eyes and Hope watched, fascinated, as it fell into her lap.

"What did you do?" Hope was almost afraid of the answer.

"When Robert's cancer came back earlier this year, I was so worried about him that I missed a few months of payments. My focus was on Robert and getting him better."

"That's why Cassidy came back. She thought it was safe since she was no longer getting payments." Hope shook her head in disbelief. "I think she was going to ask me for help. She wanted to finally be clean for Luca and needed me to watch her son while she got herself together."

But what Tessa said next had Hope's heart dropping like a stone.

"If she'd only stayed away like she was supposed to, she would still be alive."

43

TESSA

I looked across the table at Hope. She'd loved her sister so much. What would it feel like, to have someone care that much about you? Only one person in my life had ever felt like that about me. But in the end, he was just like the rest. I needed Hope to understand that I wasn't a bad person.

"I had nothing against your sister personally. When she slept with my husband, I was so hurt, but I forgave Robert. Even though it stung that he'd turned to her instead of me in his time of need, I understood why he'd done it. He needed to save her, like he did me. His cancer diagnosis made him vulnerable, and he needed to feel useful. When it turned out to be only those few times, I knew she didn't mean anything to him. He's made it up to me ever since."

"You . . . ," Hope sputtered, and I felt sorry for her. "What did you do to my sister?"

I ignored her question. "The doctors only gave Robert a few weeks, maybe months, to live. We adopted Shadow, but that was more for me than him. I realized he needed his son. That's why I took Luca. I needed to make it up to him."

"Make what up to him?" Hope's face was twisted in confusion, as she tried to work everything out.

"After your sister went away, we were happy again, for many years. We bought the RV, the biggest and best one we could find. We took so many trips in it, just us against the world." I smiled, thinking of all the carefree trips we'd taken, nothing but the road ahead of us, going wherever we wanted. "He beat the cancer the first time, and we were so grateful we were determined to enjoy life to the fullest. Everything was fine. Everything was great." I paused and looked Hope in the eyes. "Until his cancer came back. And then your sister came back."

"You killed her, didn't you?" Hope whispered this, and I could see in her eyes that she already knew what I'd done.

"I didn't mean to." My mouth drew down for a moment, because that really hadn't been my intention. "I only wanted to incapacitate her long enough to take the boy. It wasn't my fault she took more than she was supposed to. Or maybe Harry messed up, thinking I wanted it like last time."

"Harry?" Hope's voice rose slightly. "Who's Harry?"

We stared at each other without speaking for several moments. I couldn't organize my thoughts. For a second, I had no idea who Harry was. What was Hope talking about? And then slowly, a memory formed in my mind. Harry, the man whom Robert had turned to when he needed something to take the edge off the nausea from the chemo. Harry, whom Robert had turned to when I needed something to give to my parents. Something to guarantee they would overdose. Harry, whom I had turned to when Hope's sister came back to town.

"You killed my sister." She said it again.

My head cleared and I nodded, as the memories came flooding back from when I went to see Harry several months ago. My mind had been a fog of swirling thoughts at the time. I couldn't focus, couldn't concentrate. And what Harry had said to me made no sense.

"It's been a while. But I remember you." He gave me an over-friendly smile, which made my skin crawl. I shivered. I knew he was Robert's supplier. But I'd never gone to Harry before. What was he talking about?

"You wanted something for your parents, right?"

"What?" I was so confused. Harry did look vaguely familiar, but I didn't think we'd ever met. Robert was always the one who dealt with him. Even back then, when my father had almost killed my mother and me.

Harry nodded at me knowingly. "It's okay. I'm discreet. I got you covered."

I told him what I needed, still trying to puzzle out what he meant. He winked at me when I paid him. I was sweating, my shirt sticking to my back. He whispered something to me that I didn't catch, except the words "heavy" and "fentanyl." I backed away from him, and somehow, I was in my car and driving away.

"What did you do?" Hope's voice floated to me as if from far away.

I blinked and focused back on her. I had nothing to lose. Robert was gone, and I needed Hope's help if I was to be reunited with Luca. I would tell her the truth so she knew I hadn't meant to kill her sister.

When I left Harry, I drove to the motel where the boy and his mother were holed up. I knew where they were staying because I'd seen them in town one day and followed them there. I was shocked that they'd come back to the area. But then I realized it was a godsend. Robert was declining rapidly and I was desperate. Even though I had been the one to send them away, now I wondered if seeing his son would help Robert fight to stay alive.

I was going to try to slip the drugs into her car if the window was open or, as a last resort, leave them under her windshield wipers. But as luck would have it, the boy and his mother came out of their room and got into their car. I followed them to the trailway. I parked a few cars away from theirs, and when they got out, I could tell right away she was going through withdrawal. It was just like it had been with my parents. I'd seen it all before, lived with it. Hatred rose in me for my parents. Sure, they'd fed and clothed me, but often, I'd been the one who had to take money out of their wallets to get food. I had spent more time hiding from my father than any child should. They didn't care about me, only about where they were going to get their next fix. But there had been times when they'd tried to quit, to clean themselves up because the neighbors had called social services. And they'd looked and acted exactly like the woman was now.

She was slightly crumpled over, as if in pain. I remembered what my mother had told me way back when, that it felt like someone was trying to rip her guts out. The woman's nose was running, and she swiped a hand over it as she sniffed. The boy said something to her, and she snapped at him, then was immediately sorry at the hurt look on his face. She scratched at her arms, as if trying to rip off her skin, before shaking her head and putting an arm around the boy.

I recognized the signs. But she was trying so hard to stay present for the boy. I could see how excited he was, stopping to pet dogs out for walks with their owners, and running ahead before coming back to her. And then he ran way ahead because he saw a German shepherd. And that's when I made my move.

I approached her slowly, not wanting to startle her.

"You okay?" I asked in a low voice once I was by her side.

Her eyes darted to mine before drifting away, searching for her son. Seeing him far ahead in the distance, she tried to focus back on me. "Fine." But then she coughed.

"I know what you're going through." I tried to make my face as pleasant and sympathetic as possible. I didn't want to scare her. "I can help."

"I'm fine," she said again, even as she shifted her weight, her arms wrapped around her middle.

"You're not fine. Here." I held out my hand and slipped a small bag into hers.

She glanced down, and then her eyes darted around even as her posture straightened and she held herself stiffly. Then with a quick exhale, her fingers closed around it.

"I don't have any money." She didn't make eye contact, but I could tell how much she wanted to stuff it into her pocket and run off.

"It's okay. I understand. I've been where you are." I hadn't, because I would never debase myself like she had, like my parents had, but I needed her to trust me. Because how stupid would you have to be to take drugs from someone you didn't know while families walked their dogs and couples held hands and bicyclists whizzed by? Really, she was the one who had decided her fate, not me.

"Why?" That was all she said, but I knew what she was asking.

"Because someone once helped me when I needed it." No one had, but she didn't need to know that. "And now I'm passing it on." *You bet I am, you bitch.*

Robert had told me he'd done heroin with her, and that's what I'd asked Harry for. I didn't know if that's what he'd given me, or what his whispered words, "heavy" and "fentanyl," meant. Maybe I chose not to know. I saw the scene as if viewing a movie. All I knew was that I needed to knock her out long enough for me to take the boy and bring him back to Robert.

I closed my eyes for a moment while I waited for her to decide. And behind my closed eyelids, I saw Robert's face. *Oh, Robert. What I'm willing to do for you.*

"Thank you." The woman's whispered gratitude had me opening my eyes.

I gave her a nod and she pocketed the bag. Without another word, she turned away and took a few steps closer to her son. She called for him, but he was still playing with the German shepherd and didn't look up.

"I'll be right back, okay?" she called again. When he still didn't answer, she turned and practically ran back to her car, not realizing her battered patchwork tote bag had slipped off her shoulder and fallen to the ground. I frowned and shook my head, disgusted at how careless she was. All she cared about was the drugs. Just like my parents.

I leaned down and picked up her tote and then followed her back to her car. I saw her get in, her hands already fumbling to get the plastic bag out of her pocket. Satisfied that she was occupied and would soon be out of it, I turned to get the boy, the whole reason I'd planned this. Robert needed his son.

But when I turned and headed back down the trail toward where the boy had been petting the German shepherd, I saw that he wasn't there. The couple with the dog had gone on ahead and were now about a quarter of a mile away from me, but the boy was nowhere in sight. I ran down the trail, my eyes searching every person I passed, scanning ahead of me, trying to catch a glimpse of him. He had to be here somewhere. My breath came out in gasps as I jogged, since I hated to exercise and rarely did anything to break a sweat. Finally, I had to slow to catch my breath, and I bent forward, hands on my thighs, as I frantically searched for the boy. Where was he?

The couple with the German shepherd were now just ahead, and I summoned all the energy within me and ran the last yards separating us. "The boy . . . where did he go?"

They stared at me and I gestured with my hands. "The boy . . . petted your dog?"

"Oh, him." The man pointed back down the way I'd just come, toward the parking lot. "He went to find his mother. I think he went off the trail into the trees. He thought maybe she went exploring."

Oh no. Had he doubled back and I hadn't seen him because he'd gone off the path? Without another word to the couple, I turned and headed back the way I'd come. By the time I made it back to the start of the trailhead where the parking lot was, at least twenty minutes had gone by since I saw the woman get into her car. I was gasping for breath, and sweat ran down my back. I cursed, mad at myself because it had taken me so long to get back here.

I leaned over to catch my breath, and that's when I heard it: the sound of sirens getting closer. I looked up just in time to see police cars and a fire truck pulling into the parking lot. Running over to where the woman had parked, I saw that the boy was in the car with her and pounding on her chest. Her head snapped back, and then the first responders were at the car. I got as close as I dared, and caught snippets of what they were saying.

"Are you okay? Ma'am, ma'am, can you hear us?" One of them was rubbing her on the chest as another questioned her.

". . . might be an overdose . . ."

"Is this your mother?" another asked the boy. When he nodded, the first responder continued, "Does she do drugs?"

When the boy nodded again, the first responder turned and yelled to someone, "I need the naloxone kit."

Bodies moved with speed, and my view was blocked for a few seconds. But I heard clearly when someone said, "Oh shit, we don't have one . . . not replaced . . ."

"What the fuck?" someone else yelled. "Shit, this is bad."

And then an onlooker called out, "I have a kit in my car. Do you want it?"

"Get it," someone yelled at him, and I saw the Good Samaritan sprint for his car across the lot. Several minutes later, he came running up, a red kit in his hand.

And then I couldn't see anything as the first responders got to work. My heart pounded out of control in my chest. What had Harry given me? The ambulance pulled up then, and the crowd around the car got bigger as the police tried to keep people back. I couldn't see what was going on. I could hear only snippets with all the chaos surrounding her car. There was no way I could get to the boy. I stood there and cursed myself for failing to reach him in time.

". . . not responding to the nasal spray . . ."

"Move . . . give her a shot . . ."

"Mom! Mommy!"

I pushed people out of the way, trying to see. It was the boy. They were loading the woman into the back of the ambulance. I got closer, trying to catch a glimpse of the boy. When I finally caught sight of him, a police officer had a hand on his shoulder and was talking to him.

I'd screwed up my chance to get to him. And what was going on with his mother? Had she overdosed? Was it my fault? Realizing that I was still holding her tote bag, I backed away, not wanting the boy to see me clutching it. I melted back into the crowd and walked to my car, throwing her tote into the passenger seat before getting in. I'd messed this up royally, but I'd wait, watch and wait, until I could find another opportunity to finally bring the boy to his father.

44

HOPE

Hope stared at Tessa. She couldn't move, her mind still going over what Tessa had just told her. Poor Cassidy. Poor Luca.

"Why?" The question came out in a hoarse whisper. Hope had wanted to shout this, shout it loud enough that people all over the hospital would come running and punish Tessa for what she'd done, but her voice failed her. She didn't take her eyes off Tessa.

"I didn't mean to." Tessa's eyes were luminous. "I just wanted to incapacitate her."

A slow burn built within Hope until it turned into white-hot rage and she had to sit on her hands to stop herself from reaching across the table and wrapping her hands around Tessa's neck. She wanted to squeeze and squeeze until Tessa no longer drew breath. Because she finally understood how people had been driven to commit murder in the heat of the moment. She would have gladly killed Tessa right then and there.

"My poor sister. All these years, I wondered why she left, what happened to her." Hope's chest was heaving, and she brought a hand to her heart. "And it was you this whole time. The adoption." Hope stopped, as something occurred to her. "You didn't find us through the rescue site for Shadow, did you? You knew who we were."

"Yes. But I really wanted to adopt a dog. A dog just like Shadow." Tessa's eyes were imploring. "How is Shadow? Does he miss me?"

Hope sat there, speechless. She had suspected that Tessa was the one who had been terrorizing Cassidy, but she hadn't thought the woman was capable of murder. Whether she'd meant it or not, Cassidy was still dead and Luca still had no mother. Hope needed to tell someone. She should scream and bring people running, and tell them Tessa had killed her sister. But would they believe her? She had no evidence. Maybe she could just strangle Tessa with her bare hands, end this once and for all. This woman sitting in front of her was responsible for everything that had happened to Cassidy ever since Luca had been born. Hope had been blaming herself all these years, and it hadn't been her at all. But Hope didn't want to go to jail.

She couldn't sit here anymore. She had to get away from Tessa. With a loud scrape, Hope pushed back her chair so that the legs dragged on the floor and got to her feet. But before she could get to the door, Tessa's voice stopped her.

"I need Luca. When I get out of here, I want Luca back."

Hope turned around slowly, her eyes narrowing in disbelief. "What did you say?"

Tessa spoke, loud and clear. "I've been the model patient. Do you know that's what we're called here? We're not inmates. We're patients. I take my medication, I go to therapy, both group and individual, I cooperate with everyone, do what they tell me."

"What does that have to do with Luca?" Hope could feel the dread creeping up her back, afraid of what Tessa was about to say.

"I didn't think I would have any feelings for Luca. And I didn't at first. He was only a means to an end, to bring Robert his son. But something happened on our short trip." Tessa's face lit up, and her eyes got a faraway shine. "I realized I love him, as if he is my son. The thought of seeing him again is what's getting me through my time here." Her eyes focused back on Hope. "It's actually not bad in here. We have yoga, which brings Robert closer to me because we used to do yoga together. There's a book club, and other activities. The doctors told me if I keep this up, I'll be able to leave soon. Continue my therapy from home."

Hope stared at Tessa, her eyes wide in disbelief.

Tessa's eyes burned bright with a purpose as she continued. "And when I do, I'm going to petition to adopt Luca. Robert's son. My son."

45

TESSA

I watched Hope's mouth drop open in shock and I felt bad. I hadn't meant to tell her this way. But she was leaving, and I needed to let her know what I had planned. After all, Luca was more mine than hers. Hope was only the sister of his mother. I was the stepmother.

"You . . . you can't . . . ," she sputtered, unable to get the words out.

"I'm sorry, Hope. You can still see him all the time." I rested my hands in my lap. "But he needs me. He needs a proper mother, not just an aunt."

"You're not his mother. He's staying with us." She looked like she was about to pass out.

"We can talk about it more once I get out of here." I softened my voice. "We can work something out."

"No." Hope shook her head and stared hard at me. "You never answered my question before. How did you get Cassidy's letters and her phone?"

"They were in the tote bag she left behind that day on the trailway. When Luca and I were getting ready to leave for the RV trip, I saw the neighborhood boy riding his bike. I decided I'd give you her things, to make up for taking Luca. I'd been carrying them around with me, trying to figure out what to do with them."

I could see the gears turning in her head, and then she confronted me, her face like granite. "You'll never get your hands on Luca. He belongs with me."

Her voice rose with each word. Out of the corner of my eye, I saw Herman, the attendant I liked, walking by. He glanced into the room. Hope was oblivious, but I waved to Herman. He was one of the nicer ones and always tried to make things more comfortable for me.

"Don't be upset, Hope. We'll become a family." For once, I was thinking clearly. I could picture the scene in my mind. Me and Luca together, his loving aunt and uncle just across the lake. They would help me take care of Luca, pick him up from basketball practice when I couldn't. I'd have them over for dinner and watch proudly while he told his aunt and uncle about his achievements at school. I'd help him with his homework, and Shaun would be around to provide the father figure that a young boy would need. We would all go on vacations together, and Hope and Shaun would become like family to me too. The family that I never had.

"You're delusional." Hope's chest rose and fell, and I stared at her in alarm. She was working herself up, and I didn't think it was good for her. "We're not a family. Luca is ours."

"Calm down." I didn't want to be responsible for Hope having a heart attack. I already had so many deaths on my head. "We can ask Luca. He'll tell you he wants to live with me." A thought occurred to me, and I pondered it for a moment before saying it out loud to Hope. "You know, maybe your sister was meant to die. Maybe she had to die in order to bring Luca and me together."

"You did not just say that." Hope's voice came out like knives jabbing me in the chest.

I turned just in time to see the thundercloud that crossed Hope's face. My eyes widened with alarm. "I just meant, maybe this was the

Universe's way of bringing us together. That Luca was meant to be mine this whole time. Even if we had to sacrifice your sister and Robert."

Hope's chest heaved, and then without warning, she lunged around the table. In her haste, her chair went flying as she launched herself at me. I let out a shriek, putting my hands up in front of me. What was wrong with her? Why was she attacking me? But I didn't have any more time to think because Hope had landed on top of me with a thump, knocking us both to the ground, my chair going with us. I tried to buck her off, but Hope had her hands around my neck. I clawed desperately at her arms, but her forearms felt like steel as she squeezed the breath out of me.

I fought against her, kicking my feet, and could feel my heel connect with Hope's shin as my hands battered at her arms, elbows jabbing, trying to get her to let go, to let me breathe. In desperation, I raked a hand down Hope's cheek and flung my head forward hard enough to connect with hers. Her hands loosened from my neck enough for me to breathe, and I gasped in air that I so needed. She came back at me, but this time I was ready. We struggled, sharp elbows connecting with flesh, grunts coming from Hope as I pushed with all my might against her. But Hope wasn't letting up. She slapped my cheek hard enough for my head to snap back, and I screamed, trying to grab at her face, to get her off me. Hope came at me again, her hands back around my throat, and my scream petered out. But it had been enough to bring help, because suddenly, Hope was pulled off me and I could breathe again.

"What's going on here?" Herman held on to Hope, keeping her away from me.

Hope gasped, allowed herself to be dragged back. She had angry scratches down her cheek that were starting to bead with blood. She stood panting, as I struggled to sit up. Our eyes met and I could see alarm in hers. She'd just attacked a patient in a forensic hospital. I didn't want to get her in trouble. I needed her to be a part of my new family.

"It's not her fault." I turned to Herman, a big man who stood about six feet six inches, his neck as thick as a tree trunk. "I got dizzy and fell off my chair. When she came to help me, I freaked out, tried to fight her. You know what happens to me."

Herman narrowed his eyes at me, and I could see Hope looking back and forth between us. Finally, the big man broke eye contact and nodded. "You sure y'all okay?" he asked in a gruff voice.

"Yes," I said.

"I'll let you continue your visit then." He gave me another hard look and was about to leave when Hope sprang to life. With a swift motion, she picked up her purse and stalked out without another word.

Herman turned to me. "You sure you're okay, Tessa?"

I looked at him. I could see the concern in his eyes. It made me feel good, that someone cared about me. We'd become friends in the months since I'd been here. He'd told me all about his baby girl who had leukemia, and how he was working three jobs to make sure she got the care she needed.

"Yes. But I think I need some time alone." Now that I'd told Hope my plan, I knew I could work on her, get her to see that this was the best thing for Luca. I wanted to start planning our lives together, thinking of how I could make our house more welcoming to a boy.

Herman nodded and left, closing the door softly behind him. I righted my chair and sat down, focused on thinking only healing thoughts, inviting in good intentions. I couldn't wait to tell Janie what I had planned. She would be part of our family, Luca's aunt. She'd been so kind to me ever since Robert passed away, and I knew she'd be overjoyed for me to welcome Robert's son into our lives.

46

HOPE

Hope was halfway to the hospital's front door when she suddenly stopped. She veered, doing a one-eighty, and walked rapidly back toward the room where she'd met with Tessa. She couldn't let this go. She couldn't allow Tessa to think Luca was ever going to live with her. Hope would have the last word.

The big attendant watched her coming back down the hall, his eyebrows raised in question.

"I forgot to tell her something." Hope gestured into the room. "Can I go in?"

He studied her for a moment, then inclined his head. "But I'm watching you. I don't know what happened earlier." He paused, eyes searching Hope's face. "I know when she's lying."

She held up her hands. "I won't touch her. I just have to tell her something."

With another nod, the man stepped aside and Hope walked in. Closing the door behind her, she noticed that Tessa had her eyes closed, a peaceful smile on her face. Pity filled Hope, yet at the same time, she couldn't let Tessa think that Luca would ever be hers. She had just admitted to giving Cassidy the drugs that she'd overdosed on.

Maybe she hadn't meant to kill her, but that was the end result. How disconnected from reality was she, thinking that any judge would award her custody of Cassidy's child? Hope didn't know if Tessa could be charged with Cassidy's murder, if they could prove it. Tessa had already been declared unfit to stand trial. But Hope could do one last thing for her sister, and that was to protect Luca at all costs.

She waited until Tessa's eyes popped open, sensing Hope's presence. Hope gazed steadily at Tessa, wanting to make sure she had the other woman's full attention.

"I just have one more thing to say to you. I told you when I first came in that I had something to tell you. But you distracted me." Hope remained standing, gaze fixed on the other woman.

"What is it?" Tessa asked, her face open, lighting up eagerly.

Hope paused for a beat. "Luca isn't your husband's son." She let the words sink in.

"Of course he is. I explained it to you," Tessa said.

"You're wrong. My sister's best friend, Dan Stern, told me that he and Cassidy had slept together, right around the same time that Cassidy met Robert in the bar. It was only a few times, and Cassidy never told him she got pregnant. Cassidy cut him out of her life after that, probably when she realized she was pregnant and didn't know who the father was. Then you came along and scared her into going away."

"He's lying." Tessa said this with no hesitation.

Hope ignored her. "Dan had no idea she was pregnant. He moved out West soon after Cassidy stopped talking to him, so he didn't know she had a baby." Hope took a few steps away and then turned around to face Tessa. "I wanted Cassidy and Luca to stay with me. But you messed everything up."

Hope paused to catch her breath and saw that Tessa's eyes were round, hanging on to her every word.

"Robert is Luca's father."

Hope shook her head. "I contacted Dan when Luca disappeared, thinking he had information on a neighbor. I was the one who told him that Cassidy had a son." She looked away. "He was a ski instructor in Colorado, but he'd been wanting to move back to New York. He visited us back in September and I introduced him to Luca. They're so alike, down to the way they walk and talk. And they have the same cowlick in their hair. When Dan took Luca shopping one day, people kept mistaking them for father and son."

Tessa leaned forward. "No, I don't believe you. Luca looks exactly like Robert did when he was a boy. Your sister named him Luca, the name Robert wanted to name his son."

"He's not Robert's son," Hope said softly. She waited, making sure Tessa's attention was entirely focused on her. "We did a DNA test. And guess what we found out?"

Tessa didn't answer, but the way she held herself stiffly with her eyes boring into Hope's told Hope she had her full attention. Hope leaned in. "Luca is Dan's son. Not Robert's." She stared directly into Tessa's eyes. "We agreed it would be for the best if Luca continued to live with Shaun and me. He's just getting settled and used to his new room, house, school, and friends." Hope paused, watching emotions flitting across Tessa's face like butterflies dancing in a flower garden. "But Dan moved back to the area, and he's getting to know his son. Luca needs as many people in his corner as he can. He sees his father every week and they've bonded."

"No." Tessa shook her head, sending her hair tumbling. "That's not possible. He's Robert's son."

"Do you have proof? DNA tests?"

"No, but . . . ," Tessa sputtered, her mouth hanging open as the reality of what Hope was saying sank in. Disbelief crossed her face, and she shook her head again, as if trying to rid herself of the thought Hope had just planted in her mind.

"We do, and it says Dan is the father." Hope walked around the table toward Tessa.

"No, you're lying." Tessa finally found her voice. "You're lying!" Her voice was shrill, and she shrank back as Hope stopped at her side.

"I'm not lying. Dan is Luca's father." Hope stared down at Tessa. "And if I'm lying, well, you'll never know, will you?"

"No, no, no!" Tessa shook her head, again and again, and Hope waited until she stopped.

Then Hope leaned in close to the other woman's ear and spoke directly into it, enunciating every word so that there was no mistaking what she was saying.

"You killed my sister for no reason at all."

And Hope straightened, looking dead into Tessa's eyes, before she turned her back and walked out for good.

47

TESSA

I couldn't breathe. I watched Hope leave the room and sat frozen in my chair.

I couldn't think. *What just happened?* I clawed frantically at my shirt, pulling it away from my throat, gasping for breath. My mind refused to accept what Hope had just told me. I was still lost in thoughts of the new family I'd have, and couldn't understand what she meant. How could Luca not be Robert's son?

I shook my head, unwilling to accept it. I wasn't wrong. The boy looked just like Robert. Even Robert had been convinced that he was his son. The one thing I knew for sure was that Robert had fathered a son. Who was this Dan Stern that Hope was talking about? He couldn't possibly be the boy's father. *Robert* was the father.

I stood, needing air. I wanted to run to the window to fling it open, but of course I couldn't. I paced the room instead, trying to think. Hope had lied to me. That was it. That had to be the answer. But why would she do that? Tears sprang to my eyes at the thought that the woman I already considered family would lie to me. Why was she being so mean? Was it because of her sister? But things were supposed to happen this way, weren't they? Robert had to be his father.

Right?

Then my heart sank, because of course, this Dan Stern *could* be the father. I didn't know anything about Luca's mother. She'd probably slept around, for all I knew. Why had that never occurred to me? Why had I always assumed the baby was Robert's?

But no. No. I'd watched them together, and there'd been no doubt in my mind that they were father and son. I was sure. *Robert* had been sure. He'd told Janie this. He wanted his son in his life. I'd *killed* him because of this.

Where had that thought come from? I froze in place, willing my mind to clear. Robert had passed away from cancer. I was confused. My mind was muddled and swirled, like a shake inside a blender. I started to count the number of steps as I paced the room. *One two three four five six seven eight nine ten.* Turn around. *One two three four five six seven eight nine.* Turn. My steps got bigger. *One two three four five six seven eight* . . . But the memories kept coming . . .

It was two weeks before I took Luca, the day I overheard Robert talking to Janie on the phone.

"No." I heard Robert's voice loud and clear this time, despite how weak it actually was. "Tessa . . . never know. Was going to tell her . . ."

Tell me what? My forehead scrunched up. What were they talking about?

". . . but I need him. His presence . . . so much like Buddha . . . a glow . . . feel like a new man . . ." I knew Robert was talking about the boy. He'd told me how the boy reminded him of Buddha. I had been right: the boy was good for Robert.

"But what about Tessa?" Janie asked. I could understand her better than Robert. "How will you explain him to her? What if she doesn't understand?"

I held my breath, waiting to see what Robert would say. He must know by now I liked the boy. It was *my* idea to bring them together. Even if he didn't know that. But Robert was quiet for so long that I became alarmed. Had he passed out? Fallen asleep? A heart attack? Stroke? I was about to rush out of the kitchen to see if he was okay when he finally spoke.

"She . . . I knew . . . what I had to do . . ." I was confused, but then all of a sudden, Robert's voice came across, loud and clear. "You knew I was going to ask her for a divorce right before I got diagnosed with cancer. The first time. But I couldn't do it after the diagnosis. I needed her help."

My mouth dropped open. What was he talking about? It literally felt like someone had stabbed me in the heart with a knife. I must have heard wrong. I shook my head, rubbed my ears, refusing to believe what I'd heard. He'd slept with Luca's mother, but she hadn't meant anything to him. Right? What did he mean he was going to ask me for a divorce? Tears sprang to my eyes, and my lips trembled. I clamped them together, refusing to believe what I'd just heard.

And then he spoke again.

"I tried, Janie. I really did. But when the cancer came back, I knew I couldn't live with her anymore. I'm going to tell her soon. You'll take care of me, right? Let me die with dignity?"

He said more, but I no longer heard him, or Janie. I could hear my heart cracking in half as I stood rooted to the spot. All the blood drained from my face and I blinked, not willing to comprehend what I was hearing. The grief took over, and I crumpled to the ground, my muscles no longer strong enough to hold me up. I don't know how long I stayed there huddled in a ball, no tears, no sounds, nothing coming out of me. Just a hollowness as I realized our whole life had been a lie. Robert had wanted to divorce me. He didn't love me anymore. Hadn't since before his first cancer diagnosis. That was why he'd been so distant recently. He'd loved me, fixed me, and now that I was whole, he was leaving me. He wanted *Janie* to take care of him in his dying days. Not me. After what felt like hours, I was finally aware of my surroundings again. I knew what I had to do.

Quietly, I slipped out the front door, filling the empty poop bag holder with the roll I'd grabbed before I overheard Robert and Janie's conversation. Shadow was still sitting there on the front path, and he got to his feet as soon as he saw me.

"Good boy, Shadow." I stooped down to hug him, knowing he was the only one who truly loved me. I was rewarded with kisses, and I held him tight for another moment before I stood. Then, as if my world hadn't just exploded, I tugged gently on the leash. "Let's go. We're going to take a nice long walk, and then I have something I need to do when I get back."

We started down the walk to the driveway and then onto the street, waving at a neighbor who was power walking in the opposite direction.

I refused to think. I let my mind drift, focusing on only my surroundings, keeping up a light chatter to Shadow, as if he could understand what I was saying. We walked fast, and soon I was sweating, the exertion putting feeling back in my body again. We walked and walked, for over an hour, all the way to the other side of the lake, past the boy's house, but no one was about. The boy would be at school, and Hope and Shaun at work. I knew now I wouldn't be texting them later, that the boy wouldn't be coming over today to see Robert, or ever again.

Shadow and I went up and down hills, zigzagging our way back to our side of the lake, and when we finally made it home, I let him off the leash in our backyard. He ran ahead of me to our deck, and stood waiting patiently at the back door for me to open it. He ran in and I paused, one foot inside and the other still on the deck. The house was quiet. Robert must be napping. I stood still for another moment, knowing that my life was about to change forever.

When I finally went in, I closed the door quietly behind me so that it wouldn't bang shut. I hung up Shadow's leash on the hook next to the back door, and took off my shoes before walking in. I gave Shadow a treat and filled his water bowl. Once that was taken care of, I took a deep breath and walked into our bedroom, closing the door behind me softly so that Shadow couldn't follow me in.

Robert was sleeping, his breath uneven. I walked to my side of the bed and watched him, saw him as he really was. The way his cheeks were sunken and the way his skin hung off his face so that I could almost see the skeleton of his head like a ghoulish Halloween mask. His hair was all white and wispy, so thin I could see his scalp. His lips were chapped, and his body barely made a lump in the bed under the sheets. He was propped up with two pillows, and there were two more on my side of the bed.

Oh, Robert, how I loved you. You were my whole life, the only person I have ever cared about in my entire life.

I picked up one of my pillows and walked with it around the bed to his side. I didn't hesitate.

At the last moment, his eyes flew open and met mine. His eyes widened, but then understanding dawned. I gave him a gentle smile and brought the pillow down over his face with purpose. I pressed down, my mind completely blank, devoid of all feeling as I focused on the task at hand. It wasn't hard. He was so weak he barely put up a fight, and within moments, it was over. He was still. I held the pillow down for a few more minutes just to make sure. When I finally lifted it, I let it fall from my hands onto the floor as I looked at my beloved Robert.

He was gone. He'd been dying anyway. I was finally ready to face the truth, to believe what the doctors had been telling me. All I had done was help him along. Because he'd betrayed my love.

I stood there, memorizing his face.

Goodbye, Robert. I loved you.

I traced a finger down his cheek, touching him for the last time.

And my name is Tessa. Not Tess.

I sat with him for a while, not moving, not talking, not touching him. I just sat and thought of our life, and then finally, I stood because I knew Shadow would need to go out. And then my mind let go, because I couldn't face that I had just killed my husband.

I stopped pacing. My eyes dilated as the thought took root, deep in the recesses of my mind, where terrible thoughts dwelled and where I did terrible things to people. What if I'd killed Cassidy and Robert for no reason at all?

I was a good person. Wasn't I?

"Robert!" I looked up, as if I could find him somewhere above me. "What have I done?" The last word ended in a wail, and then I collapsed to the ground, no longer able to stand upright. A sound filled the room, a strange keening sound that I didn't know was coming from me until Herman flung open the door and rushed to my side.

"Tessa, Tessa . . ." He said more, but I couldn't hear him over the roar in my ears as I realized what I'd done.

I'd killed Robert. The doctors were right. They kept saying some sort of trauma or guilt had triggered my thinking Robert was still alive and that things were great with us again. And now I knew what that was: I'd killed Robert, and my guilt had conjured him up. I took Luca to make it up to Robert. I wanted us to be a happy family. But we weren't. Robert was gone, and I was all alone.

If I hadn't done what I had, we might have had a month, two, maybe more together. But he'd told Janie he was leaving me. I couldn't bear it. I couldn't take it. The keening sound got louder and louder, until it was all I could hear. And then my mind shattered, my head bursting until all my cells went flying all over the room. They spattered Herman, and spattered the people now running into the room, hovering over me.

"No . . . ," I howled, the single word loud and mournful, drawn out until I gasped for air.

I couldn't take it. This wasn't supposed to happen. Bright lights flashed behind my eyes, and then nothing.

Darkness.

Robert.

My love.

Where are you?

48

HOPE

Hope had walked out of the room, past the big man, and was headed for the front door, when she stopped again and turned around. The man watched her until she stood in front of him.

"You should call Janie. Tessa is going to need her."

The man regarded her, and then his eyes flew toward the room. He looked back at Hope, and with a nod, she turned and left.

She wasn't sorry for what she'd told Tessa, but she wasn't inhuman enough to leave Tessa alone. Tessa was Janie's problem now. Not Hope's. She heard the howls behind her as she exited the hospital. Her heart stuttered, but she didn't stop. She steeled herself and walked with determination to her car. She was sorry for Tessa, but even more sorry over what Tessa had done to her sister. All these years, Hope had thought *she* was the cause of Cassidy never being in touch, not getting to know her nephew as he grew up. She'd spent all these years thinking Cassidy had hated her so much that she'd stayed away.

Hope finally had her answers, her closure where Cassidy was concerned, and she would not allow herself to doubt her actions. So what if they hadn't actually done a DNA test? Dan very well could be Luca's father. He'd finally confessed to Hope recently that he and Cassidy had been together. He'd thought this was it, that they were finally going to be a couple. But Cassidy had pushed him away, avoided his calls and texts after that. Dan had been hurt, angry because he'd thought Cassidy had led him on. He'd moved away to try to forget her, and when she'd started calling and texting again, he hadn't responded.

The estrangement had been his fault. But after a year or so, he'd regretted the loss of their friendship. By then, Cassidy had disappeared from all their lives, and she never answered any of his attempts to reconnect. He'd suspected Luca might be his but hadn't been ready to face what that meant when he'd so recently found out Cassidy was gone. He'd been mourning Cassidy, regretting the estrangement and his part in it. Regretting not having known she'd had a child who could very well be his.

Hope got in her car and knew she would ask Dan if he'd be willing to do a DNA test. She had a feeling he would. He was wonderful with Luca, who adored him. Whatever the results, Luca would stay with her and Shaun. They'd never wanted children, but had been granted the privilege of having Luca in their lives. She'd always mourn Cassidy, but she would honor her sister's memory by caring for her son.

With a determined nod, Hope pulled out of the parking spot, heading home to her family. She would protect what was hers.

AUTHOR'S NOTE

According to the New York State Department of Health, every five and a half minutes, someone dies from a drug overdose. Some of the characters in this book are affected by substance use disorder, commonly known as addiction. While I did use the disorder as a plot device, this is a topic I don't take lightly. Much effort has been made to ensure the density and the dynamics of addiction were portrayed both tenderly and accurately. Much like the experiences of the characters in this book, overdose is a growing concern, taking over 107,000 lives in 2021 in the United States alone. The effects of the disorder range from the terror Tessa's parents rained on her to Cassidy's fight to stay clean for her son. While their stories are fictional, the consequences of their struggles are very real. I hope Cassidy's story helps others see the complexity of addiction and gain compassion for those walking the journey of addiction and recovery.

I am grateful for the heroic work of so many first responders, treatment professionals, preventionists, and harm reductionists who have worked to reduce the negative outcomes of these substances. Thank you to my friend Lauren Johnson, MA, M-CASAC, who has shared her expertise with me. For more information on treatment for substance use disorder, peer recovery advocates, and access to the life-saving medication naloxone (Narcan), please see the links below:

www.nextdistro.org
www.samhsa.gov
www.heal.nih.gov

ACKNOWLEDGMENTS

I am eternally grateful to my agent, Rachel Brooks, who has been through so many ups and downs with me in the past five years. I couldn't have asked for a better partner and champion for my writing career, and I'm so grateful to have Rachel and BookEnds Literary Agency in my corner. Here's to many more "Chipotle on You!" in the years to come.

Thank you to my brilliant editor, Jessica Tribble Wells, who understands how my thriller brain works and is such an enthusiastic supporter of the twisted stories I concoct. It is the greatest honor to get to work with you on another book. Thank you also to my developmental editor, Andrea Hurst, who once again pulled stuff out of me that I wasn't sure I was capable of. You have a gift for helping me flesh out the story I really wanted to tell. To Ploy Siripant, the genius behind another stunning cover, I am in awe. A huge thank-you to the rest of the team: Miranda Gardner, Kellie Osborne, Jill Schoenhaut, Heather Rodino, Michael Jantze, Stef Sloma, and Sarah Shaw. And thank you to Ann-Marie Nieves of Get Red PR for being the best publicist ever.

I turned to many experts for details about police procedures, addiction, and RV life. To the following people, thank you for sharing your expertise with me. Any mistakes are my own. Ryan Korzevinski, Brian Cregan, and the state police officers in my town, thank you for walking me through what would happen if a nine-year-old boy disappeared from his driveway. Thank you to Lauren Johnson MA, M-CASAC, my neighbor and friend who told me more about substance misuse and addiction and why having a naloxone kit and learning how to use one is so important. And much thanks to Lisa Yount for providing all the details about RV living, including detailed videos (with Little Bubba!), and sharing her experiences with me.

To Joan and Henry Kazer: thank you for being my inspiration for Tessa and Robert. Although you are nothing like the two of them (thank goodness), Joan's love for true crime prompted me to model the couple after you. I had so much fun imagining what could be since there isn't a nicer couple out there and I'm blessed to know you both!

Thank you to my lake community for providing the inspiration for the setting of this book, even though I took liberties with the geography of our community. You may recognize some names in the book. ☺

Many thanks as always to my mom and dad for always being willing to watch our son and three dogs when I have a writing deadline. Thank you to my husband, Jim, for reading every one of my books and accompanying me to all my author events. To our son, Lakon, the best PR/marketer I could ask for, always willing to get people to "buy Mommy's books" and help me sign them. My author events wouldn't be the same without him in the front row taking pictures and videos. And as always, I must thank my writing companions, Lokie (who went to the Rainbow Bridge before this book came out), Mochi, Cash (and Pinot in Heaven), who do the best job of supporting my writing by snoring at my side.

And last but not least, to all the readers out there, I couldn't have this dream career without you. Thank you from the bottom of my heart.

ABOUT THE AUTHOR

Photo © 2020 Dave Cross Photography

Lyn Liao Butler is a Taiwanese American author of thrillers, upmarket fiction, and rom-coms. Her most recent thriller, *Someone Else's Life*, was an Amazon bestseller, and her second book, *Red Thread of Fate*, is a finalist in the WFWA Star Awards for 2023. Before becoming an author, she was a professional ballet and modern dancer, and is still a fitness and yoga instructor. For more information visit www.lynliaobutler.com.